The First
Warm Evening
of the Year

Also by Jamie M. Saul

Light of Day

The First
Warm Evening
of the Year

Jamie M. Saul

WILLIAM MORROW
An Imprint of HarperCollins*Publishers*

THE FIRST WARM EVENING OF THE YEAR. Copyright © 2012 by Jamie M. Saul. All rights reserved. Printed in the United States of America. No part of this book may be used or reproduced in any manner whatsoever without written permission except in the case of brief quotations embod-ied in critical articles and reviews. For information address HarperCollins Publishers, 10 East 53rd Street, New York, NY 10022.

HarperCollins books may be purchased for educational, business, or sales promotional use. For information please write: Special Markets Depart-ment, HarperCollins Publishers, 10 East 53rd Street, New York, NY 10022.

FIRST EDITION

Library of Congress Cataloging-in-Publication Data has been applied for.

ISBN 978-0-06-144972-7

12 13 14 15 16 OV/RRD 10 9 8 7 6 5 4 3 2 1

For my brother, Lawrence A. Saul
And in memory of William T. Braman

PART I

Marian

One

THE FIRST TIME I SAW MARIAN BALLANTINE SHE LOOKED like a burst of bittersweet among the winter branches in her bright red coat and orange scarf, her hair thick and dark, the way certain secrets are dark.

She extended her hand, which folded over mine, and said, "Not what you expected, was it?" Marian might have known that there were more than a few other things to which she could have been referring, besides the circumstances for my arrival. I might have even believed that she was nothing more than a pleasant distraction from the unpleasant purpose for my having to be there, except I was aware of more than just her presence. It was her face, mostly, illuminant from deep within her eyes, and more complete than a simply attractive face, more involved. It was a welcoming face, which made me think for a moment that she'd mistaken me for someone else, or she thought she might have known me from some other time. It revealed the certainty of recognition and familiarity.

No one had ever looked at me quite like that before. That's when I fell in love with her.

A FEW WEEKS BEFORE, IN THE MIDDLE OF A SLOW MORNING IN March, I was alone in my apartment. According to my date-book it was the last week of winter, but I was feeling the "damp, drizzly November in the soul" that Ishmael talks about and sends him sailing toward his rebirth of wonder. For the past month or so, the rumblings of discontent, an emo-tional stasis had settled in. All the things that used to give me pleasure were unsatisfying now. I had a lucrative career doing commercial voice-overs for television and radio, with the kind of freedom that most of my friends envied; a relationship that allowed me an autonomy that other men seemed to desire— my girlfriend, Rita, was the least possessive person I'd ever known—and that I once wanted, too.

I couldn't quite locate the reason why I now felt so unset-tled, as though my collar were always half a size too tight—and it had been a long time, it seemed, since work or relationships provided me much satisfaction.

This morning I'd decided to rest all considerations of heart and mind, feeling that loafing away this delicious lazy day and its unblemished and undemanding time was just what I needed to pull myself out of the doldrums.

Outside my window the sun had broken free of all clouds. A smattering of people crossed the street against the light, hailed taxis, ran after buses, walked the paths of Central Park, beneath the sad, bare trees and dreary lawns. I stood and watched Manhattan's anonymous society and felt a sense of well-being. I was one of them, at peace with myself and the city. The gloom of the morning had passed when the doorbell rang and my doorman handed me a registered letter with a Shady Grove, New York, postmark and the return address of an attorney named Frank Remsen.

I recalled the name Shady Grove, but why, I didn't know. It couldn't have been from a book, since it was a real place, and I was sure I'd never been there, but a registered letter from a lawyer, even if I had remembered the town, was the sort of thing to fill me with apprehension, which was why the letter remained unopened while I finished my coffee and allowed myself the illusion that this day still belonged, complete and inviolate, to me.

Then, I sat down and slowly peeled open the envelope.

I read the letter once, and a second time, and even then I wasn't quite sure what to think. It seemed like such an unusual request: Mr. Remsen was writing on behalf of Laura Stevenson, who was requesting that I act as executor of her estate. There was nothing in the letter saying why Laura wanted me to do this, and nothing at all about Laura, except that she lived in Shady Grove, New York, hoped I remembered her, was aware that this was coming out of nowhere, so I could certainly decline, and would I please call Remsen with my answer at my soonest convenience.

I stared at Laura's name, not because I didn't remember her, and not because I needed time to make my decision. I knew Laura Stevenson, or had known her, twenty years before, when she was a student at Juilliard, and I at Columbia. Her name was Laura Welles back then. Why would she want me to act as her executor after all these years? And what was so urgent about it?

I walked into my bedroom, opened the daybook on my desk, and checked my appointments, but I'd already dialed Remsen's number.

I told him I'd just received his letter. "And it's all very vague."

There was silence at the other end, as though I'd given the wrong response, but it didn't last long.

Remsen said, "I thank you for getting back to me, Mr. Tremont."

"My father is Mr. Tremont," I told him. "Call me Geoffrey."

"Laura was aware that you'd have a few questions, Geoffrey—"

"She can get in touch with me herself. Even after all these years."

"She wanted me to ask you, and she didn't want to see you— Well, actually, she didn't want you to see *her*."

"You said didn't."

"Laura died," he said. "A week ago. There really isn't very much—" Remsen began.

I only then realized that I'd turned my back to the phone, and was staring at the floor. "Wait a minute." I kept looking down. I had a feeling of disbelief, because in my mind, I could recall a girl named Laura Welles, and all I could think, as irrational as it was, was that girl should still be alive.

"Can you tell me how she died?"

"Cancer. Lung cancer."

I took a moment before saying, "What about her husband? When I knew her she had a—"

"Her husband passed away some years ago, as have both parents. Laura had no children."

"What about the brother?"

"You know Simon?"

"I've met him."

"Laura hadn't stayed in touch with him." Remsen cleared his throat. "There was some trouble years ago. She had her reasons."

I knew about those reasons and remembered the spring in '86, but I said nothing about it to Remsen.

"But that was then," he was saying, "so who knows? Anyway, I should tell you I notified him a couple of days after the funeral. He wanted to know how to find you. I said I'd have to check with you first. He didn't leave a number or anything."

I was aware now of the room feeling hot and airless.

"When would I have to take care of this?"

"At your convenience. Of course, sooner would be better than later." He had the kind of voice that made me think of those men who go bald before they're thirty. "For what it's worth," he said, "it isn't much of an estate. Her house and furniture. Nothing terribly complicated. All you have to do is make sure the people and charities receive what she specified for them, that her house is sold for a fair market price, and the money's donated to the high school music program where she taught. Basically, that's it."

"A music teacher? When I knew Laura she was a jazz musician and lived in Paris."

"She moved back here after her husband died. This is her hometown. She taught at our high school for the last ten years or so."

I'd already turned around, and had a pen in my hand.

"I'll need her address," I said, "and directions. I can't leave town until Tuesday."

Remsen said it could wait until then, and told me how to get to Shady Grove and find Laura's house.

I hung up the phone, sat on the edge of the bed, and tried to remember Laura Welles.

I wish I could say that my mind was ripe with memories, but I hadn't given Laura very much thought in all these years. Although we'd been good friends, close friends, when we were both in school, we hadn't stayed in touch once she'd moved to Paris. I suppose we might have kept up if we'd lived closer to each other or had the convenience of e-mail like we have now. And now there were things that I wanted to remember about her. Not the broad things—how she looked, what neighborhood she lived in, things we did with our friends. The smaller things. What we'd done on a specific afternoon, what we'd talk about late at night over a beer, what was important to her, and what she shook off. Anything that might have conjured Laura Welles for just a minute, given texture to the sadness I was feeling, and held more than this pitiful context.

I am not blessed with the deepest memory—when I was in the theater, I could always remember my lines and cues and marks, but the exact year of a show, or where we played, I couldn't say—and I didn't do much to keep up with people from my past or any of my old friends from school, including Laura, and all that was left were a smattering of recollections, parties we'd gone to together, nights at the West End, over on Broadway, where we used to eat inexpensive food and listen to jazz. I recalled one night when we seemed to be doing a lot of catching up and gossiping, so it might have been when we'd just come back from summer vacation, and we were laughing a lot; although it could have been almost any time, since the West End was one of our haunts, we always had things and people to talk about, and we always made each other laugh. It might have been just before the start of our senior year, when Laura sublet a studio apartment in the same building where I was living—I was staying in my brother Alex's apartment while he did his residency in Chicago—Laura and I certainly would have been happy about that.

I remembered that we used to go to some of the downtown clubs and stay out all night, sometimes all weekend, and we went to the theater and concerts once in a while. And one night, in someone's apartment near Lincoln Center, looking out the window at the people on their way to the opera, maybe, or the ballet, Laura said she liked watching them from up high like that. She said most things looked better from a distance.

Two

I T'S ABOUT A TWO-AND-A-HALF-HOUR DRIVE FROM MANHATTAN to Shady Grove, all of it pleasant and scenic along the Parkway and state roads, where Shady Grove nestles into the New York–Massachusetts border just south of the Berkshire Mountains. This is the corner of New York State where Old Dutch meets New England and each neutralizes the other, leaving a little town that might be mistaken for a dozen other little towns in the region. A week after Remsen's call I was driving down a main street of pleasant if unexciting stores, the local bank, a spacious town square that even in late morning seemed to be in the midst of a habitual nap. And I had to wonder why Laura would come back here to teach high school music after New York and Paris. I couldn't reconcile that Laura with the one I had known in Manhattan.

Remsen met me at Laura's house, handed me the keys, and the inventory of what was going where and to whom, and left me there alone.

It was a small two-story place, set back from a neat lawn, three steps up to the front porch. There really wasn't much to do. Laura had packed most of her personal things, or maybe she'd had someone do it for her. The closets had been emptied of clothes, upstairs and down, and the walls were all bare—I could see the light stains of picture frames. Lined up in orderly rows in the living room were dozens of boxes labeled in a clear, feminine handwriting, clothes and books for a town thrift shop.

The furniture was still there, a sofa with two deep cushions, two soft chairs, coffee table, and end tables with a matched pair of lamps.

I walked to the back hall and into the dining room where there was a small drop-leaf table of no particular age, four matching chairs, and a glass bowl that might have been used for flowers. The kitchen still had plates and cutlery, a little table by the window. Outside the back door was a garden, which was in disrepair, maybe because of a harsh winter and not from neglect.

Upstairs were two bedrooms, with quilted bedspreads, and delicate lace curtains. The larger bedroom had flowered wallpaper, the smaller bedroom was painted pink and white.

I went downstairs and got to work, not that there was much for me to do.

In a corner of the room was a fairly large carton marked: "Scrapbook and photographs," along with two violins Laura had left to someone named Marian Ballantine; and a stereo system and a box of old LPs that Laura had bequeathed to me, which, she'd explained in her will, we had listened to together and, if she remembered correctly, I liked. But what the songs were, where or when we'd listened to them, what they might have meant to her, or what she thought they'd mean to me, she hadn't said.

There was also a box with photographs, some in an envelope with my name, and the rest I was to give to Marian Ballantine.

The entire house looked like the kind of place where someone's grandmother lived, delicate and tidy, not fussy, but in strict order. Except for the cartons, and the slight accumulation of fine dust that had settled on the furniture and floors, and the absence of the more personal touches, it seemed as though at any moment Laura might walk in, with a fresh bouquet for the table.

It didn't take me long to make a full account of Laura's things, and a few minutes later I was sitting on her couch, holding a photograph of the two of us looking young and painfully optimistic, taken, so the inscription on the back read, at "Bradley's" the first time she sat in with the Mel Stevenson trio. I remembered that night, at least the part when Laura sat in, and I recalled that no one ever called Mel Stevenson anything but "Steve." There was another photo of Laura, Steve, and me sitting at a table in a jazz club; two photos, both of Laura and Steve standing next to a piano, Laura wearing a tuxedo and a smile, Steve in suit and tie, hair combed back over his forehead, looking very cosmopolitan; and two framed photographs: Laura when she was a teenager, standing outside a large house with another teenage girl; and one of her sitting on the steps outside Juilliard. I held onto that photo, and stared at the expression on her face. It was an expression I'd seen often when we were friends, an amused expression, and private, but in a moment she would tell you *all* about it. I had no trouble remembering that and how much I enjoyed being around her.

I wanted to believe that Laura had known that I'd do this for her, that she'd wanted this to be between the two of us. That she'd wanted me to sit with the empty closets, the stripped walls, the tokens of her life; but what I found rather remarkable was, whether by accident or intent, she'd managed to lay bare everything and bare nothing at all.

Then, a moment later, I wasn't thinking about empty closets and bare walls, or anything else about Laura Stevenson, whom I had never known. I was thinking about my friend, Laura Welles, who had died at the age of forty-two. Anything else that I might want to consider at the moment was quite beside the point. Which was what I was still thinking about when I walked outside and saw a woman standing there, in a bright red jacket, an inviting expression on her face, shivering in the cold.

That's when Marian introduced herself, explained that she'd come by to get the few things Laura had left to her, extended her hand, and said, "Not what you expected, was it?"

I said that few things were, but I wasn't sure to what she was referring.

She smiled. "All this," and made a circle in the air with her hand.

I said, "Considering that I've never been anyone's executor before, I really didn't know what to expect. It's a bit confusing."

"I told Laura more than once that she could depend on me to take care of this, but she said she didn't want her friends to have to bury her twice, that you were the closest thing to a friend who wasn't still involved with her life. I must admit, I didn't like it. I told her it was very risky to ask someone she hadn't seen in all these years. She said you were the most trustworthy person she'd ever known, and the most reliable, and you were always there to help her out when you two were in college. She thought you might be willing to help her again."

It was the first day of spring and a cold morning. Dormant gardens were visible under the few inches of weathered snow. Empty bushes sagged like skeletal arms beneath the muted sky. Marian was still shivering. She pulled up her coat collar and put her hands in her pockets.

"Not that Laura was sure you'd do it."

"Why wouldn't I?"

"Why *would* you?"

"Because I loved her."

She took a step back, as though she needed to put a little distance between us. She appeared to be surprised and unsettled by my answer.

"Not like that," I said. "I genuinely loved her."

Marian's face softened. "I know what you meant." She took a step closer, said, "Laura understood that," and walked me over to the house.

We sat on the front steps. The cement was cold, but the sky had cleared, and a moment later we were warmed by a circle of sunlight.

Marian was leaning forward, her arms resting on top of her legs, staring down at the ground and looking pensive and sad, and I wanted to say something to let her know that I understood her sadness, or was trying to. That I was thinking about the face I'd seen in those photographs, which was how I remembered Laura: as the twenty-two-year-old girl I had known, and it was that girl who had died, and I realized that it was her who I was here to mourn.

"I'm not here as a stranger," I said.

I saw Marian watching me out of the corner of her eyes.

"When I met Laura I had a girlfriend at Colby College," I said, "and I'd gotten the noble idea not to fool around while she was gone. Laura and I started going places together, our freshman year, and I liked her. She was very urbane, certainly compared to the other girls I knew. I always had the sense that she knew who she was." I shook my head. "I'm not doing a good job with this."

"I've known—knew her all my life. That's a pretty good description of her."

"After a while, it wasn't about being noble. The girlfriend and I broke up and Laura and I remained friends. Girlfriends came and went. And Laura's boyfriends."

"And the two of you remained friends."

"I guess we did."

Another minute or more passed, before I asked the more obvious questions about Laura's death, and the more indelicate ones.

"There was nothing sudden about it. If that's what you're asking. She had time," Marian said, "to prepare for her death, and to prepare her friends."

"That sounds like Laura."

"It wasn't enough time." Marian sat up straight. "It's never enough time, is it."

We stayed outside, sitting in the warm sunshine, and continued to talk about our friend Laura, who studied classical violin at Juilliard, and whom I hadn't seen in twenty years, who taught music at a local high school, and who, Marian said, had found a sort of sanctuary in her hometown.

"I've always liked the idea of her, even after we'd lost touch," I said.

Marian turned to me.

"I can't say I was ever aware of thinking that, or that I thought about Laura all that often, but I liked the idea of her. Of having a friend who was a jazz musician and lived in Paris. I liked the idea of knowing her."

Marian was still watching me.

"A long time ago," she said.

"But she and Steve did live in Paris and were jazz musicians, right?"

"After Steve died Laura moved back to Shady Grove. Nine years ago."

"A *music* teacher?"

"She stopped performing."

"And they gave her a job at the high school?"

"Laura and I always kept up with each other, so when she told me she wanted to move back and what she'd like to do, I told her about the job opening up at the high school."

"Is that what you do? Teach?"

"*Me*? No. I'm a gardener. Actually I own a nursery, and do *other* people's gardening. It's not the most exciting thing in the world."

"What is?"

She shifted on the steps, secured one of her coat buttons, when she saw me looking at the yellow pickup truck parked at the curb, at the logo BALLANTINE DESIGNS.

"And you're also a landscaper?" I asked.

"My husband, Buddy, was. He did the landscaping and I did the flora."

"Here in Shady Grove?"

"Around the region."

"And this is where you're from? Shady Grove?"

"Are you really that interested?"

"Why shouldn't I be? You and Laura both grew up here?"

"We grew up and she grew out."

"For a while."

"And when she came back, we settled right back into our old friendship."

I nodded my head in the direction of the truck. "And the landscaping? You and your husband—"

"I gave it up after my husband died."

"Oh. I'm sorry."

Marian said, "He died the year before Laura moved back. Laura used to call us 'the young widows of Shady Grove.'" The way Marian said this made me think I'd been making her feel uncomfortable, and I apologized.

"That's all right." She put her hand on my arm. "Hey, let me tell you a story Laura told me about you." She gave me a quick glance as she said this.

"Is it embarrassing?"

She shook her head, kept her hand on my arm a moment longer, and asked me, "Does the name Neil Billson sound familiar?"

I needed a moment. "Was he that weird guy who was always following her around?"

"He told her he was crazy about her. Laura told me he was just plain crazy. This was just around the time she met you."

"Did he have long hair, and always needed a shave?"

"All I know is, you told Laura that he was a messed-up guy, and she agreed. She said he never became menacing or anything, but he did get on her nerves and made her feel creepy. Maybe he thought his persistence would wear her down. Finally she told him, first of all that she didn't like him, and second, to back off. But he kept calling her. You told her that you'd say something to him, but she didn't want you to get involved."

"I remember Laura wasn't very worried about it. She was sure that it would run its course and he'd get discouraged. But I didn't like it."

"You saw him at some party or something, and told him you were Laura's brother, and that Mom and Dad were coming to Manhattan to meet him and find out what his intentions were—"

"I actually used the word *intentions?*"

"So the story goes. And everyone in the family hoped he liked big weddings and big families because Laura did. And you were all anxious to set a date." Marian let this settle in, then smiled at me. "You were always coming to her rescue, weren't you." She leaned back on her elbows, turned her face to the sun, and said, "In a few more weeks you'll be able to smell spring. That's really delightful." She said she always looked forward to the change of season, and *The Old Farmer's Almanac* predicted spring would come early that year. She said, "The fragrance of spring in the air delights me." As though this was what I was also looking forward to, or should have been. And suddenly I wanted us to have that in common, watching for the approach of the new season. I wanted to be there with the scent of her hair, aware only of how it felt to sit this close to her, like dancing in drifting sunlight with a piano playing in a distant room.

I didn't know Marian before that day, yet I felt that I'd known her for a very long time. How familiar she seemed to me, yet it was the *unfamiliarity* that felt so compelling. I'd been stuck in the horse latitudes and it felt as though Marian were the change in the weather that I'd been trying to locate, the shift in the breeze.

And then there was her laugh.

Marian had just said, "The crocuses will be coming up, and the daffodils and tulips," and told me that she had all sorts of gardens around her house. "You should see them in summer. The birds, and the flowers. It's like an explosion."

I told her I'd like to.

She looked at me as though she might have misunderstood *my* intentions.

"I have a boyfriend," she said.

I said, "That's nice."

"No. I mean, if you think I was flirting with you. I have a boyfriend." There was a slight stammer when she said this as though she was uncertain, either of the boyfriend, or the necessity of telling me about him. While I felt a tug of disappointment.

But I recovered quickly enough to tell her, "I was *hoping* you were flirting with me, and unless your boyfriend is hiding in the bushes with my girlfriend, I think we're safe."

Her laughter sounded like water in a dream.

I thought of Laura and Marian spending their summers together, and maybe they laughed that same way. I was going to ask her that, and tell her that she surely must be used to men flirting with her, which was just a way to keep on flirting, only now I was thinking about how she and Laura must have felt all those years after their husbands had died, and what they must have felt when Laura got sick, and the reason for my coming up there, and maybe what they talked about on those summer days wasn't so funny.

For the second time since we'd met I wanted to apologize, but Marian was smiling at me again, and there was that welcoming look on her face. She had her hand on my arm again and I felt the warmth of her fingers through my sleeve and I moved my hand to cover hers, but she stepped back and asked, "So what happened to the girlfriend at Colby, anyway?"

"She broke up with me," I said.

"Did she meet someone else, or did you?"

I didn't answer right away, and when I did, I told her the truth. "I didn't love her enough."

Marian tilted her head, squinted her eyes, just a little bit when she looked at me. There was brittleness in her voice when she said, "I've been keeping you out here too long." She stood up and offered to help me get the carton with the photographs and scrapbook, and Laura's violins.

I asked if she was sure she wanted to be inside Laura's house.

She said, "I'll be fine," and we walked in together.

We went to the corner of the living room and before I picked up the carton, Marian said, "I always liked that picture of the two of you."

"You've seen that picture?" I asked.

"Oh sure."

I looked over at the two violins. "She was a hell of a musician," I said.

"They both were. My husband and I visited them in Paris a few times." She looked around the room. "It's like it never happened. I mean standing here with all her things around, it's like—I still expect her to come walking down the stairs."

I heard the wind outside and felt it blow through the house, as though it were already taking possession of the rooms. I turned toward Marian. She seemed to have sunk into her coat and looked small.

I might have asked, "What is it?" Or else I was thinking that and it showed, because Marian said, "This is the first time I've been here without her." She looked around, her eyes stopping on the blank spaces on the walls. "We spent many nights sitting here talking about—" Marian walked over to the window and looked outside.

"Tell me something about Laura," she said, with her back to me. "I don't mean something you two did together, but something else you remember about her. That you liked about her."

I thought for a moment, then told her one of my favorite things about Laura: "She held people accountable for their behavior," I said. "More than accountable. Responsible. Her friends, especially. She thought what you did, the way you acted day-to-day *mattered*, and she let you know, she was straightforward about it. You always knew just where you stood with her. It made it easy being her friend. And she was game. She was up for just about anything. I *really*—"

Marian was crying.

I didn't know the protocol for watching a person you hardly know cry, so I walked over to her and refrained from making any of those insipid, sympathetic sounds people make in these situations.

She cupped her hands over her face and whispered, "I'm sorry. I'm really sorry."

"There's no reason to be sorry."

I put my hand on her shoulder. She turned, moving a little closer and pressing the palm of her hand against the front of my coat. I didn't know if she wanted to keep me away or wanted to touch me, maybe she didn't either, but before she could make up her mind, I took out a fairly respectable hand-kerchief and closed her hand around it. As she wiped her eyes I pushed a few damp strands of hair away from her cheek, and walked her outside.

"Let's get away from here," I said. "This can all wait. I'll buy you a cup of coffee or something."

Marian shook her head. "Someone's coming by to help me with this stuff. I have to be here. But you don't."

We were walking out the front door while she said this, and she kept on walking and sat on the running board of the pickup. I sat next to her. She did not slide away.

"Well," Marian said, "you've seen me laugh and seen me cry. My entire repertoire in under an hour."

"I doubt that's your entire repertoire," I told her.

She shifted around to face me, reached over, and brushed the back of her hand against my shoulder.

"Dust," she said.

I'd turned to face her without thinking about it, without reservation about how close we were sitting. I might have been smiling at her. Marian looked like she was about to smile at me. Then the look on her face changed, the corners of her mouth turned down, and her lips grew tight. She looked past my shoulders and moved away from me.

A car had stopped at the curb, a few feet behind the pickup, and a man got out.

He was about our age, tall; a big man, with a broad, square chest, and wide shoulders.

He said, "Looks like I got here just in time," nodded his head at Marian, while at the same time he said to me, "You must be Geoffrey."

Marian said, "I'm sorry. Eliot Wooten, Geoffrey Tremont."

Eliot shook my hand, and quickly turned back to Marian. "I was afraid you wouldn't need me."

"Oh. No," she said. "The stuff's still inside," just before she blew her nose and put my handkerchief in her coat pocket.

Eliot unlatched the back of the pickup, looked at Marian again. He must have just noticed that she had been crying, for there was now an expression of sympathy on his face that was so total that for a moment I thought he suspected himself of causing her tears, then it changed, and there was another expression, one which I was incapable of identifying. As we walked to the house, Eliot looked as though he were in a great hurry to be done with this.

It was when he opened one of the violin cases and picked up the instrument that I noticed Eliot's hands. They were lean, with long, elegant fingers, the kind of hands that made me think he was a musician, which is what I told him.

He said, "The best I can do is 'Chopsticks' on a piano, and barely that. I just wanted to have a look. Marian's the only person Laura trusted to care for it."

"You knew Laura?"

"Sure."

"From before or after she came back?"

"Both," he said. "We all—people around here kept up as best we could with her career. It was kind of surprising that she came back. But you know how it is. You think you're doing something for the short term, and next thing you know it's nine years later and you're still doing it. But hey—" He looked at the boxes of records that Laura had left for me, and the stereo, and offered to help me fit them into my car.

When we were outside, after we'd loaded up my car, and put the violins and the carton with the photographs and scrapbook in the back of the truck, Eliot turned to Marian, and again I couldn't read his expression. He hopped onto the back of the truck bed, pushed the box into a corner, talking while he worked, although I wasn't listening to what he was saying, only to the way that he said it.

There was a noticeable timidity in his voice when he spoke to Marian. A stiff-necked sound, a formality. He reminded me of someone who was watching his step, a man afraid of losing his balance.

It was only after he invited me to be his and Marian's guest for dinner, and Marian said yes, I really should join them, that I realized Eliot was the boyfriend. I managed to grin and say, "Why don't *you* be *my* guests? I'm staying at the Bradford House. Their restaurant looks pretty decent."

"The Bradford?" Eliot said. "Then you have to be our guest." He patted me on the shoulder.

Marian looked pleased by the offer. "Of *course*. You *have* to. Eliot's a part owner of the place."

She gave his arm a squeeze, and it was I who felt like the man a little off balance.

Three

T HE DINING ROOM AT THE BRADFORD HOUSE WAS NOT VERY
large, with a separate pub just beyond a small alcove,
about twenty tables, most of which were occupied,
soft green tablecloths, votive candles. As unassuming as the
rest of Shady Grove.

The menu was better than the standard grilled meats and
fish, and lacked the pretensions of a lot of small town restaurants when they try to mimic big city menus. The service
was quiet and attentive, perhaps because of Eliot's presence,
although there seemed to be a sincere attempt to please.

Most of what we talked about was how difficult Laura's
last year had been. But I was surprised how impersonal
Marian sounded now. She seemed anxious not to say too
much. Nothing more about the life Laura lived in Shady
Grove when she wasn't teaching music. Nothing about Paris
or Laura's marriage. Or about the illness that killed her. Even
when Marian said, "Laura called it ironic payback from sit-

ting in those smoky clubs," she seemed anxious to get that out of the way, interrupted Eliot before he got to speak, and managed to change the subject, telling me that Eliot owned a hardware store in town and, only after I asked, that she and Eliot had been seeing each other for nearly ten years.

Eliot ordered the wine. He told me that their wine list was quite exceptional. By Shady Grove standards, anyway.

After our waiter came back and poured, Eliot raised his glass, watched Marian and me raise ours, and said, "Shady Grove may look like a dull little town, but don't be fooled. It *is* a dull little town."

I was aware that Marian's laugh was not at all as vibrant as it had been when I'd heard it outside Laura's house. And that same caution that I'd heard earlier in Eliot's voice was now in the expression on his face. Even when he made his joke. Had I not known otherwise, I would have thought he and Marian hadn't known each other very long, or very well.

Maybe it was just the way the two of them behaved in front of other people, the way a lot of couples behave when they're with a stranger. There was none of the playfulness and when Marian stroked the top of Eliot's hand and said, "He's a very good magician, you know. For the children at the hospital." She sounded patronizing. It made me uncomfortable to be there. I wanted the Marian I'd been alone with to come back, and for Eliot to go away.

Later, while we were eating, Marian said, "Laura told us you'd been a child star."

"Hardly a star," I said.

"But you *were* an actor."

"That's right."

"That's pretty glamorous stuff," Eliot said.

"Not that glamorous."

"Not glamorous enough," Marian said, "if you left it."

"Or maybe I'm not about glamorous things."

"Is *that* what you're not about."

If we'd been alone, I would have thought that Marian was flirting with me, or at least being more adventurous than I would have expected, unless I misread what I was hearing. I'm apt to do that.

"Sometimes it's just time to quit," I said. "My voice was starting to change. The theater was certainly changing. Nineteen seventy-six was not a vintage year for child actors, and unless I wanted to go out to Hollywood, which my parents were set against, it was time to get out and get educated."

"Didn't you miss it?" Eliot wanted to know.

"Not really."

"And now?"

"I still don't miss it."

"I mean, what do you do now?"

"Voice-overs."

"Like commercials?"

"And cartoons, I mean, *animated features*, and teasers, you know, lead-ins for television. Sometimes movie trailers."

"Have I heard you?"

"Probably."

Eliot asked me to tell him some of the work I'd done, I named some of the accounts. He seemed satisfied with that.

I wanted to buy them after-dinner drinks, so we got up and went into the pub room.

The place was crowded, three deep at the bar, the rich hum of voices, people moving about with drinks in their hands from one circle of talk to another. Eliot started looking around for an empty table, but Marian wanted me to meet a couple of Laura's friends, who were sitting on the opposite side of the room, and Eliot was left there by himself.

The two of us slipped through the crowd to a table in the corner. Marian introduced me to Jennifer Morrison and Kate Callahan, who thanked me for helping Laura. They must have said more than that, but I never heard it. Marian's hand was brushing against my wrist, not quite settling on it, more like warm breath than flesh, and that was all I was aware of. Until Jennifer's voice, or maybe it was Kate's, broke the spell, talking to Marian about spring gardening, Marian asking me if I'd tell Eliot that she'd only be a minute more, and I was walking across the room without her.

Eliot was standing near the bar with four other men, laughing at a joke, coming back with one of his own. He seemed calmer than he'd been when Marian was around. His voice was solid, steady, as though he'd finally found his footing. He introduced me, but all I wanted was time to think about what had just happened between Marian and me, if, in fact, anything had happened at all.

I needed to take inventory of the past few minutes, but Eliot was now walking me to a table by the window, telling me what a great place this was, more like a club than the local bar, really. That it gave people the feeling of belonging.

"It's important to feel part of something," he said. "Don't you think?"

I pressed the tips of my fingers against the spot that Marian had touched, as though I were taking my own pulse.

Yes," I said—I didn't know what I was saying—"that's important."

Once we sat down, Eliot lifted his hand for the waiter, and

asked me what I wanted to drink. I asked shouldn't we wait for Marian. Eliot said there was no telling how long she'd be, besides, he knew what she liked, and ordered her a Grand Marnier.

Maybe that was his way of letting me know who was who in the cast. Anyway, it was enough to stop me from thinking about her.

The television above the bar was dark. There was music playing, but not so loud that we had to talk above it. Eliot said they had live music here on Saturday nights, jazz usually. He used to hope Laura would come in and play, but she never did.

Marian was still talking with her friends when the waiter brought our drinks. Eliot left his drink alone, and I didn't touch mine, either.

"She didn't always do this, you know." He raised his eyes and stared past my shoulder. "Her gardening business. That's what she's probably talking to Jennifer and Kate about. She takes care of their gardens. Theirs and a lot of other people's. She used to do landscaping with her husband." He took a sip of his brandy, waited for me to take a sip of mine. "But she gave that up. She just does gardening now. It must be what she likes doing or she wouldn't be doing it, don't you think?"

I heard Marian's voice before I saw her, and I turned around with a bit more eagerness than her appearance required. She was still approaching us, already apologizing for taking so long, offering a thin smile, looking at neither Eliot nor me. She was about to sit down when a woman a few tables away stood and shouted Marian's name. Marian told us she *really* did have to talk to her about her spring schedule and was very, very sorry, in a way that made it clear that this was not the first evening that had been interrupted like this, and walked away.

"She was crying before, wasn't she?" Eliot asked. "She's very sad about Laura, and I think Laura's death brought back the sad memories about her husband."

"Did you know him?"

Eliot turned his head and nodded toward the front window. "Out there is one of the most beautiful town squares you'll ever see. It was in magazines. Won awards. Buddy designed it. Everyone knew Buddy. He was a hell of a guy." Eliot didn't say this with acrimony, nor like a jealous lover, only with a tone of failure.

ON THE WAY OUT OF TOWN THE FOLLOWING MORNING, I REALIZED what it was that I'd been hearing in Eliot's voice that past evening. It was the voice of a man alone in love.

Four

IF I KEPT A LIST OF PEOPLE WHO MAKE ME FEEL BAD ABOUT myself, Simon Welles would be at the top.

It was the morning after I'd returned from Shady Grove. I was tired from the drive, from carting my inheritance from the parking garage, and when the doorman phoned to tell me that Simon was in the lobby I could have sent him away, but we did share some history, and he was Laura's brother, so I let him come up.

He looked about twenty-five. Of course he was much older than that. He had wild, curly blond hair, a subtle suntan, and a quick smile that was not, as I recalled, necessarily a sign of amusement or pleasure. But what was most noticeable were his clothes, his thin cotton shirt, his light khakis. The wrong clothes for the wrong climate.

I asked him what he wanted and why he came to see me.

"Why shouldn't I? Maybe I want to reminisce."

He walked into the living room, and I followed him. He

started toward one of the chairs, changed his mind, walked over to the window, and stood looking outside. I could see Central Park over his shoulder. Even with the sun shining, the trees and everything around them looked dreary and gray.

"You wouldn't happen to have a cigarette?" Simon kept his back to me.

"I don't smoke."

"Of course you don't." He stayed at the window. "The last time we met, you let me sleep on your couch."

"Pass out," I said. "As I recall."

"Do you also *recall* the occasion?"

"It was the day your sister got married."

"The day *after*. You were very understanding. You gave me twenty-five dollars. I was broke and you felt sorry for me, coming all the way to New York for Laura's wedding just to be a day late."

"Not so understanding. You asked for fifty."

He leaned his hip against the wall, hands in his pockets. I sat on the arm of the chair.

"My only sister is dead." He kept his face turned toward the window. "She made *you* her executor. The last time I spoke with her she said if I had any questions about her will to ask you." He turned to me now and showed that smile.

"When was that?"

"When I saw her. Last year sometime."

"You came a long way just to ask me about your sister's will. You could have phoned."

"What makes you think I hadn't planned on coming to New York anyway?" Then he looked himself over, shrugged, and said, "You wouldn't have any coffee around, would you?"

"Not made."

"Never mind. By the time you made it, I wouldn't be in the mood. Has anyone called, asking for me?" His eyes never stopped moving while he spoke, looking at the wall, the floor, at his watch, at me, then out the window again.

"Why would anyone call *me* looking for *you*?"

"Oh, I gave your number to a few friends," he said, and still looking out the window he told me, "I want to stay in my sister's house."

"I have nothing to do with that. Talk to her lawyer."

"I went to high school with him. He's a moron."

He stared outside a little longer, said, "She was my *sister*," walked past me, into the foyer. "If someone named Howie Greenberg calls, if *anyone* calls, I was never here."

He opened the front door. "This apartment is too big for one person. You must get very lonely here," and Simon let himself out.

For the past twenty years, I hadn't given Simon Welles any thought. I used to tell myself that all the blame was his because of what he'd done to Laura during our college days, the way he'd treated her. But I felt no more generous toward him now than I had then, which was why I tried not to give him any more thought after he left my apartment.

I did think about my girlfriend, Rita, about calling her, but I didn't want to see her just yet. Most of that day, I thought about Laura and, when I could no longer hold myself back, Marian. It occurred to me that I was having the fantasy life of a teenager.

❧

Three days later, I still hadn't called Rita. She'd left me a voice mail the day after I'd come back home, but I was in no mood to see her.

I was still thinking about Marian. Sometimes, I'd imagine meeting her by chance in a restaurant here in town, she with her friends, me with mine, in one of the places I like to go for cocktails. She'd be seated at a small table. I wouldn't notice her at first, not until I heard her laugh, and when I looked over, she'd be there. Then I changed the scenario: She was meeting *me* for drinks. It was our first date. I'd be early and already seated. I'd turn toward the front of the restaurant and Marian would be walking in, and even though she'd never been there before, she looked like she'd been coming there forever, because Marian impressed me as someone who never looked awkward or out of her element; and even though I was as familiar with this place as I was with my own apartment, being with Marian changed all that. It was like I'd never been there before. Not until Marian walked in.

This was a hell of a thing to imagine, romantic fantasies about a woman whom I hardly knew, who was another man's girlfriend.

Not that all I did was moon about Marian. I had a lot to keep me busy those three days: Twelve hours at the recording studio. An evening at the theater with friends. Lunch with a new account. Drinks with some Hollywood people, who were considering me for the voice of a cat. Drinks, this time with friends, and dinner. And an evening with my brother, Alex, who had returned from a spa looking uncharacteristically relaxed, and in formidable good humor.

I would not say that my brother had an inordinate amount of secrets, and while I was never loath to speak my mind with him, I was also aware that there were limits to just how much he was willing to tell me of his personal life and his relationships. Even a vacation at a desert spa was off-limits, but this night Alex appeared ready to step up to the microphone and take questions. To ask him to cede center stage just to hear about my *affaires de coeur* would have been not only inconsiderate and insulting, but annihilating in a way that my brother, a psychiatrist, would have understood and resented. Plus, there were few things more enjoyable than listening to Alex when he was in the mood to puncture inflated egos.

He gave a thorough and piquant rundown of "the small coven of middlebrow narcissists and their idyll among the cacti. Self-absorbed, self-entitled . . . Fortunately, they preferred their own company. Sort of like volunteers for a chain gang." He put his hand on my shoulder and gave it a firm squeeze. "But really, it was *very* pleasant, even if I did feel that any minute Virgil was about to appear and point out the more *attractive* accommodations of this southwest ring of hell." He looked quite satisfied with himself after he said this.

We were in a taxi, on our way to supper with our aunt Sukie, our father's younger sister and our only blood relative still living in the city. We were both quite fond of her, and Alex liked to make sure that we saw her at least every month.

Traffic was slow that night, but I didn't feel impatient. I was glad to spend the extra time with my brother.

"Did you meet anyone?" I wanted to know.

"The man of my dreams? Afraid not, my friend. Although I did manage to shake five pounds off my ass, and have a pretty good time." He leaned forward and checked on the lack of progress on the street. "And, by next week, I'll be my miserable old self again, and it will be as if I'd never gone away." He turned toward me. "You know what I'd really like? I'd like to come home at the end of the day and someone's waiting for me. Someone whose company I like, and who likes mine." He smiled. "Otherwise it's all just distraction."

That wasn't the first time he'd told me this. I don't know if I was going to say anything, or what it would have been, but Alex raised a finger to stop me. "*You* are in no position to talk to *anyone* about relationships."

I knew that tone of voice. It always made me think of tweed rubbing against bare skin, and whatever I'd have said, whatever I might have offered, Alex would have turned to me with a look of antipathy, as though I'd not only exacerbated what he was feeling, but confirmed his lowest opinion of himself, and would I please just disappear. But that passed. Alex was smiling again, saying, "Tell me what happened in Shady Grove."

I told him about some of it, and asked him to tell me what he remembered about Laura.

"I met her your senior year, right?"

"Was it?"

"She was really quite stunning. And she spoke impeccable French."

"You *remember* that?"

"She eloped with a jazz musician, didn't she?"

Traffic started moving a little faster, and when we were a few blocks farther along, I told Alex about Marian, and he told me he wasn't in the least surprised.

"She falls into your three basic food groups, doesn't she."

"Only two."

"Three." He counted on his fingers: "You're attracted to a woman who's got a boyfriend, which, along with your own, shall we say, *situation* with Rita, poses no threat of your actually having a relationship with her. Two: Since you can't act on your infatuation—"

"It goes *deeper* than infatuation."

"It still makes her and your feelings about her ultimately disposable."

I couldn't argue with him, so all I said was, "I guess I'd just better forget about her."

"And forgetting about her is the *third*."

IT WAS AFTER ONE IN THE MORNING WHEN ALEX DROPPED ME OFF. The phone started ringing as soon as I was in my apartment. It was Simon's Howie Greenberg, wanting to know if Simon was there—but not before apologizing for calling so late. He was in L.A., and the time difference had confused him.

When I said that Simon wasn't here, Howie told me, "Well, if you're smart, you won't believe a word he says"—his voice wasn't loud but it was firm—"or you'll never get rid of him."

I was about to hang up.

"And whatever you do"—his voice was louder now—"don't *sign* anything."

I told him I'd be sure not to, and again was about to hang up, when I heard him yell for me to wait. "And tell the little fuck I want the two months' rent he owes me and the seventy dollars he *stole* from my wallet. Oh yes." And the line went dead.

Early the following morning Simon called. He said it was urgent that he see me. I told him I was still in bed.

"By the way, one of your *friends* called. Howie Greenberg."

"What did he say?"

"Why the hell do you do these things to yourself? You're better than that." I hung up and went back to sleep.

I'd told Alex that I might as well forget about Marian, but I could not forget about her. Not that I did anything about it, except go on imagining meeting her places, spending the night at my apartment, or a weekend at one of the little boutique hotels in town. Maybe an entire week, showing her the city, hearing her laughter, seeing the same expression on her face that I'd seen the first time; and feeling the agitation of attraction, when her hand might touch my wrist as it did that night; all the nerve-wracking uncertainties of a new romance.

But I was really no better than Alex's narcissists. Marian's closest friend had died, and the best I could do was flirt with her and indulge an infatuation. Worse, the *fantasy* of an infatuation. I never really stopped being aware of that. Yet, I still kept thinking about her. Even when I was with my girlfriend, Rita D'Angellis, the *situation* to which Alex referred.

A FEW NIGHTS AFTER I SAW ALEX, RITA AND I HAD DINNER AT A small Vietnamese restaurant on the Upper East Side, sharing a plate of salt and pepper squid and a couple of beers, a ritual of ours.

Rita and I had been seeing each other for about three years in what we both considered as exclusive a relationship as either of us was interested in having. Rita edited cookbooks for a large publishing house, and whatever restaurant we went to, the staff knew her and made a fuss. It was always a good time.

After dinner she asked me where I'd been. I started to answer that she knew I was going up to Shady Grove.

She said, "No. I mean tonight. *All* night. You've been somewhere else." I said I wasn't aware of my mind being on anything other than her and she told me, "Just know that it's showing." She took a short swallow of beer, leaned forward, and grinned at me.

"Do you remember the first time you heard the word *dysfunctional?*"

I didn't.

"The first time I heard it was back in the eighties, when I was a summer intern over at Doubleday. I was reading a submission, one of those memoirs that people were writing back then. The writer referred to her mother, who was *horrid*, by the way, as 'dysfunctional,' and that word's always had a very negative connotation for me ever since. But sometimes it's not so bad." She refilled her glass. "I'd say *we* have a dysfunctional relationship, and it's worked out well for both of us."

"Dysfunctional."

"You sit here with your mind somewhere else, maybe you're thinking about your work, maybe you're thinking about how bored you are and would rather be somewhere else. Who knows? Most women would be offended, hurt even, but I'm not. I don't take it personally. If you wanted to tell me what you're thinking, you'd tell me. And if it were reversed, you'd just let me have my moment, and we'd go on from there."

"That's how we like it," I said.

"It's how we like it." Rita wasn't speaking much louder than a whisper, but she must have thought she was, because she lowered her voice even more and leaned closer to me. "I'd say that's pretty dysfunctional, at least compared to what most people want."

"I didn't realize you'd given it this much thought."

"Not that much, actually. It just came to me."

IT WAS ABOUT FOUR IN THE MORNING. WE WERE IN BED, IN RITA'S apartment. Rita was asleep, one bare leg stretched outside the covers, her breath warm on my face. I enjoyed looking at her tall, lean body, all graceful angles, always so responsive. We'd never gone through that period of adjustment that begins most relationships. We never commented on it, either. We simply enjoyed each other, and took that for granted from the start, much the way we took for granted our being to-gether; never any spasms of doubt and worry if the phone didn't answer, or if a week went by and we hadn't seen each other or spoken—I was pretty sure that Rita went out with other men from time to time. I occasionally went out with other women, although neither of us was stupid or reckless enough to be promiscuous.

Rita turned in her sleep. I could smell the night on her skin. I let my lips touch the texture of her hair. The covers slipped away. I could see her body exposed in shades of black and white. The bend of her arm, the tilt of her neck. I thought how everything about her was lean and spare. Her apartment, her life. And I liked that. I liked Rita, liked being with her. Yet, if I woke in the morning and she'd already gone to work, it wouldn't have bothered me that she'd left without saying good-bye. If I didn't wake up in time to see her leave, Rita wouldn't have been at all bothered by that, either. If, right then, I'd decided to get dressed and go back to my apartment, Rita might be surprised that I wasn't there when she woke up, but she wouldn't have been troubled by it. It was being unattached to each other that kept us together.

I'd thought about this before, but not in a long time. I wouldn't have that night if Rita hadn't mentioned it. But as I lay there I realized that I wanted to miss Rita when I left in the morning and I knew I wouldn't. I wanted her to miss me. I wanted my happiness to balance and be balanced by the happiness of a woman I loved.

Five

T HE FOLLOWING DAY, A SMALL PACKAGE ARRIVED AT MY apartment with the handkerchief Marian had borrowed, clean and folded, with a note thanking me, saying she wished we could have met under happier circumstances.

I held the handkerchief up to my nose, and inhaled the scent of Marian's laundry soap, pressed it against my cheek for a moment, then carefully refolded it, as though it no longer belonged to me. When I left my apartment a few minutes later, the handkerchief was in the inside pocket of my sports coat.

It was a bright afternoon, warm for the first week in April. I started walking to the corner of Seventieth Street, when I heard someone call my name. I turned and saw Simon sitting behind the wheel of a caramel-colored Mercedes, an SL280, early '70s. His arm was resting on the window frame, his chin was resting on his arm. He had a day's beard and he looked tired.

"Get in," he said, "and I'll drop you off."

"I'm going around the corner."

"I'll take you."

I thanked him, but no.

"I tried to come up to see you, but your doorman wouldn't announce me. Did Howie scare you that much?"

"What's on your mind?"

"I want to talk to you."

I told him I could live without that. He got out of the car, anyway, without bothering to roll up the window.

I noticed that he was wearing the same clothes he'd worn two weeks before. He reached across the front seat, pulled out a gray overcoat, and put it on. The coat was too large for him. He wrapped it around his body like a robe.

I started walking away. He came with me.

"Buy me a cup of coffee," he said.

"You better not leave your car there. It'll get towed."

"It's not my car."

"It's *some*body's car."

I kept on walking and he stayed with me.

He asked, "What happened to my sister's things?" a little out of breath.

"What things?"

"Don't be an asshole."

"She didn't own much, and what she did she bequeathed to people."

"What people?"

"Why do I think you're playing me?"

"Look, I just need a little closure here. And since you're re-sponsible for taking care of her . . . *possessions*—" We turned the corner onto Madison Avenue. Simon nodded at the coffee shop across the street. "A cup of coffee. Come on."

After we went in and sat down, and Simon ordered a cappuccino, he said, "It was completely by accident that I even found out Laura was sick. The day before I came out here Remsen called and told me she'd died. Can you imagine?"

"I thought you'd seen her in Shady Grove. You said you even spoke to her about the will."

He watched the waitress put down the cup, stirred in a spoonful of sugar, all the while keeping the spoon from touching the rim. I noticed the sweet effeminacy in the way he did this, the way he sat, angled snugly in the corner of the booth, the overcoat still wrapped around his body. When he looked at me, there was a slight turn to his mouth, as though his smile were warming in the wings. When he saw me watching him, he flashed it at me. I imagined it was this same smile that had gotten him into the driver's seat of the Mercedes, and I wondered if he expected it to get him inside his sister's house.

"I missed her wedding, and I missed her funeral."

"Maybe you can ask Marian," I told him. "Maybe she'll help you."

"Marian? Marian Thayer?"

"Ballantine."

"As in *Buddy* Ballantine?"

"You were never up in Shady Grove. You never saw Laura or spoke with her," I said. "She never told you to get in touch with me."

"I beg your pardon?"

"You were lying to me."

Simon didn't even flinch at this, and he didn't bother with an answer. "I saw them when they came out to the Coast to play some of the clubs," he said. "Laura and Steve. They were so in love, I found it unbearable."

"Stop being evasive," I told him. "Tell me what you want."

It was a few minutes after two, the lunchtime crunch was finished, and only three or four people were sitting in booths and at the counter. Simon's eyes never stopped moving, looking around at each person as though he was expecting to see someone he knew—or hoping he wouldn't—looking out the window at the street, then past my head in the direction of the front door. Then at me.

"I'd really like to see my sister's house, some of her things. Before you give them away."

"I'm not giving anything away. Ask Remsen. I have nothing to do—"

"I'm sure you don't know what you're talking about. Do you know that *Remsen* didn't let me go to her funeral? The son of a bitch kept me away."

"How could he keep you away?"

Simon lifted the cup, looked into it, and put it down. "By not telling me she died until it was all over." He took a quick peek past my head. "Did you get to look through Laura's stuff?"

"Let me understand this. You ran out on your roommate, came to New York without any money and apparently no change of clothes, all because you want *what*?"

"Another cappuccino." He was speaking to the waitress now. "I can only wonder what they—" He watched the waitress walk away, didn't quite sit up, but pulled himself, just a little bit, out of the corner. "I don't want anything. Not from *you*. I only want to go to my sister's house one last time, look at some of the things that belonged to her, just to get some closure."

"The last time I saw you, you were running away. My guess is you're running away from something now."

"Because I want to spend a little time at my sister's house?"

"Wouldn't it be easier to leave this alone?"

"Now who's being evasive?"

"I know you're after some*thing* because chances are some-one's after *you*. You know what I'm talking about. Howie Greenberg calling in the middle of the night? That car?"

"Don't lecture me about my life." Simon glanced down at his hands, just for a moment. "God forbid I should have any feelings about my sister. That I might actually want some small token—"

"Contest the will, if you want."

"This is going to take more than a cappuccino." He made eye contact with the waitress and asked for a menu. "These people—look, Geoffrey—oh crap." He sat up and leaned forward.

The waitress came to take Simon's order, I asked for a fresh cup of coffee.

"You and I were never friends," I told him. "I'm not your friend now."

"What do you know about Laura and Steve?"

"Your sister entrusted me to take care of her estate. Not to take care of you."

"That's not all she entrusted you to do."

"Do you *ever* know what you're talking about?"

"Do *you* ever know what I'm talking about?"

"You're acting like this is the first time we've met. Like I have no recollection of you. And I'm looking at you and seeing what an irresponsible mess you are. And I don't think that's much of a change since the last time I saw you. Tell me I'm wrong."

The waitress brought over my coffee, and placed the sandwich Simon had ordered on the table. Simon gave it slow consideration and before he took a bite, he said, "You're a very abrasive person, Geoffrey." He bit into his sandwich. "I grew *up* with these people. I don't need you. I can go there without you."

"So go."

He took another bite of his sandwich. "Whether you like it or not, you and I have history together."

"We have no history."

"I was hoping you'd be a lot more rational about her."

"What are you talking about? Can't you just follow a conversation?"

Simon went on eating, and when he stopped he was staring at me, probably because I was staring at him. I could see Laura in his face. The high cheekbones, the soft, full mouth, even the way he lowered and raised his eyes, and that made me think of the times Laura and I had sat in coffee shops like this one. And I didn't know which was more unsettling, that I was missing Laura or that seeing her in Simon's face made me feel sorry for him and how pitiful he looked.

Just for a moment I wanted to help him with whatever he was after, or whatever trouble he was in; but my impulse to get involved with him did not last.

Simon was staring at that spot behind my head again. "You're a lot more like Laura than you think."

"Meaning?"

"She went back to Shady Grove. For Christ sake."

"Her husband died—"

"School's out. Get the fuck on with it." He wiped his mouth. "You really should know what you're dealing with." He pushed his empty plate to the corner of the table. "I've got to get out of here." He left me to pay the check.

When I walked outside, Simon was smoking a cigarette and looking into the window of a clothing store.

"You didn't get what you wanted," he said.

"I didn't want anything."

"You were going around the corner. I assumed it was to get something."

I crossed the street and left Simon blowing a mouthful of smoke at his reflection.

All that I wanted was to get away by myself. Fly down to a beach somewhere, sit in the sun and drink cold beer. I wanted to be a stranger to everyone I met, and not have to know about other people's lives and their inconsolable sorrows.

THAT SAME NIGHT, I WENT OUT FOR DRINKS AND SUPPER WITH MY agent, Roberta; my friend Nancy Shapiro, a partner with an ad agency here in town; and Nick and Amy Brennan, whom I'd known for a couple of years. I'd always liked when the five of us got together, but tonight felt different.

We met at Keens, over on Thirty-sixth Street. Roberta mentioned my trip to Shady Grove, and all they wanted to talk about was how mysterious it was, how fascinating.

Nick and Amy knew someone-who-knew-someone who'd had a similar experience not too long ago, and found out that he was the father of a child he'd never known about. Was it possible that Laura and I . . . Could there be a diary hidden in the house that explained Laura's reasons . . . Was she secretly in love with me and could that be the meaning to the music she'd left . . . Maybe one of the violins was a Stradivarius and worth millions, or both of them . . . Maybe Laura had stashed money somewhere in the house. I should have looked around . . .

Some other time I might have appreciated this, even added my own speculation. Their talk would have amused me. Tonight it sounded frivolous and disrespectful. A violation of Laura's death. I wanted to talk to people who'd known her when she lived in Paris, who'd known the two of us when we were in college, and not have to listen to my friends joke about a woman they did not know and about whom they knew nothing; and while they went on telling me all the things they thought Laura may have hidden away in her house, the things she may have intended when she asked me to help her, I thought about some of things I could have told them about Laura Welles.

It was no accident that Simon once spent a night on my couch all those years ago, and it wasn't because he was late for Laura's wedding, nor was it a matter of my largesse. It was more a matter of his being misled about the details. I never liked what Laura and I did to him that day, but she was my good friend, and I helped her, although it meant that I didn't go to Laura's wedding, either, which was something I would have done otherwise.

Simon had come to town not the day after, but on Laura's wedding day, unannounced, running away from someone or something, which was not unusual as far as I knew, and what I'd come to know about Simon before I'd ever met him I knew from Laura. My impressions of him, my opinions, were made of Laura's impressions and her opinions, like seeing Simon's reflection in the store window, and no more substantial. Laura never told me much about their childhood. To me, Simon was just Laura's beautiful younger brother, a talented seventeen-year-old being groomed for a career in ballet. Laura raved about him the first time I met her.

But I'd only seen him once or twice, the whisk of his body hurrying up and down the stairs, when Laura and I lived in the same building.

It was during our junior year. Laura and I liked to meet at least once a week after classes at a coffee shop on upper Broadway. One afternoon, when it was still winter, she told me that Simon was coming to the city for the weekend. She was hoping Simon would follow her to New York when he graduated high school, and she wanted to show him around Juilliard. She was very excited about my finally meeting her brother.

Laura borrowed one of my futons to sleep on so Simon could have her bed. She'd bought fresh flowers and groceries.

I didn't see or hear from Laura that entire weekend. I went down to her apartment Monday night. When she opened the door, the futon was rolled up against the wall.

Simon had shown up at her apartment late Friday morning, in wrinkled clothes and in need of a shower. He offered an unenthusiastic hello, dropped his shabby overnight bag in the living room, and was about to leave when Laura grabbed him and sat him down. He seemed distracted, wouldn't tell her what was bothering him.

Laura told me that she'd managed to convince Simon to clean up and have lunch in the apartment with her. She started talking about the things they might do that day and for the rest of the weekend, but Simon cut her off, said he had an appointment downtown, and he'd be back in a few hours. Laura waited for him the rest of the afternoon, all that night, and all day Saturday. Simon still hadn't shown. When he walked in on Sunday morning, his eyes were bloodshot, he smelled of stale beer. He wouldn't say where he'd been or tell Laura what was going on. He lay on her bed and slept for the rest of the day. Early Monday morning while Laura was still sleeping, Simon took the bus back to Shady Grove.

Laura called her parents that same morning, but they didn't seem at all upset. They assured Laura that Simon was going through one of those sulky teenage phases and would grow out of it by summer.

Laura didn't talk to me again about Simon and I didn't ask questions. I knew if Laura wanted to talk to me about her brother she didn't need my invitation. And that same year, she'd met Steve, and Simon and his problems seemed to fade into the background.

If Laura did mention her family at all it wasn't to talk about Simon. Her parents were not at all happy to hear that their daughter was seeing a jazz pianist, twelve years her senior. They had not, her father reminded Laura, sent her to Juilliard so that she could waste her talents on jazz and a jazz musician. It was bad enough that Simon was being so selfish, Laura had better stop thinking only of herself and come to her senses. They insisted that she end the relationship. Laura insisted that she would not.

Laura told me that she felt as though her parents were asking her to make a choice, and it wasn't an artistic choice of jazz or classical music, but choosing them over Steve.

It was during the autumn of our senior year that Simon showed up again. One night after a gig at a club down in the Village, Laura brought Steve and a few of his friends back to her apartment to wind down. Simon appeared at the door, looking ragged, he'd been drinking and was apparently too high to notice that there were other people there besides Laura, or what he was interrupting. He did manage to stagger into the living room, knock over a few glasses and plates, get sick in the bathroom, and pass out on Laura's bed.

In the morning, Simon told Laura that he'd dropped out of college and was running away. He didn't explain why he'd dropped out. He wouldn't answer any of Laura's questions. Laura doubted that it would do much good for her to go back home with him, but she would face down her parents for both of them, if Simon would only talk to her about what was troubling him. All Simon would tell her was that he knew he was letting her down, letting their parents down, and what he wanted was to be left alone, damn it. And he walked out of the apartment.

Laura told me it wasn't only Simon who was letting down her parents. It was breaking her heart knowing that her parents were disappointed with her, and to hear the disapproval in their voices. And it was breaking her heart to see her brother so lost and troubled. She was frustrated and angry with her entire family. Simon wouldn't let Laura help him and he was incapable of helping himself. Her parents wouldn't try to be less rigid and allow that Laura's needs and passions were separate from theirs.

I told her she wasn't accountable for anyone else's happiness but her own. She was twenty-two, for Christ sake, and that was too young to feel responsible for solving everyone's problems, or to be made to think she could. Her parents and Simon shouldn't be laying this all on her. At least, that's what I remember telling her.

That same year, Simon came to Laura's apartment three more times. He'd always been drinking, and never wanted to talk. He'd just drop off his overnight bag, the few times he brought one, leave, and when he came back, usually early the following morning, he'd pass out on the couch, or make it no farther than the living room floor.

He never said where he'd been, never said where he was going. All that Laura knew was what she saw. And now she couldn't even talk to her parents about him.

The last time Laura told me about Simon was also the last time she saw him.

It was early spring, our senior year. Laura said it was a typical Simon appearance.

Unannounced and uninvited. He was twenty years old by then, and nothing about him had changed much, boozy breath and bloodshot eyes. He did tell her that he hadn't seen their parents for nearly a year.

It was this visit when Simon got into the trouble Remsen had referred to when he called me that morning in March. He'd taken three blank checks from Laura's checkbook, made out payments to himself, forged her signature, and cashed the checks, overdrawing against her account, and bouncing all three. This was, of course, before the Internet and online banking. It took days for Laura's bank statement to come in the mail. Laura didn't find out until a week after Simon had left the city.

We were sitting in her apartment when she told me this, when she said it, it was as though a stranger had been visiting her these past few years and not her brother. Simon had not only embarrassed her in front of her friends and Steve, she said, but had stolen money from her. And how could he not know that he'd destroyed whatever bond they'd had. She said she could never trust him again.

That was the last time I heard Laura talk about Simon. Until her wedding day.

It was Commencement Week for Juilliard and Columbia. My parents were in town for a few days leading up to my graduation, and the day after, so I didn't get to see Laura until her commencement. I went with Steve.

A few days later, Laura was married in a no-frills City Hall ceremony, just a few friends, late in the morning. I was dressed, about to leave my apartment and meet the bride and groom downtown, when I heard someone banging on Laura's apartment door. I stepped outside, looked down from the top of the stairs, and knew at once it was Laura's younger brother, ragged, disheveled, slamming his fist against the door, kicking it, hollering for Laura to open the hell up and let him in.

I walked to the edge of the landing and told him Laura wasn't home. The first thing Simon Welles ever said to me was to mind my own fucking business. His words were slurred, his eyes half-closed. I repeated that his sister wasn't home. She'd gotten married the day before and had already left for her honeymoon.

Later, I would tell myself that Simon had brought my response on himself, otherwise I would have told him the truth. But truth is temporal, fastened to temperament, determined by disposition. I wanted to believe that what I'd decided in that moment was not premeditated, that I was already predisposed and had chosen Laura's side, and no matter what Simon had said to me that morning, or anything else he might have done, I would have told him that lie. I knew that Laura had not told him about her wedding, that she wouldn't want him there. That's what I told myself that morning, watching Simon staring at the closed door, seeing his disconsolate expression. That I was protecting my friend. That was my truth.

It was a hot morning. Simon was wearing a soiled and wrinkled tropical shirt that he hadn't bothered to tuck in, over faded jeans, and scuffed loafers. He was smaller than I'd imagined, about five six or seven, thin, unshaved. But even in those dirty clothes and three days' beard, there was no hiding that he was a beautiful boy.

He turned and leaned his back against the wall, wrapped his arms around himself, looked at me, and wanted to know just who the hell I was and how the hell did I know so much about his sister. He walked up the stairs toward me while he said this, introduced himself, mumbling his name. When I told him mine and that I was Laura's friend, he stepped around me, pushed on my apartment door, and went inside.

I was already calculating how long it would take me to get downtown by cab or if I still had time to take the subway, and said that I had an appointment and I wasn't going to leave him alone in my apartment and he'd have to leave now.

He walked across the floor, saying more to himself than to me that he couldn't believe that he'd missed Laura by one lousy day, and how could that happen? He said he couldn't believe his life. I told him again that he'd have to leave, put my hand on his shoulder, and started leading him to the door. He shook me off, sat on my couch, asked me if my air conditioner was working, and I told him that there was no reason to turn it on, I was on my way out and so was he.

His body sagged and he told me that none of this should have been any surprise, and covered his face with his hands. I had the very uncomfortable feeling that Simon was crying. He asked me if I would mind leaving the room. I pointed out that this was a studio apartment—*my* studio apartment—and I sure as hell wasn't going to sit in the bathroom.

He raised his head and looked about as miserable as Laura had described him, then turned and stretched himself across the couch. He said this was the worst day of his life, he couldn't think clearly, and would I please just let him stay there until he could get his head straight.

I was starting to wonder how the hell I was going to get rid of him, when the phone rang. It was Laura, telling me I'd better hurry or I was going to be late. I managed to let her know that my friend Simon had dropped by and I didn't think I could keep our appointment. I remember the sound of her breathing at the other end. She asked me if Simon knew where she was and I said no. She asked me to please not let him ruin her wedding. I said I was sure that wasn't going to happen. Laura thanked me and hung up.

When I looked back at Simon, he was sitting up, shaking his head and asking me if there was any way he could get in touch with Laura, did I know when she was coming back.

He started pacing the floor. I told him again that he had to leave, which sent him back to the couch, where he sat down and glared at me, pushing his hands through his hair, his eyes red with tears now. He wanted to know if Laura told me anything about him, and what a complete wreck he was. I didn't answer. He said he really couldn't bear to be alone right now and would I mind just sitting with him for a few more minutes.

He asked me if I'd ever felt like I'd fallen into a hole and didn't know how to find my way out. Then he stretched across my couch again, and fell asleep. I tried to wake him but he wouldn't open his eyes, wouldn't move.

I had taken Laura's side because she was my friend, and I didn't doubt the rightness of what I was doing. But Simon was just a frail lost kid, all alone. I took off my jacket and lay it across his shoulders, took off my tie, kicked off my shoes, and turned on the air conditioner and sat in the chair, while Simon slept on the couch.

It wasn't until long after dark that I managed to wake Simon. I got him out of my apartment only after I explained that the couch was a pullout bed and only one of us was going to sleep in it tonight and it was going to be me.

I watched him walk down the stairs. He stopped for a moment and stared at Laura's apartment door, a sorry-looking kid in rumpled summer clothes. Then walked down the next flight of stairs and out to the street.

I'd missed the small party Steve's and Laura's friends had for her, but I did see the bride and groom the following day, gave them their present, and took them out for supper. Just the three of us. Laura asked me about Simon and about my day with him, and I told her all about it. It was a solemn evening.

The next day she and Steve flew to Chicago for their first gig as a married couple.

THAT NIGHT AT KEENS, I COULD HAVE ALSO TOLD MY FRIENDS HOW Laura learned to speak such impeccable French. She'd spent

the summer after her junior year in Paris with Steve, playing jazz, playing house in his apartment in the Marais. Her
mother and father forbade her from going. I remembered her
telling me they could forbid it but they couldn't prevent it.
That was the last time I heard Laura talk about her parents.

Not that any of this was important. What *was* important
was this: I wanted to touch whatever it was that had made
Laura and me close friends, what had made us trust each
other. I wanted to touch the quality of her person. I wanted to
feel what it had felt like when we were students, and what it
felt like to hang out with her, to feel the pleasure of her friendship, the texture of those times, the content of her being. But
there was something within me, an emotional indigence,
which made this impossible, and which I now found uncomfortable and inconvenient.

Later that evening, when I was alone in my apartment,
I wasn't thinking about Laura, but about Marian standing
outside Laura's house, and what Alex had said about distrac-
tions. I felt that urge to get away. Not to a remote beach somewhere, sitting alone in the sand with a cold beer. I wanted to
drive up to Shady Grove.

Six

ABOUT FIVE MILES NORTH OF SHADY GROVE, JUST OFF County Road 8, a dirt road cuts through a state forest. Alone on the four miles of this road was the bluestone driveway, just as they'd told me at the gas station.

A few yards from the bottom of that driveway, along a growth of woods, was an old barn and, parked in front of it, the yellow pickup. A long flagstone path curved left from the barn leading to the side porch of Marian's house, an old farmhouse with a small, oval flower bed fanning out and away from the side porch, stretching to four larger flower beds.

About fifteen feet from the right of the house, a smooth lawn opened to a woodland park, and I could see winding paths, hedges, deep stands of trees and gardens of various sizes that seemed to expand rather than recede toward an expansive vanishing point, like a phantasmagoria. I wondered if it was one of these gardens that Marian had described that day when I fell in love with her outside Laura's house.

Marian must have heard my car pull up. She was stepping off the porch just as I started walking across the driveway. She wore faded jeans and a gray sweater the color of pale smoke. Her hands were in her pockets. When she said hello, she sounded neither surprised nor displeased to see me.

I could have made up a dozen excuses for my coming there, but I told her the truth.

"I haven't stopped thinking about you since we met," I said. "And it's scaring the hell out of me."

Marian smiled at me, turned her head toward the house, and said, "Let's go in."

I followed her to the side porch and into the kitchen. She invited me to sit, and we sat facing each other across the table.

There was a small desk to the left of my shoulder, above it on the wall a picture of a man who I assumed was Buddy, tan and aesthetic—not the way I'd imagined him—lying face-up on a white-sand beach.

There was a shelf with cookbooks next to the door leading to the pantry, and above it a round clock that read four-thirty.

I looked at the arrangements of platters and ceramic pitchers on the shelves of the corner cupboard, the two framed watercolors on the wall next to a window, then I looked only at Marian, at the way her hair was parted on the side and swept across her forehead, like a boy's, and which would have been too masculine except for her eyes, which revealed a deep femininity. I may have noticed this before, but that was the first time I was aware that they were not the kind of eyes you could look at in haste. You had to take some time to see them, see the depth within them and her interest in what was happening.

Her chin was a put-up-or-shut-up chin. And I wanted to be sitting with her in a restaurant in the city, in a dark corner booth, just the two of us telling each other cautionary tales because we both were aware of what was at stake, even if there was really nothing left to lose.

And then, I wasn't thinking about anything, except how happy I was to be seeing her, and all I wanted was to be there with Marian.

She leaned forward and rested her hands on the table. I could smell her perfume. She looked at me as though she were making a calculation. It was the sort of expression that, if I'd known her better, would have made me ask what she was thinking, but I met her eyes with silence.

We stayed like that for a moment longer, before Marian asked, "What do you want?" in a way that was neither challenging nor inhospitable. "I don't mean right this second. I mean— You don't need me to tell you what I mean."

"I have a girlfriend in New York," I told her, "who's smart and attractive, and who likes that we don't live together, that we don't want to get married and are too old to have children. When I get back to the city, she won't even know I was gone. Or if she does, she won't ask me where I've been. She's been my girlfriend for three years. Until a few weeks ago, *that's* what I wanted."

"What does that have to do with me?"

"Because I don't want that anymore." I leaned a little closer. "I want to know what you like for breakfast on a rainy Sunday. And what your hair smells like in summer. I want to hear your laughter at the funny parts of a movie and tell me what kind of day you had because that's what we do. I want to know what it's like to kiss you over and over again. And it's driving me crazy to think that will never happen because you think what you have is enough for you."

Marian had been leaning closer while I said this, and when she spoke, her voice didn't sound all that firm. She moistened her lips with the tip of her tongue before she said, "I *have* what I want. You've met my boyfriend, and I get along with him just fine. I have my business, and this house that I come back to every day. That, Geoffrey, is enough for me. And— why should you care so much about what is or isn't right for me?" Before I could say anything more, she said, "You're not one of those people who gets a charge out of complicating other people's lives, are you?" She still seemed to be having trouble finding her voice.

"I don't want to complicate anything."

"Because one thing I don't want to do is complicate my life."

"You mean, what you don't want *me* to do is complicate your life."

"That's what I said."

"No. You said the one thing *you* don't want to do."

"Either way." The expression on her face made me think of the way she had looked standing in the middle of Laura's living room.

"What I want right now," I said, "is to hear you tell me what it's going to look like outside in the summer. And tell me slowly, so I can memorize your voice. And I want to come back here and see your gardens with you."

Marian stood up, walked around the table, and stood behind me. I turned my head and saw her hands resting on the back of my chair. She'd moved a little closer to me now, and I could feel the soft warmth of her torso near the back of my neck.

She said, "Summer is still a long way off. But I'll tell you. If you like."

I turned my head toward her. Her face looked a little flushed.

I told her, "Yes. I'd like that very much." My voice wasn't any firmer than hers.

She took a step around and leaned her hip against the side of the chair. "You probably saw the woodland garden when you parked your car. Buddy and I started building that right after we got married. If you walked in you'd be able to see the trillium that's starting to come up, primroses, and soon the spring bulbs will start blossoming, you know, daffodils, crocuses . . . Around the side of the house, the lilac bushes start flowering, but not until late May." She raised her eyes toward the door. "And white peonies. In the moonlight, they give off their own light. Which is why you plant them."

There was a change in Marian's voice, an airiness, a pleasing enthusiasm; and when she described the shapes of the gardens, an animation. I wished that I could see what she was seeing.

She brushed her hand across the back of the chair, just below my shoulders, as though she were daring herself to touch me, at least I enjoyed thinking she was.

Marian was speaking slowly now, telling me about the different grasses that came back every year, and what flowers appeared in June and July. "The delphiniums— tall and spiky. You'd recognize them if you saw them. A *true* blue. A very hard color to achieve in the garden palette."

"They're your favorites," I said, leaning my head back and

turning just enough to look at her. "Or maybe roses. You *must* have roses."

"I've talked too much." She pulled the sleeves of her sweater over her wrists and said in a tone that was more playful than I'd have expected, "What about you? What great loves have *you* lost over the years, Geoffrey?"

"I've never loved anyone enough to miss them when they're gone."

"Then you were never really in love."

"That may have changed."

"You're a dangerous man, Geoffrey, saying dangerous things."

"I don't know when I'll have the chance to say them again."

She grinned. "It isn't like Laura didn't talk to me about you and your collegiate conquests."

"My conscience is clean."

"Claims the condemned man as they march him to the gallows."

"Condemned without a fair hearing."

She wasn't grinning now; in fact, all expression had come to a halt. "If I told you to go back to New York. Today. Now. Please don't think it's because I don't appreciate your . . . Well, your being interested in me. God, that sounds so immodest. But I really don't want to get involved with you."

"Because you think I'm a dangerous man?"

"I want you to go back to New York and forget about me."

I told her, "I don't know if that's possible." She was still standing close to me, but she looked as though she were about to tell me to get the hell out of there. What she said was, "I don't know what you think is happening here," and pressed her lips together in a tight smile, "but I'm sure you're not a person who assumes what he wants to about people to fit his own—" She walked away from me and leaned against the side of the sink. "Buddy had a cabin in the Adirondacks. With a lake. He used to go ice fishing in the winter. He loved ice fishing."

"That's very solitary."

"He usually went with his friends. He didn't the last time." She crossed her arms over her chest and stared down at the floor. "The cabin had an old gas heater. Propane. A wind blew the flame out during the night and Buddy died in his sleep from carbon monoxide poisoning." Her voice was as flat as winter ice, and she hurried her words with what sounded like a great fatigue, and sorrow.

"I sold the property and never went there again. Buddy was thirty-two years old." She turned her face to the window. "So, if you came here thinking that I was someone you might be interested in, someone who might be interested in . . . a stupid, avoidable accident, alone in a crappy little cabin." Marian did not turn around.

I couldn't keep staring at the back of her head, I didn't know where to look, so I glanced at the desk just behind my shoulder. Along with the telephone and laptop was a stack of envelopes, all with the letterhead that bore the same logo that was on the pickup truck. It made me think of the hotel stationery you take with you for a souvenir, a reminiscence; and I wondered if Marian's life was nothing more than reminiscences and souvenirs; living in the same house she'd lived in with Buddy, driving that old truck. Like a fly in amber.

I looked up and saw Marian staring at me.

She said, "People in town used to say that one of the joys of spring was watching Buddy's designs come back to life. It's still one of my joys. You won't understand this, probably, but having that to look forward to is part of a routine, one of the habits of living. Like the year that Buddy died, it was attending to the business of being Buddy's widow. And after that was finished, it's anything I can do to—I don't know— It's all—"

"A distraction?"

She opened her eyes a bit wider, as though she'd just been revealed.

"I don't know what I was doing when we were at Laura's. You can think I was flirting with you, if that's good for your ego. Okay, I *liked* flirting with you. Maybe it was the tension of the moment, but whatever, it wasn't me. And if that's who you came up here to be with, it's not me. Anyway, what I'm telling you is that you can't just step into my life as though nothing went on until you showed up."

I got up and stood next to her. She stepped away from me.

She said, "I'm *trying*—the day of Buddy's funeral, there were a lot of people in the house. I didn't want to be around anyone, so I sat out there." She pointed to the porch. "Eliot came out. He didn't say anything. He just stayed with me. It was cold, and I wasn't wearing a coat. I liked the way the wind chilled my blouse and my skin. It seemed like the most appropriate way to feel. I kept on thinking the same thing, over and over: That I couldn't remember a time when I didn't know Buddy. I asked Eliot to burn down the cabin for me. I never wanted to see it again. Eliot said he couldn't do that, but he'd clean it out, sell it for me, and I wouldn't ever have to go there again. And that's what happened." She said, lowering her voice, "If it wasn't so dark outside, you'd be able to see all the gardens we built together. We were supposed to do more." She looked over at me. "Just about this time of year, Buddy and I would prepare the furniture for outside. We'd start putting down mulch. He used to say that I had a better feel for the gardens than he did. That women were closer to the earth, the soil, than men. Now I'm going to tell you why I'm telling you this." She closed her hand around my wrist, and I put my hand on top of hers. "This really has as much to do with Eliot as it does with Buddy—it has *more* to do with Eliot and me, really. You see, as long as I've known him, and that's a long time, Eliot was just someone who was always around. He was just a guy in high school, then he was the guy who owned the hardware store, the guy who entertained the kids in the hospital with his magic tricks. Then he was the guy keeping me company after Buddy died, when I visited my friends, so I didn't feel like a charity case, an appendage. Then we started meeting for lunch once in a while, then dinner. As far as I was concerned, Eliot was just doing a good deed." The tone in her voice went deeper than simple kindness. "I can remember the year and the day when I first kissed Buddy, and where we were. I can remember the first time we made love. But not the first time Eliot and I went out. Or what we talked about or where we went. What I always remember, the thing that I am most aware of is this: I prefer loving Buddy to loving anyone else. I prefer missing him to being with anyone else. Not from a sense of loyalty, but because no one compares to him. And I'll never want to replace him. Eliot knows it. He's told me that he knows this, and it doesn't matter to him. That's a hell of a thing, Geoffrey. I should have told him from the beginning that it shouldn't—it shouldn't be enough for him. It shouldn't be enough for *anybody*."

"You can still tell him."

"It's too late for me."

"It's not too late."

She shook her head. "Are you ever afraid of growing old? I mean, actors worry about losing their good looks, of course, unless you're George Clooney. But what you do for a living really doesn't have much to do with the way you look. Only the way you sound."

"I'm sure I should be offended."

"No. I only meant . . ."

"I'll know it's time to leave when they offer me the Depends account."

Her laughter was the sound of complete appreciation.

"I think youth is overrated," I told her, "and vastly over-marketed."

"You're right about that. But don't you ever worry about it?"

"The consequences, I suppose."

"And you won't try to recapture your youth by dating twenty-somethings?"

"I don't complicate other people's lives, and I don't try to recapture my youth with twenty-somethings I wouldn't have been interested in when *I* was twenty-something."

"You know, I can't believe that."

"Which part?"

"It's different for men."

"Different, not easier."

"Anyway, I'm too old to take chances."

"Chances?"

"You come here and say you can't stop thinking about me, and expect me to—what *do* you expect me to do?"

"What do *you* expect you to do?"

"What would you have done if Eliot had been here, you know, when you first got here?"

"I wasn't thinking about that, actually."

"You didn't consider that before you drove up?"

"It's a long drive. I thought about a lot of things. Maybe I would have told him I had to see Remsen and thought I'd drop by and say hello. Maybe I'd have told him what I told you. I really don't know."

"I'm not so sure I believe that. You impress me as a man who always knows what he's doing."

"I told you I've changed. And I've never been so over my head before, and yet so confident about what I want."

She went to turn on a couple of lights. I liked feeling her body heat when she went past me and watching her move in her sweater and jeans. Supple and assured. I enjoyed the way the expression on her face changed, the intonation in her voice, not only when she'd made the "condemned man to the gallows" comment but even when there was no levity, when she talked about Buddy and Eliot. When she talked about her sadness. No matter what Marian was saying, there was the same familiarity that she'd shown that day at Laura's, the look of recognition in her face that had made me so certain about what I was feeling and saying to her.

I said, "Don't you ever do anything on the spur of the moment?"

She didn't answer right away, but looked like she was making that calculation again.

"About two years after Eliot and I started seeing each other, I went over to the hospital to pick him up, to go out for dinner. He was still upstairs doing his magic act for the kids. I decided to go up and watch. I'd never done that before. He was always downstairs waiting for me. I didn't go into the room. I only stood in the doorway watching him make coins vanish, little plastic birds materialize. Magic. I saw a kind of assurance that he never seems to have when he's around me, more masculine, and comfortable with himself. But I think it was the expression of pleasure I saw on his face that I couldn't remember ever seeing before. For the first time since I'd known him, I was able to separate Eliot not just from the person I'd seen around town most of my life, but from the person I'd been going out with for two years. You see, Geoffrey, until that evening, I thought I'd understood our relationship. I thought I understood Eliot. I'd always had a clarity of feeling, but I was wrong. It was only after I saw him up there that I really understood that Eliot was doing more than a good deed there at the hospital, or being with me; and if I hadn't gone up there to see him, I might never have realized it. I mean it took me that long to realize that Eliot *wanted* me to love him more than I could. And it made me, makes me, very sad. Is that what you meant by doing something impulsive?" She did not say this with bitterness. "There were times when I'd go back to the hospital to watch him, without him knowing about it, hoping I might get close to what I'd felt before. At least it was a feeling. *Something.* Maybe I thought I might convince myself— It comes down to what Eliot and I are willing to settle for. Like when he learned his first sleight of hand. He was still a kid and thought he was going to learn *real* magic, but all it was was a trick. Well, a trick isn't magic, but it was what he wanted."

Marian came over to the table. She didn't sit down, only put her hands on the back of her chair.

"I'm not saying Shady Grove is teeming with available women, but Eliot could have the pick of the litter. Instead he's with a forty-two-year-old widow who's still in love with her dead husband, which may not be the bottom of the barrel, but it's not exactly top of the line, either. A few years after Laura moved back, she said she wished she could fall in love the way she fell in love with Steve. Just once more, she said, before it's too late. She didn't want to re-create the life she'd had with Steve, she just wanted to *feel* that way again. I told her I wished I had her courage."

She said, "Laura told me some people hear the music and some people don't. She said maybe it was because she'd lived in Paris, but she didn't think a person could live without love. She wanted to hear the music again." Marian stepped back and walked over to the window, and stood with her back to the panes and wrapped her arms around herself. "That's when Laura first called us the young widows of Shady Grove. She said she couldn't stand the idea of it." She straightened up and let out a deep breath. "I told Laura I could never fall in love like that. Loving someone that much and losing him, again." She shook her head. "That's not it. Not all of it. If I'd gone up there with Buddy, he'd still be alive. I'm sure of it. I didn't have to like ice fishing. All I had to do was be there with him. Guilty is just the beginning of how I feel. Guilty for that. Guilty for what I'm doing to Eliot. And I'd feel guilty if I left him, after all he's done for me. Guilty for even thinking about you with Laura not even dead for more than—I'm a guilty mess, Geoffrey. And that's not for you."

I said, "When I looked at Eliot that afternoon when he came by, when I saw how he looked at you, I saw a lonely man alone in love. You're just as alone, and I want to take you away from that feeling and the fact of it, and, believe it or not, I find that intimidating."

She smiled at me now. "Tell me about your girlfriend," she said.

I listened to myself describe Rita and our relationship, and it sounded as though I were talking about two people I barely knew; as though I were recalling something told to me by someone else. Our relationship sounded so slight and without purpose that I felt like apologizing, or offering further explanation, but a moment later it wasn't an explanation I was thinking about, or Rita, or Buddy and Marian. I was thinking about Marian and Eliot, because I realized that Marian and I had a lot in common, and I wondered if she knew it.

"Does she buy things for you?" Marian asked. "Did she buy the cologne you're wearing?"

"My cologne?"

"It's very nice. Did she buy it for you?"

"I buy my own cologne. We don't buy things for each other."

"Well, it sounds like a very New York romance."

The word *romance* made me think Marian was making a joke.

"Why would you think I'd joke about something like that?"

"I suppose I suddenly find it laughable."

"And living in New York?" she asked. "Is that laughable, too?"

"It's what I know."

"I've only been there a handful of times. Laura never wanted to go back there after she moved here. Although she said if you can't live in Paris, live in New York City. Well, I don't know about living in Paris, but I think New York is a very hard place. I don't mean hard difficult, although it *is* that. I mean, *hard*." She rapped her knuckles on the table. "It must wear you down after a while."

"When it does, I leave."

"Like today?" She grinned at me again, and I thought about telling her that it wasn't at all like today, and about the past three weeks fantasizing about meeting her again somewhere in the city, and all the times I'd felt compelled to see her, but I figured that I'd scared her enough.

"You know, I was in New York for Laura's wedding."

"*You* were at the wedding?"

"That's right. I wound up being their witness while—I know what you did for her with Simon. And, no, if you'd been there fate would not have been tempted." She sounded like she enjoyed saying this, and letting me know. "I was with Buddy."

Outside, the full moon spread its light across the ground, making everything look silky and unreal. I wanted to stand out there with Marian, hold her in my arms and feel her body against mine. Hold her in the cold until we couldn't bear it, and wait, just a moment longer, so we could kiss.

I was bewildered by what I was thinking and by all the things I was feeling. I didn't know what the expression on my face was, but Marian was still smiling at me.

"You're very good at keeping secrets."

"I think you're giving me too much credit."

"I bet if I asked you not to tell anyone what I've told you today, you wouldn't."

"Why don't you ask me in twenty years."

She stopped smiling now. "What I said before, about your being dangerous. I meant it."

"I never doubted you."

Marian and I walked down the flagstone path in the cool night breeze. As I started to open the car door, she stood just behind my shoulder and said in a low voice, "Bacon on buttered toast, and very strong coffee with cream."

"What's that?" I asked.

"What I like for breakfast on rainy Sundays," she said.

The full moon was high above the trees. The wind began to pick up, making a deep and rushing sound through the branches, like ocean waves. It made me think of those tempest-tossed characters in mythology and Shakespeare who wash up on unfamiliar shores, their sudden arrival inducing transformation. They are no longer who they were only moments before. That's how I felt with Marian, listening to her, talking with her.

As I drove away, with her face barely visible in the rear-view mirror, I was incapable of imagining what I might do that would allow me to forget Marian Ballantine.

Seven

I LEFT SHADY GROVE THAT NIGHT FEELING EVEN MORE UNSET-
tled than I had before I'd seen Marian. What had I accom-
plished except upsetting her life? There was no pleasure
to be had from that.

I was the only car on the dark country roads, and I drove
until I found a bed-and-breakfast, about thirty miles from
Shady Grove, near Great Barrington, Massachusetts. I wasn't
ready to go back to the city, not just yet. I didn't want to be
so far from Marian. Not that I had any intention of lurking
about Shady Grove, appearing in the grocery store, showing
up at the house again. I just liked the idea of Marian being
nearby. At least for the night.

But I didn't go back to New York the following day, either,
or the next three days. I drove around the Berkshires, sleeping in strange beds, walking quiet streets, looking through
antique stores and book barns, shopping for clean clothes. It
was fine weather for early April. The spring sunshine had

a restorative effect. I didn't even mind the static of my own company.

I thought perhaps this break was just what I'd needed and I could go back to the city and my life with a feeling of renewal, and satisfaction. I'd had my visit, I could shake off my doldrums.

Instead, I thought about Marian most of the time, the way she looked with the sun backlighting her hair; and when she described her gardens, even when she made her case for never seeing me again, the way her voice welled and faded.

One afternoon, while I was having my lunch, I noticed a couple sitting a few tables away from mine. I watched the man reach across the table and touch the back of the woman's hand with the tips of his fingers; with a graceful sweep she pushed a few strands of hair away from his forehead; when they spoke to each other, how enthusiastic their faces were. It made me think of Simon talking about Laura and Steve. Telling me: "They were so in love, I found it unbearable."

I thought of the way Marian's hand had brushed against my wrist while she introduced me to her friends. And how I liked the way we touched when we spoke to each other. Then I was thinking of the way Rita's legs lay exposed in the gray light of her bedroom after we made love, and would I ever want to make love to her again?

THAT AFTERNOON I WENT BACK TO NEW YORK CITY. I'D ALWAYS liked coming home to my apartment after a trip, whether I'd been gone a few weeks or a few days; the perfunctory greetings from the men in the garage, the doormen. The comforting rituals, gathering the mail, playing back messages on the answering machine, reading e-mail. Just like that, the routines of life waiting inside the apartment, like an obedient dog.

One of the messages was a last-minute invitation to a friend's apartment for a party, and I decided to go. I wanted the distraction.

It was a relaxed Sunday gathering in the apartment of Richard Davidson, whom I knew through work. It was nothing very formal, Bloody Marys, Mimosas, and finger food, in one of those spacious Upper West Side apartments with long hallways and high ceilings, a view of the Hudson River and, on this particular night, filled with dozens of people and that exhilarating sound of tinkling ice cubes and adult conversation.

I was sipping my drink and talking to Felicia Robeson, a choreographer I'd known for a few years. She'd come back from Mexico about a week ago, and was telling me, "My mind just refuses to leave the beach," when Amy Brennan came over, kissed Felicia on the cheek, then me, and wanted to know, "How's that executor business coming along? I still think it's *so* intriguing."

"Not that intriguing," I said.

"What's intriguing?" Felicia asked.

Amy answered the question.

"You know," Felicia said, "I'd trust Geoffrey with *my* last remains."

"That's a grim thought." It was Richard, our host.

"Are you still going on about that?" Amy's husband, Nick, had now joined us. "What's happening with it, anyway?"

"We're about to find out," Amy said.

"Is there something I should know?" Richard asked.

"Absolutely nothing," I said.

"Then why is everyone talking about it?"

"Who's *every*one?" Felicia answered.

Richard squeezed Amy's arm, said, "I'm too sober for this conversation," walked to another circle of people, while Felicia and I went over to the bar for refills.

I asked her, "What's the occasion, anyway?"

"Richard's celebrating his daughter's divorce."

"Oh?"

"He never liked the son-in-law."

"The daughter must have come over to his side."

"She's quite happy about it."

"How long were they married?"

"Eight years. She's in Maui. Having her own celebration."

There was laughter coming from somewhere down the hall, and laughter closer to us; a gentle swirl of perfume . . . a woman's hand resting on my shoulder . . . a voice introducing itself . . . "How have you been . . ." "What have you been doing these days . . ." "I haven't seen you since . . ."

Outside the open window, the setting sun floated above the New Jersey Palisades, holding off the dark for a few minutes more, for we had entered the time of longer days. I listened to the jagged noise of the city lifted on the air and into the room, adding its voice to the conversations.

A dark-haired man came up behind Felicia, wrapped his arms around her waist, kissed her on the neck, and said, "You're just going to have to have dinner with me soon. It's been way too long."

"Yes." She turned to face him. "Much too long."

"You come, too," he told me.

"I'll make sure of it."

Then he whispered in Felicia's ear and walked away.

"I have no idea who that was," Felicia told me.

"Never saw him before," I said.

"He has very soft lips."

Amy came back to tell us, "When you two are ready to leave, find Nick and me."

None of this was alien to me, not the noise, not invitations from strangers, nor the conversations going on around me, and if I didn't know the evening's subject, I was no stranger to the context.

"Are you having a good time?" Felicia asked me.

"I always have a good time."

"You *do*. Why is that?"

About an hour later, Felicia and I found Amy and Nick, and the four of us took our small piece of the party downtown to Nick and Amy's place, where we had a few more drinks, some Chinese takeout, and more conversation.

Then Felicia told us about her new show, a flashy musical. Amy was excited about the work they were doing on their apartment. Nick thought there was nothing wrong with the apartment the way it was . . . and they talked about a trip they were planning, Oslo, Copenhagen . . . and did Felicia and I want to go with them, and of course, I should bring Rita.

Felicia said she'd be too busy with the new show. I said I'd have to see what I had scheduled, and was my choice of companion limited to Rita. Everyone laughed, but a quick, discernible sense of discomfort and regret passed through me because I wasn't making a joke. For a moment, I wanted to tell my friends about what had happened between Marian and me in Shady Grove and to declare, "I've met someone under the most unusual circumstances, and I can't get her out of my mind."

THE NEXT MORNING, I PHONED RITA. THAT NIGHT WE WERE IN MY apartment, sitting together on the couch, Rita wearing a gray sweater and black stretch pants, hair pulled back and tied in a French knot. Her shoes were off, her bare feet were tucked under her legs. She was sipping a glass of wine, her lipstick traces stained the rim.

She put the glass on the coffee table, and moved closer to me.

I told her, "You're looking very chic tonight."

She said, "Don't try sucking up to me. You took your sweet time returning my call."

"I was out of town. I drove up to Shady Grove."

She turned and brushed her lips against my cheek, laid her head on my chest, then pressed her hand against the back of my neck; her flesh felt soft against my flesh. She raised her face to mine, her mouth parted. Her dark red lipstick appeared like liquid in the lamplight.

"It's good to be back," I said.

"How long were you gone?"

"A couple of days."

"That's not very long."

"It seems longer than that."

She moved her mouth close to my ear. "You should have told me you were going."

"Oh?"

"Then I could have missed you. It's nice knowing some-one misses you when you go away."

She uncurled her legs and stretched them past the edge of the couch. I turned and when I kissed her it was one of those moments when in an instant the mind flashes a myriad of considerations—when all that was happening was noth-ing but a kiss. Just a kiss. Something we'd done countless times before. Only now I was aware of both the assurance in our actions, and the assumptions, and I wanted to reacquaint myself with those assumptions. I wanted to reacquaint myself with all the things that I liked about Rita.

The way she said, "Wouldn't it make you worry if I started keeping my clothes here?"

She said this after I told her that I'd like her to spend the night, and she said she'd have nothing to wear to work tomor-row. Then she put her head on my shoulder.

"Would it worry *you*?" I asked back.

"Maybe I should try it sometime. Like Grace Kelly in *Rear Window*, showing up with her little Mark Cross overnight case." She laughed. "My clothes popping up in the corners of your closets like mushrooms? Wouldn't it make you feel just the worst kind of claustrophobic? I bet it's bad enough seeing my toothbrush."

This made me think about our "very New York romance," which seemed most desirable at the moment. It also made me think about Marian and if she would ever declare a thing like that, living alone in her cozy country house with the sweet gardens outside. I didn't know her well enough to be certain of anything she might declare about sharing her closets and with whom, but I knew Rita, and no one's clothes cluttered her closets, no desires for sweet gardens and a cozy country house cluttered her brain. It was that dissimilarity that made Rita so attractive to me at that moment. It was what I wanted to reacquaint myself with.

She lifted her head, kissed me on the mouth, then said, "I was just thinking how much I like you."

In the morning, while the coffee brewed, Rita stood wearing only my bathrobe, phoning her assistant to make sure there was nothing on her morning schedule.

I poured coffee for us, and we went into the living room. Rita sat in one of the chairs while I pulled back the curtains, looked out the window for a moment, then sat in the chair nearest to her. Rita wasn't quite smiling at me, but her expression was not quite lacking amusement, and there was an aspect to it that I wanted no part of.

She kept on looking at me, while I tasted my coffee, then with that expression still in place said, "Tell me, darling, about last night. You didn't happen to take the vow of celibacy while you were away?"

"Just tired. That's all."

"Being an executor seems to have taken more out of you than you expected."

ALEX'S OFFICE WAS IN A GROUND FLOOR APARTMENT ON SEVENTY-eighth Street and Park Avenue. It was quite modest, the waiting room in the front and the office at the end of a short hall. There was a small kitchenette in between. Not that I'd ever seen him use it for anything more than boiling water for his tea.

The blinds were always down, which gave the sensation of

stepping into perpetual twilight, even when the lights were on. There were three old and comfortable chairs in the room, the one Alex sat in was behind and to the left of the patients' couch, the other two chairs were separated by a drum table. A built-in bookcase filled one of the walls, and several abstract paintings covered the others, with a desk and phone in the far corner between two windows.

It was after eight in the evening. Alex was supposed to have finished with the day's last patient, and we were going to have dinner together, but when I got to the building, the doorman told me Alex had gone out, and said I should wait inside. He unlocked the door and turned on the lights in the waiting room and closed the door for me. I let myself into the office, turned on all the lights, and sat in what looked like the most comfortable chair.

By the time Alex showed up, it was nearly nine-thirty. I'd flipped through all of his magazines, and was reading a book I'd taken from the bookcase.

He managed to say hello, but he was already standing at his desk, looking through his appointment book, writing with one hand, unbuttoning his coat with the other. There were lines around his mouth, and dark rings under his eyes. All vestiges of his two weeks at the spa were gone, and what had taken their place looked exhausted and worn out.

He lay down on the couch, still wearing his coat, and closed his eyes. I was certain that he was falling asleep, but all he did was yawn and turn his head toward me.

I said, "A day at the clinic?" As much an expression of sympathy as an observation.

"*Clinic*? No. Two hours with the masseur and a mani-cure, which left me barely enough time to rush over to the most *wonder*ful cocktail party, from which I just couldn't tear myself away . . ."

"Sarcasm will get you nowhere."

"You think I don't get *invited* to cocktail parties?"

"At least try to keep your eyes open when you ask that."

"A lot of parties."

"You probably have to turn people down, you get invited to so many."

"That's right."

"Well, I'm glad we got that cleared up."

He sat up, slipped out of his coat with no small effort. Then he narrowed his eyes at me, the way a marksman would, and said, "You *saw* her. That friend of Laura's." He adjusted one of the pillows and lay down again. "Did she come to New York, or did you go up there?" Before I could answer: "You went up *there*. I heard it in your voice when you called. So? What happened?"

"That all depends on what you mean by 'happened.'"

He laughed. "So that's what our little get-together is for."

"You're a very smart man."

"That all depends on what you mean by 'smart.'" He yawned again. "Would you mind very much if we went up to my apartment instead of a restaurant?"

"I love your apartment."

"Don't overdo it."

ALEX'S APARTMENT WAS ON THE SEVENTH FLOOR IN THE SAME building as his office. At first glance, you would think no one lived there, or at best that the occupant was never home.

The only room worth talking about was his study, designed for comfort with two soft sofas and a couple of overstuffed chairs.

Alex had changed his clothes, and was now wearing a pair of wrinkled khakis, a frayed oxford shirt, and a pair of slippers; and while we ate ham and cheese sandwiches, a beer for me, ginger ale for him, I told him about the things I'd been doing since we last saw each other.

"Let me understand this," he said, "you slept with Rita and couldn't get it up?"

"Didn't even try. I wasn't interested."

"Oh, that's too bad. I'm writing a paper on conflict and impotence, I thought I could use it."

"Sorry to disappoint."

"You never disappoint me, Geoffrey."

Alex got up, brought our dishes into the kitchen, and came back with two generous slices of coconut cake on fresh plates, handed one to me, sat down, took a bite, looked pleased and took another bite.

I wasn't in the mood for cake, and put my plate on the coffee table.

"Later, I mean after Rita left and I was alone," I said, "I realized how dishonest my actions were. Then I started thinking about Marian, and that I was dishonest with her, too. Don't you think?" Alex didn't say anything. "And then I started thinking about what Marian told me about Eliot, and what I'd asked her to do by my driving up there. Only now I could understand what she was talking about, because I feel the same way about Rita, not the way Marian feels about Eliot, but a responsibility to her, to our relationship, and I can't walk away from that."

"The feeling or the responsibility?"

"You know what I mean."

"No wonder you feel conflicted." He took another bite of cake. "You're worried that you're not the person other people think you are."

"What if it turns out I'm not the person *I* think I am?"

"You don't really see that as a possibility."

"Whatever's going to happen, I know I can't fold myself back into my life."

"I only wish I had your kind of problem."

I said, "I wish you did, too. I'd love to hear you tell me about some guy you were shacked up with for three days at the Plaza, and now you're going crazy because he hasn't returned your calls. Or because he *has*, and what are you going to do?"

"When I was younger, maybe that would have been appealing. But that's not the case. So, let's not even talk about it." He said this in that tweed-on-skin way, but I spoke past it.

"Instead of filling your time with clinics and committees—"

"It's not that simple."

"It's not that complicated."

He lay down on one of the sofas.

"Do you remember the first time I told you I was gay?"

"We were going somewhere, weren't we?" I said. "In a car, I think."

"My old Karmann Ghia. You were sixteen. It was Christmas break and I was driving you home from school. When I told you, you said it was no big deal, and besides you'd already figured it out. Do you remember what I said to you after you said that?"

"Word for word?"

"I told you that if it ever be*came* a big deal, if you ever were bothered by it, or ashamed, you should tell me." He was speaking to me the way I imagined he spoke to his patients, the way he probably sounded that day in the car. "I also told you to remember that it had less to do with sex than you think. I told you that because I didn't want you to worry that I'd get AIDS, but what I wanted you to understand was, what it all comes down to is having the capacity to love another person. I'd say that's what I'm dealing with now. What you and I have always been trying to deal with."

"Katlin Mallory. I was telling Marian about her. My girlfriend, sophomore year in college. Marian asked me why we broke up. I said because I didn't love her enough."

Alex sat up and looked over at me. The expression on his face made me think of a man who'd just received an unexpected package in the mail.

"You told her a lot in under an hour," he said.

"I only just figured it out—and realized that it mattered to me—I've never loved anyone the way Marian loved her husband or Laura, Steve. No one mattered to me like that. Not Rita. None of my girlfriends. No one except you."

"You don't have to tell me that."

"I want to."

"I mean, I already know it."

"And I mean, I want to tell you."

He nodded his head, and puckered his lips, and there was a look of amusement on his face. "It seems Marian's unleashed a well of emotions in you."

"Wouldn't that be nice." I sat up a little straighter.

His expression grew a bit more somber now. "But that's about you," he said, "not me. Your experiences are not mine."

"It's what you just did that I'm talking about."

He said, "Come again?" with more than a slight tone of indignation.

"Keeping people at arm's length. Keeping *me* at arm's length. You do it all the time. We both do, and not only to each other."

Alex took off his glasses, placed them on the end table, and rubbed his eyes.

"Wouldn't you say you already know why we're like that?" I said. "Or do you think we're both too blocked to have any real insight and just accept it as the way we live our lives?"

"You want an answer, or an explanation?"

"I think you and I have been after the same thing, and the only difference is, you reached your point of frustration a lot earlier in life than I have. Why do you think we've never talked about that? I don't mean clinically, I mean—"

"Just what do you think it is that we're both after?"

"Passion," I said. "When I was talking about wanting you to go crazy over an unreturned phone call, I was also talking about myself. I like this feeling, feeling a little bit crazy."

"Back at the Plaza, are we?"

"I think you already have passion in your life," I told him, "for your practice, your patients, really, and when you feel an attraction to someone—when you start to really care for someone, the other relationships are threatened. It creates, to use your word, conflict."

"Which creates an emotional impotence?"

"So, it seems I've always known I wanted relationships with women who I'm dispassionate about," I said, "or who are inaccessible, because anyone who tries to get close feels intrusive to me."

Alex said, "Which is one of the things you and Rita have in common."

"But *you* want to feel close to someone," I answered, "or so you say, except then you find it conflicting, so you distract yourself with your practice, which is the very thing that makes having what you want conflicting."

"Do you ever think that I'm content with that? So what if I commit myself to my profession? It's still a vital aspect of life. I have my patients, and my friends when I have time for them."

"If I said that to you, you'd say it's just misdirected feelings," I told him. "Substitutes for more substantial relationships. What some people do with their pets, or their mistresses. How's that for an explanation?"

Alex leaned on his side. "You at least always manage to have a girlfriend."

"Variations on Rita, that's all," I said.

"That's nothing to dismiss."

"Choosing the wrong people?"

"They're exactly the right people. For the kind of relationship you want."

"While you choose not to choose anyone at all. Why is that?"

"My reasons are my reasons," he said, "just as yours are yours."

"Well, all of that's changed as of a few days ago."

"You've lost me."

"When I was younger," I told him, "I was happy to be happy. When I got older, I was content to be content. But all of that changed when I was with Marian. Being content just isn't satisfying anymore. It's what I've been feeling for—you know, stagnating, stuck in the horse latitudes? That feeling's been percolating for a while now, but I like thinking Marian's made me realize that I want to go back there and be with her again."

"A woman who wants nothing to do with you."

"She's been living in perpetual mourning since her husband died," I said. "And now she's stuck in a dead-end, repressed relationship with her boyfriend."

"You find that attractive?"

"I find pulling her out of her emotional rut attractive."

"Maybe *I* should create my own myth of a broken heart," he said.

"The man who got away?"

"The man who never *was*." Alex got up to straighten a lampshade on the other side of the room, came back, and sat on the sofa. "It would seem," he said, "that we're talking about something a little more significant than former girl-friends and current ones."

I lay down on the floor, propped a pillow between my head and the bottom of the sofa.

I said, "Maybe we should blame our parents." And we both laughed.

"Yes. For being negligent enough to wait until we were both adults before leaving the city."

"What about early childhood influences?"

"Convenient, but cowardly."

Alex asked if he could get me a beer or something, and walked out of the room. He came back with a glass of club soda in his hand, went over to the window, looked downstairs, and down on the sofa again.

I was thinking about, trying to remember, actually, when

Alex and I had started having these conversations, all the evenings and all the talks, the two of us, in this room. I was thinking about how close it made me feel to him, how important it was to feel that. But I said nothing, and I had to wonder what inhibited me from telling Alex how much I loved talking with him, and if I shared his aversion to the emotional trespass.

I sat up and looked over at my brother. He was turning the ice cubes around his glass with his index finger and staring at me.

"The truth is, I'm stuck with the life I have," he said.

"Stuck, but not trapped. The solution," I told him, "would be for you to get past thinking you need to find someone who doesn't threaten the relationships you have with your patients, or make demands on your practice. I'm thinking you want a deeper relationship than that."

"From explanations to solutions, all in one night?"

"With a bit of resistance thrown in from my big brother."

"What do you want from me? You're the one who thinks he's in love, not me."

"I'm thinking about you falling in love. Really in love. Not that it would hurt if you shacked up with some guy at the Plaza for a few days in the meantime."

"If you're going to have fantasies about my sex life, I'd appreciate it if you made it the Carlyle. It's so much classier than the Plaza."

"The Carlyle it is."

"And you still have to tell Rita about your sudden change of heart."

Eight

I N A CORNER OF MY BEDROOM CEILING THERE WAS A SMALL OVAL just a little bit brighter than the rest of the paint. Maybe it was bleached from the sun, maybe it was just one of those mysteries of apartment life in Manhattan. I spent most of the day lying on my bed staring at that spot, thinking about the things that Alex and I had talked about the night before, thinking that later in the afternoon I'd take a cab crosstown to Lincoln Center, to Juilliard, where Laura and I used to meet when her classes were over. I would have even gone uptown to the West End—only it had closed down years ago. I'd never gone out of my way to see these places again, and I didn't know why I wanted to see them now. Maybe it was an attempt at changing something about the way I'd been living; not a bold-stroke change but something small, something slight, like that oval of bright paint in the corner of my ceiling.

That night, I met a few friends for supper in Chinatown, friends who didn't know about Laura and Shady Grove, whose company was fun, whose conversation was easy, with about as much depth as my coat pocket. I enjoyed being with them. I always did.

Telephones that don't ring were never my concern, but when I got back to my apartment, I wanted my phone to ring with Marian's voice on the other end. She'd say it was coming up on the middle of April, time for her to start working in other people's gardens, or just about that time. She'd describe what she was planting and what it would look like. We would speak to each other the way we did that first afternoon at Laura's. I would feel a lightness within me, and hear that same lightness in Marian's voice, playful and flirtatious. Did Marian ever think, just for a moment, that she wanted her phone to ring with me at the other end?

I thought about her and Eliot, and what they would be doing this spring. Did they make plans the way a lot of couples do? And I thought about Rita and what we might want to do together a month from now, or even next week. But what I really wanted was that phone call from Marian. I fell asleep thinking about that call and how good it would feel to hear Marian's voice.

In the morning, when the phone did ring, most of it was business: copy to review for a voice-over I was doing for a charity benefit, studio time, but not too much, breaking up the rest of the month, a handful of days in midtown. Lunches with accounts, with my friends. Drinks, dinners into the weekend, people who didn't know about my being Laura's executor, and a few dates with those who did. I was surprised by how much I wanted to talk about Shady Grove. Not about Marian and what I was feeling for her—some of these same people knew Rita or knew people who did—nor any of the things that Alex and I discussed, and certainly not Laura's death. I wanted to talk about the day I spent in Shady Grove. I liked remembering that, even the night when Marian and Eliot and I went out to dinner, in spite of the awkwardness. But there was no one to tell these things to.

I was experiencing feelings that until recently I'd been unfamiliar with. The nestling anticipation, the restiveness and indecision. It wasn't at all unpleasant, not all of it, anyway. I enjoyed the uncertainty.

Sunday afternoon, while it rained outside, I was alone inside my apartment, in the room I used as an office, and decided to assemble the stereo system Laura had left to me. It was quite impressive, top-of-the-line twelve-inch steel turntable, a tone arm that rode across the records at a gram and a quarter, a powerful amplifier, two speakers that must have been custom-made and were huge by today's standards. It all looked much too expensive for something Laura would have owned when she was a student, and too outdated to be available when she was older. I assumed that it had belonged to Steve.

And then there were the record albums. Two dozen of them. In their original sleeves. Collections of American standards by legendary songwriters, sung by legendary stylists, spinning at a civilized 33⅓ rpm.

It was music I had always liked and had always listened to, and while I had no great rush of where or when I might have listened to these particular songs, I assumed it was somewhere in New York City with Laura.

I decided to play one of the cuts. An hour later I was sitting on the floor, sipping a whiskey and water, and still listening to the music Laura had wanted me to hear, and when I finished my drink, I turned up the volume and continued listening while I cooked my dinner, then listened to more music while I ate.

Songs of and about love. Love at first. Love at last. Love again. Conquering love. Surrendering to love. Brazen about love. Secret about love. Happy, beguiled, and through with love. The wit, the clever rhymes, the tight melodies and harmonies, and not a verse or lyric that was new to me; but until this night I'd never considered all of the anguish and enjoyment, conflict and delight contained in their scores. When the music stopped, I wondered why Laura had wanted me to hear them.

I wondered if Marian knew why, and would this be the excuse I needed to call her—or just send her an e-mail.

Would I have sounded foolish? And why should I care what I sounded like?

I'd have said, "I was sitting around thinking about you and thought I'd listen to the love songs Laura sent me. I thought you might know why?"

And Marian would ask: "Why you're thinking about me?"

"Why Laura left me all these love songs."

While Ella Fitzgerald sang "In the still of the night" and gazed from her window at the slumbering moon, I gazed from my own window, and felt like someone in love.

While the stereo kept playing that warm, honey-butter sound on vinyl, and the tone arm floated across the steel platter like a memory, I wondered if that was all Laura had intended to leave me, the solitude of reminiscence.

⸎

IT WAS DARK OUTSIDE BY THE TIME I'D TURNED OFF THE MUSIC, washed my supper dishes, and poured myself a second drink. I sat in my office, no longer trying to figure out hidden meanings and intents, just listening to the rain splashing against the windowsill and the small sounds rising from the street below.

The phone rang. I felt the flurry of anticipation, as though Laura's music had taken up residence inside my head and anything was possible. Even Marian was possible.

I let the phone to ring a second time and a third, while I prepared myself for the sound of Marian's voice, prepared my own voice, before I lifted the receiver.

"I really *am* sorry for not calling you sooner."

The voice was quite familiar, it took me only a second to recover and to wish that I could have found some comfort in that familiarity, as I had other times when Rita called, but all I felt now was deflation and the urgency to remove that from my voice when I replied that it was quite all right.

"I've just been so incredibly busy," she said.

"As a matter of fact, I've been incredibly busy, too. You know, late nights at the studio, mediocre takeout."

"*That's* unacceptable, Geoffrey. Next time call me. I'll see to it that you get a great meal."

That was what Rita had always been able to offer, the charms of the excellent meal, prepared by the excellent chef, and never second rate. I was not averse to those charms that night; but there was the twinge of sadness while I listened to her tell me in one breath why she'd been so busy and why she hadn't been able to call me and why she was so sorry and why she was never too busy to make sure I had better than mediocre meals when I was working late. Which made me feel only regret for all the things I'd been thinking before she called, and the disappointment and the disenchantment I'd been feeling while she talked to me, which was why I told her, "I'd like to see you when things slow down."

"Things have already slowed down," she answered.

"Then how about tomorrow?"

I didn't want to have dinner with her. I didn't want to be alone with her in a restaurant, or in either her apartment or mine. I was not about to navigate my way around an evening that ended with us in bed together.

"Let's meet around lunchtime, in the park."

"The *park*?"

"Central Park is beautiful the day after a rain."

"I'm all for beauty."

The following afternoon, I met Rita at the park entrance on Sixtieth Street. She kissed me on the lips and put her arm through mine as we stepped around the street vendors and the tourists they attract, and walked down to the pond.

It was a cool day, even with the sun shining. Rita was wearing a light green jacket over a black skirt and high heels. Urban and sophisticated, two of the things I'd found attractive about her.

The rain had left behind a smattering of puddles, but we were able to find a dry bench with a view of the Gapstow Bridge. After we sat down, Rita started telling me about the work that had been keeping her busy, and the new author she'd just signed. A celebrity chef from Charleston, South Carolina.

"I'm going down to see him at the end of the month. Why don't you come with me? We'll make it a long weekend."

When I didn't answer, Rita pulled her head back and

crossed her arms over her chest, turned her head away from me, then back, the smoothest, most elegant double take I'd ever witnessed, and said, "Oh shit."

I told her what had been going on during these "incredibly busy" times and about my conversations with Marian and Alex.

Rita said, "It was only a matter of time before one of us wanted something else."

"Three years is more than 'a matter of time.' "

She shrugged her shoulders. "It's just like you not to try to fake it."

"It's just like you not to hold that against me."

"The other night. I should have known then."

"Even I didn't know it then."

"Regardless." She pushed a few strands of hair away from my forehead. "Which took longer, deciding to tell me, or figuring it all out?"

"Don't ask me that."

"Then help me figure it out now. You're not breaking up with me because of another woman, but because she helped you understand how unhappy you are?"

"Made me think about how I've been living my life."

"And how unhappy you are?"

"This doesn't have to do with happiness."

"Unsatisfied, then. And how does she feel about this?"

"Are you sure you want to know?"

"And you think you're in love with her. Is she in love with you?"

"I have no idea."

"That's no small matter. And I can't say I don't feel any less insulted."

I said, "I feel like I'm about to go over a cliff."

Rita said, "Thanks for not holding my hand while you do it." She rested the tip of her chin on my shoulder. "I wish you still wanted what I want."

I pressed the side of my face against her cheek.

She said, "I think I lack some gene or something, because I've never wanted that great marriage, that total partnership."

I said, "You never make me feel tied down."

"It may be that I lack the imagination to want anything more than what I have at the time."

"Or you don't want to feel beholden to anyone."

"I like it just as it is."

"I didn't come to this easily."

"Who wants easy?" She sighed. I felt the warmth of her breath on my eyes. She said, "I've always believed that everything in life is transitory. And yet, I never like endings." Her voice was soft, but not sad.

"Thanks for letting me off the hook."

"You were never on the hook." She put her hand inside mine. "It's very strange, the thought of not seeing you again."

The sun was strong and hot against my face. The light illuminated the dark red strands in Rita's hair. At that moment I was only aware of how beautiful she looked.

She said, "I think we shared a taxi."

"A taxi?"

"The night we met. I think we shared a taxi."

"Was it snowing? I seem to remember snow."

"I'm very fond of you," she said.

We sat for a while longer, Rita's hand in mine.

She said, "I'm not quite ready for our afternoon together to end. Let's walk a little while. Walk me back to my office."

Rita held onto my hand as she stood up, then put her arm through mine while we walked up the stone steps and out of the park. She stroked the cuff on my coat with the tip of her fingernail. "I wonder what it will feel like the next time I hear your voice on a commercial?"

We crossed Fifth Avenue to Madison, then headed downtown, as though we were just any couple on the street, in no particular hurry. Looking in store windows, our reflections looking back at us. How compatible we appeared—a metrosexual couple—through the displays of clothes, shoes, and cosmetics, arm in arm.

I said, "I'm being cruel, aren't I?"

"Not the way you mean. Not intentionally."

When we reached the doors of her building, Rita took hold of my lapels, pulled me close to her, and kissed me on the lips, as though it were just a kiss, as though we were sure to kiss each other again tonight.

She said, "I wonder how long this will last. Whatever's going on with you. With the two of us now, I suppose."

"You'll go to Charleston as planned."

"You're going to be hard to replace." Rita lifted my hand and held it against the front of her coat. "Oh well, what's the point of having a heart, if you're not going to use it?"

Nine

I T SEEMED LIKE THE TIME TO FIND THE NEAREST BAR, GET drunk, and confide in the bartender, as if pouring me a whiskey made us old friends and I could talk to him about feeling untethered and reckless, and how appealing that seemed until a few minutes ago. Except, I rarely drank in the afternoon, and never made a practice of telling my sorrows to strangers, bartenders included. Instead, after I watched Rita get onto an elevator, and tried to remember exactly what I had thought I would accomplish by breaking up with her, I started walking.

I must have been walking for quite a while. I was way over on First Avenue past the U.N., over by the little plaza on Forty-seventh Street, under the bare trees. The street was filled with traffic, the sidewalks were deep with the postlunch brigade, I stepped into the current, the man on the street—I liked the idea of that—melding into the crowd and heading uptown.

Sometime after that, I took out my cell phone, called Alex, and told him what I'd done.

He asked, "When did *this* happen?"

"Today. An hour ago. Longer than that. I suppose I should tell our friends. Maybe Rita will. I don't know . . ."

He said, "This is too important for the phone. I'll come over to your apartment."

"What time is it anyway?"

"Almost two-thirty. I'll try to make it as soon as I can."

I was aware of the chill in the air, but not much of anything else. I was just trying to move along, keeping pace.

I walked west to Park Avenue, uptown to Seventieth Street, and west again to my apartment on Fifth. When I entered the lobby, there was Simon, sitting in one of the chairs, reading a magazine. I started laughing.

"How do you manage," I said, "to appear at the absolutely worst times?"

"A talent and a curse?"

He'd shaved since I last saw him, and his clothes were pressed and might have even been new, but there was still that tired look about him when he stood and walked over to me, speaking as he approached: "I really have to talk to you."

"Some other time. I'm having a bad day."

"Why are you such a hard-ass? All I want is your help, Geoffrey."

I started to walk away from him. He followed me all the way to the end of the lobby and over to the elevators, talking to my back as we walked.

"It's been twenty years for you," he said, "for me, it's been every day of my life."

"I don't know what the hell you're talking about."

"My sister—"

"Not today."

"Can you possibly think that I like embarrassing myself this way?" He looked over at the doorman. When I got onto the elevator, Simon got on with me.

When the doors opened and I stepped off, Simon stayed with me all the way to my apartment. He was still talking.

"Five minutes," he was saying. "Ten at the most."

"For what?"

"Not out here," he said. "Give me a break. Okay?"

I unlocked the door and let him in.

After Simon settled himself into one of the living room chairs, folded his jacket on top of his legs, he said, "I once told you you don't know what you're dealing with."

"Did you come here to see if I remember things you've told me?"

"You have to tell Remsen that I can stay in my sister's house. At least let me go inside for a little while. I've got to get some closure on this."

"I told you before, I have nothing to do with that."

"You've got more to do with it than you know."

"You're giving me too much credit," I said. "And too much responsibility."

He slumped deep into the chair, reached into his jacket for a cigarette, put it back and rubbed his eyes with the heels of his hands, at the same time telling me, "I'm sitting here thinking: What can I say to get you to help me?"

The intercom buzzed. The doorman told me that Alex was on his way up. I opened the front door and went back into the living room.

"We'll have to continue this some other time."

"What other time? *This* is the time."

Alex walked in, said, "So, tell me all about—" saw Simon sitting there, and that was all he said.

"This is my brother. Alex, this is Simon Welles."

"Laura's brother?"

"Simon was just about to lecture me on the importance of closure."

"Are you familiar with the term?" Simon asked Alex.

Alex took off his coat and sat down.

Simon was watching me while he told Alex, "What I have to say is for Geoffrey alone."

"This is your only chance," I said.

"Your brother?" Simon lifted his chin toward Alex.

"Say what you want to say," I told him.

"Don't believe everything they told you about me." Simon was speaking to Alex.

"They?" Alex asked.

"They don't know the whole story."

Alex said he didn't know there was a *whole* story.

Simon now looked over at me. "Twenty-some years ago, you meet Laura Welles, and she's smart and beautiful, and oh so talented. You're great friends. And that's all you know."

"What's your point?" I asked.

"The Welles family history. By the time you met my sister she was already fully formed, or nearly, but you never knew the two precocious Welles children. The performing monkeys growing up in the shadow of Tanglewood."

I saw Alex lean back in his chair and press the flat part of two fingers against his lips, and all that I was thinking about was getting Simon out of there so I could speak with my brother.

"You see," Simon was telling me, while he looked everywhere but at me, "Laura and I, each in our own way, broke
our parents' hearts. Laura by running off with Steve, and—
well, after summer workshops and leaping across the appropriate stages, the plan was for me to plié my way behind my
sister all the way to Juilliard, fast-tracked to wasting my youth
making auditions and ending up in the chorus of *Coppélia*."
He shook his head. "Laura had the real talent, and she was
smart enough to know what was right for her."

"She fell in love," I said.

"Well, there's that. I suppose. So there we were, Laura and
I—there everyone was, really, family, teachers poised to send
us off to New York. Only there were two minor technicalities
where I was concerned: I wasn't good enough, and I didn't
want it badly enough. My parents wouldn't listen to me. Just
because I had some talent I was supposed to— Sometime
I'll tell you all about the pater familias and the Arts." Simon
leaned forward. "I didn't know how to talk to Laura about
it. Or maybe I was afraid to. I mean when I started freak-
ing out about it. All I could do was get drunk and high and
alienate her. I was young, scared, desperate. So desperate that
I thought if I did something really egregious, I'd be able to
wriggle my way out of it. And everyone would realize they
were mistaken about me."

"You forged some checks."

"A gesture that seems to have defined my life. You look
bored." Simon was speaking to Alex. "Am I boring you?"

"When did you run away from home?" Alex answered.

Simon looked over at me. "What makes him think I ran
away from home?"

Alex said, "You ran away, didn't you?"

Simon was still looking at me. "My parents' advice to me was—they thought I couldn't make the commitment or the sacrifices, but what's the sense of doing either if the love isn't there. Or the talent. They didn't believe that. I don't mean they thought I was lying, I mean, they didn't understand. They thought that I lacked the drive, the ambition, that *they* had *for* me." He looked back at Alex. "Is there something else you're just dying to ask me?"

Alex grinned. "Are you through telling us why your parents never understood you?"

Simon turned and grinned back at Alex.

"When the smoke cleared, I tried to get back in the good graces of my family, first at Bennington, and when that didn't work out, the nearest community college, which also didn't go according to plan. I don't know why."

"Why it didn't work out, or why you expected it would?" Alex asked.

"I'd like you to stop annoying me," Simon answered, "and let me finish talking with Geoffrey." He got up and walked across the room, pulled back the curtain and looked out the window. With his back to Alex and me, he said, "I'm going to be forty years old and still don't know why I do most of the things I do." He turned and looked only at Alex while he said, "Maybe I'll get it figured out the next time Self-Awareness Week rolls around."

I'd been watching Alex through most of Simon's monologue. I didn't know what my brother's face looked like when he was with his patients, but I guessed that it looked much the way it did while he listened to Simon. Not just curious but concerned. I supposed a psychoanalyst analyzed regardless of the venue. That was what I thought at first.

"Eventually I ran away from Shady Grove," Simon was telling us, "hustling around—not *that* kind of hustling, faking my way into one job or another. I was only eighteen, nineteen years old, so you can imagine the shit I had to do." He came back to his chair, sat down, and folded his coat over his lap again. "Sometimes I crashed with friends, sleeping on dorm floors, finessing meals in dining halls, doing whatever . . . Finally, I came to New York. Which is where you come in, Geoffrey."

"My couch and twenty-five dollars."

"And the next thing I know, Geoffrey's telling me that my sister's married and out of the country." He shook his head and frowned at me. "I knew you were lying to me, that day. I didn't know she was getting married, I found that out later, but I knew she didn't want me anywhere near her, not then. I know what you did for her."

I spoke to the expression I saw on Alex's face. "I told Simon that Laura had left the country, when in fact she was downtown getting married."

Simon told Alex, "He also used to cover for her when she was off somewhere with Steve and my parents got curious."

Alex was sitting forward, his elbow on his knee and his chin resting in the palm of his hand, as though he were studying, scrutinizing, not only what Simon was telling us, but Simon himself. He looked unhappy.

"I think that's what I envied the most." Simon was talking to me. "When we were kids, Laura and I always confided in each other. We talked about everything. And then she went away, and not only had I lost my closest friend, but she met you and confided in you and she didn't need me anymore. And I still wanted to be the person she could tell things to, instead of you." He felt around the inside of his coat pocket again. "I've often wondered if you were the brother substitute. The *good* brother. You know, leaving the theater at a young age, the way I left dance? Only without the angst." He took out the cigarette and this time placed it between his fingers.

"So, what do you think?" Simon was speaking to Alex.

"Was I supposed to think something?" Alex sat back now.

"About what I've been saying."

"What have you been saying?"

"I mean," Simon told him, "shouldn't your brother at least *try* to help me out here?"

"This is between you and Geoffrey. What makes you think I want to be involved?"

"Isn't that why you're sitting here?"

"I came to see my brother."

"And you have no opinion?"

Alex folded his arms behind his head.

"I have lots of opinions."

"About what I've been saying."

"How could I not have an opinion?"

"Don't you think Geoffrey should help me out?"

"I think you're full of shit."

"I don't think you're qualified to have that opinion," Simon told him.

"I don't think you're qualified to question my qualifications."

Simon put a cigarette in his mouth. "You're a funny kind of brother," he told Alex.

"You should see me at parties." There was a sly smile on Alex's face. If it had been anyone else, I'd have thought he was flirting.

"You think I'm lying?"

"Is that what I said?"

"Why would I make all of that up?"

"*Did* you make it all up?" Alex asked.

"I liked you better," Simon answered, "when you were bored with me."

Alex said, "Something tells me you'll be boring again before long."

Simon gave Alex a flashy little smile and said to me, "Mind if I have a cigarette out on your terrace?" and walked away.

"And that," I told Alex, when Simon closed the terrace door, "is Simon Welles."

"He's kind of sweet. In a damaged sort of way."

"Didn't you just call him a liar?"

"He's being less than forthright. I didn't say he was lying, I said he was full of shit, which he is. He's not that desperate to stay in his sister's house. But he's trying to find out what you'll do for him. And I'd like to find out, too."

"Did I miss something?"

"What could you miss?"

"You're interested in *Simon*?"

"Interested as in how? If you mean professionally, he's pretty standard."

"Interested as in what was just going on between the two of you?"

"Just because I don't think he's lying?"

"I could leave the two of you alone if you like."

"Did *I* miss something?" Alex looked at his watch, then in the direction of the terrace. "Anyway, I came here to talk to you."

I told him: "My problems aren't that important at the

moment. I prefer watching you and Simon." And I did enjoy watching Alex circling Simon, albeit rhetorically. I was pleased that my brother seemed to enjoy the sparring and sniping, even if it was with someone as screwed up as Simon Welles.

"Simon is the *last* thing I need right now," Alex said.

"He might be fun. And you just might need to take your mind off your—"

"You are no judge of what I need. And certainly not of what's on my mind." Alex stood up and grabbed his coat. "It's foolish to even consider—I don't want to talk about it."

"Other things have been more foolish."

Alex's lips were pressed close together, and his eyes were narrowed.

"I'm not saying you have to do anything about it," I told him, "but isn't this what we've been talking about? Taking a chance—"

"Just mind your own damn business."

Simon came back into living room, not quite closing the terrace door behind him.

"Did you make up your mind while I was away?" he asked.

"If you want to stay at Laura's, talk to Remsen about it."

"You're a mean son of a bitch, Geoffrey." Simon turned to Alex. "I'm going downtown, can I drop you somewhere?"

"Yes," I said, "can he drop you somewhere?"

Alex said, "I have to talk to my brother."

I said, "I doubt that Simon has the cab fare, but so what? We'll talk tomorrow."

I started to laugh as soon as they were out the door.

I didn't hear from Alex the following day, but I did get a call late that same morning from Amy Brennan reminding me that I had a theater date with Nick and her that night. I didn't say anything about my breaking up with Rita until we'd seen the show and the three of us were having drinks at the Algonquin.

I told them, "What I find most remarkable is that it seems never to have happened."

They thought I was talking about the breakup. I said I was talking about the entire relationship. That I'd realized just how insubstantial it was.

"Like speaking into an empty paper cup."

They didn't understand how I could feel this way. After all, Rita and I had been such a good-looking couple. What more did I want? What more did I expect?

But wasn't that the point? That it wasn't a matter of what I expected. It was a matter of what I wanted.

I wanted to talk about Laura's love for Steve and Marian's for Buddy. And tell them about gardens and spiky flowers and tall grasses. And that I'd known Rita for three years and could walk away from her without regrets or sorrow, but I couldn't shake my heart loose from an afternoon with Marian, and I couldn't sleep nights, aching to see her again.

I wanted to talk about the willingness to be made mad with love and by the loss of love. But it wasn't about grief, it was about passion. That's what I wanted, the willingness to be made mad with love, if just for a little while.

But I didn't tell them, not when all they could think to say was that my breakup with Rita was crazy. After all, we got along, always had a good time, and looked so good together. And I was just being cuckoo.

Amy said this was all too depressing. I wasn't behaving

like the Geoffrey she and Nick knew and liked so much, and could I please come to my senses, change the subject, and enjoy our evening together.

When I was alone in the taxi, riding back to my apartment, I was thinking not about this particular evening but the night at Keens when I'd just come back from my first trip to Shady Grove, and the way my friends spoke about Laura; how amusing they thought they were, how annoyed I was with them; and last week, the easy conversations with pocket-depth; and wasn't that just like the Geoffrey my friends knew and liked so well, wasn't that what they expected of me, to enjoy the nights, and the people who were part of those nights.

My friends were sure to call, and, oh yes, we really should . . . and just as soon as . . . Which made me feel as adrift as I'd felt after I'd walked away from Rita, unmoored from all the things that I'd found so comfortable and benign. And I didn't mind.

Leaning back in the cab, watching the city lights roll by on Madison Avenue, I thought about the heart's autonomy. That it didn't matter whether or not a person was willing to fall in love. Willingness had nothing to do with it. It was a matter of having no other choice.

While I was quite at ease with this insight, looking into the hearts of Laura and Marian, and into my own, I wasn't ready to share it with anyone else, just in case, as happens with most late night revelations, it would dissolve with the first rays of sunlight or the sound of a human voice. The only person I would have risked speaking to was Alex, had I been able to get him on the phone.

Alex didn't return my call that night, or the next day. I

didn't hear from him the following day or the day after, either. Not that I was exactly lying fallow. There was my work to attend to, a stray ticket for a concert at Carnegie Hall, and several evenings alone, enjoying the pleasure of my own company and counsel.

I was adrift but no longer becalmed, staring at an endless horizon.

When Alex stopped by the apartment on Saturday morning, I was in my pajamas, sitting in the living room, drinking my coffee.

"You're a tough man to get ahold of these days," I told him.

He sat down but only on the edge of the chair, and didn't bother taking off his coat. It made me think he had a cab downstairs with the meter running. Or maybe someone was waiting for him.

"As I recall, the last time I saw you, you were on your way out of here with Simon Welles."

"I'm really sorry for running out on you like that."

"There's nothing to be sorry about. You weren't running out on me, and you don't owe me an apology."

"You're very kind."

"A busy week?"

He unbuttoned his coat and leaned back in the chair.

"I want to hear all about it," I said.

"What day is it?"

"You left here with Simon. I haven't heard from you . . . *Talk.*"

"It's not what you think."

"Talk."

"Aren't you getting a little personal?" he said.

"That must have been one hell of a taxi ride."

"You've got a dirty mind."

"You seemed amused by it the last time I saw you."

"That was before."

I had to laugh. "This really is great. Simon. Of all people."

Alex was not laughing with me. "Get dressed," he said. "I have to get back to my office."

"*All* week?" I asked.

"You can walk me there."

"You walked all the way over here *from* your office just to ask me to walk you *back* there?"

"I have *no* idea *what* I'm doing. It's wreaking havoc with me, my schedule. My commitments . . ."

"Of course," I said. "Your *commitments*."

"Really."

"I know . . . I know . . ."

"And besides—"

"You and Simon." I clucked my tongue. "I should be surprised."

"It's not *me* and *Simon*."

"Does Simon know that?"

"Stop or I'm leaving." Alex was smiling now, and looked as though he enjoyed my teasing.

"Not without me in tow."

"Then get dressed. Do you have any tea or ginger ale?"

Alex walked to the kitchen. I went to my bedroom and got dressed. When I came back, Alex was still in the kitchen, standing near the stove, watching the kettle boil. In the bright sunlight his face looked pink and smooth, the skin lying soft and settled on the bone, the way it does after a night's deep sleep.

I poured myself a second cup of coffee, and hoisted myself onto the countertop.

"He wanted to know about me," Alex said. "I can't remember the last time anyone wanted to hear me talk about myself—except professionally, and you, but that's different." He turned off the flame, opened a canister, took out a tea bag and put it into a cup. "We talked. After we left here. For hours." Alex repeated the word *hours*.

"That's what we did after we left here," he said. "That's what we've been doing most of the time. I'm too old to bother with other people's bullshit, which is just about all Simon's about, but not when he talked with me." Alex took a sip of tea. "He fell asleep on my couch." He raised the cup toward my face. "And don't say a word."

"Have I said *anything*?"

"I know what you're thinking."

"Actually I'm still getting a kick out of the idea of you and Simon."

"I came to talk seriously with you, not hear about what you do or don't get a kick out of." He took another sip, put the cup on the counter, and said he wanted to get out and walk. "You have the wrong impression of him," he told me.

Outside, walking up Fifth Avenue, Alex said, "I realized something, Geoffrey. It's the oddest thing. Well, not odd really. Something I've been aware of, as you know. I'm tired of being alone. I don't mean tired as in I don't like it or it's wearing me down. I mean tired as in it's become uninteresting."

"Was it ever interesting?"

"And *time* consuming. I think I enjoy his company."

"You *think*?"

We walked east to Madison Avenue and continued uptown. Alex stopped to look in the window of a clothing store.

"He's just so damned defended all the time. Like the port-cullis comes down. Then he goes into his routine. It's so obvious what he's doing, no wonder you get impatient with him. *I* get impatient with him." He turned away and we kept on walking.

At Seventy-second Street, we crossed the street and walked to Park Avenue.

Alex said, "He's the way he is for a reason."

"Aren't we all."

"Don't be such a smart-ass. I know you're thinking he's trying to con me. That's how he sounds even when he isn't trying. That's the way he's been living his whole adult life. It's the only way he knows how to get what he wants. Or what he wants at any particular moment."

"And you think you can change him? Fix what's broken?"

"You know I have good judgment about people, and I don't just do things without giving them a lot of thought. And you have to trust that I haven't all of sudden changed in the past five days."

"So you *do* know what day it is."

It was another block before Alex said, "You really should help him."

I shook my head. "I'm not getting involved in that."

"I want you to listen to me, okay? You kept him away from Laura's wedding, you don't have to keep him away from her life. Your obligation is over."

"Is that what this conversation's about?"

"He hasn't had time to properly mourn his sister's death.

Going to Shady Grove will give him a chance to do that. Otherwise, all he's going to do is keep revisiting that experience."

"I don't usually argue with you on your home turf, but this time I can't agree."

"He's going to keep repeating it without ever having a real chance to get over it."

"Are you his shrink now, too?"

"He's not bullshitting about wanting closure." Alex pulled his head back, as though he needed to get a better look at me. He said, "Simon's right. You can be a very abrasive person."

I told him I had no idea what he was talking about.

"You're no longer Laura's protector, only her executor, and your job does not require that you protect Marian, either."

"You think I'm protecting Marian?"

"Your resistance is staggering." Alex took a deep breath, and as he exhaled, said, "You treat him like he's some kid who once stole your bicycle."

"Have you heard about the roommate he ran out on? And the vintage Mercedes he left on the street?"

"What he told us the other night about the trouble he got into—I think if that had been all there was to it, just some stupid adolescent mistake, but it was more involved than that, and more involved than what he told us. What he said, that he and Laura were like performing monkeys, wasn't completely off the mark. They were two *very* talented kids living in the shadow of every arts performance in the Berkshires."

We were a block away from Alex's office now. He leaned his hand on my arm to slow me down.

"They were enrolled in music school and dance school when they were much too young, performed at recitals and things like that. It was a small town, so they got noticed and were considered pretty exceptional. Simon referred to Laura as a 'virtuoso' more than a few times when he talked about her. For a time, and this was before they were even in their teens, there weren't a lot of people their age they could talk to, they really only had each other to keep them sane. It wasn't that their parents were putting undue pressure on them, or living vicariously through their children. It was in the mix, sure, but Simon doesn't think that was all there was to it." Alex pulled me to a stop. "You weren't supposed to cheat yourself, squander your talent. That's the message they got from their parents. The theme, if you will, of their childhood." He said, "If Simon had shown a talent for plumbing, or medicine, it would have been the same. It so happened he could dance well, and was being told how wonderful he was by his dance teachers, the other kids in his dance class, everyone, parents included." He hadn't let go of me yet, gave my arm another squeeze, and we started walking. He didn't say anything more for another few minutes until we'd come to his building and were inside the vestibule.

The doorman handed Alex a stack of mail, and unlocked Alex's door for us. We walked through the waiting room and into the office. While Alex sat at his desk, I sat in one of the chairs on the other side of the room. Alex didn't say anything for a moment. I thought he'd lost track of what he was telling me until he said, "Simon was a thirteen-, fourteen-year-old kid living in his tight little world and feeling the drive and pressure, not to mention the competition to 'make it.' Do you remember what it was like for you in the theater when you were that age? Well, Simon hated it. He thought that everyone was wrong about him, and he was a fraud. Laura, however, was taking everything in stride." Alex began sorting his mail. "Laura was already breathing rarefied air before she was sixteen and liking it, and certainly not lacking for confidence in her achievement. She had her own group of admirers, teachers, other music students, a secure circle of friends."

"And Marian was one of them?"

Alex tossed the rest of the mail aside, and looked over at me. "Simon was feeling nothing but miserable." He sounded miserable when he said this, but there was more in his voice than unhappiness. I suppose if I'd been alone, or if Alex had stopped talking for a moment, I might have been able to remember some other time when he spoke to me about someone the way he was talking about Simon, except there had been no other time.

He leaned back in his chair. "Okay, comes his senior year in high school, Simon passes his Juilliard auditions, most of his friends would have traded places with him in an instant, and the ones who wouldn't were part of the competition and envious—and oh, let's not forget he was hitting his sexual stride and realizing he liked boys instead of girls, which may have been acceptable among the young dancers he was around, but it had to remain unmentioned and under wraps with the family and the rest of little old Shady Grove."

The telephone rang, Alex lifted his finger and picked up the receiver. He stopped talking to me long enough to reschedule one of his patients. When he put down the phone, he said, "So now . . ." He folded his hands behind his head. "Simon was not only conflicted and scared, he had his very own secret life to deal with and there was no Laura to talk to, she was already at Juilliard, and he did what any panicked teenager would do. He ran away. Got on a bus and went to see his sister. It was her sophomore year—isn't that the year you met her? He says Laura tried to get him to talk to her, but he felt so ashamed of himself, and knew he was disappointing her, so all he did was self-destruct, slowly, and right before her eyes. And when she offered to help, he was sure it meant getting him to change his mind and go back to dancing. There seemed to be no way out for him, and that scared him even more." Alex's voice never seemed to relax, and I was having a hard time identifying just what he was working toward.

He stood up, came over to the couch, sat, leaned back against the cushions, but he got up again to open the shutters, then sat in the chair facing mine.

He said, "You see, Geoffrey, as far as his parents were concerned, his friends, his teachers, even Laura, Simon's talent was a given, and therefore his love for dance must have also been a given. If Simon wanted anything less than artistic success, well, it was just plain negligent. At least that's what he was hearing from his parents. How could he do that to himself? Simon's fear that he might not be good enough was a *real* fear. But it was beyond his parents' comprehension. They told him that he may not be as good as he wanted to be *now*, but in time he would be, by the sheer will of his desire." Alex raised his voice, "He really does believe that you and he have that in common. That you left the theater because you had real fears about your talent. I think it's good that he thinks that. It makes you less intimidating to him."

"Why do I intimidate him?" I didn't wait for an answer. "I still don't get it."

When he looked at me I could see that Alex was not pleased with what I'd said.

"What it really came down to is something you can understand and what you two *do* have in common: Simon didn't love it enough. Laura dearly loved playing the violin. I don't think she could understand how anyone could not love the thing they were most talented in. And I don't think she appreciated that Simon was convinced that he wasn't as talented as people thought he was, or she thought he was, and eventually everyone would realize that. He had real fears of failure and humiliation. And he felt trapped by a plan, a course, set out for him by other people. And when he came to New York and saw his sister, he felt that he'd let *her* down. Then that passed and what he had left was his anger."

"Are you speaking professionally?"

He laughed at that. "I'm not so sure I'm totally objective. I don't—"

There was another phone call that Alex said he wanted to take. I thought he looked relieved to catch the break, and I didn't mind the interruption, but when I started to leave the room he put his hand over the mouthpiece and asked me where I was going, as though I might be running out on him. I mouthed the word *coffee* and went into the kitchen.

I stayed there for another minute or so. I was thinking about the way Alex was acting, and if I'd never heard my brother speak to me the way he was speaking to me today, I wondered why. What was Alex trying to tell me? What was I hearing? That he was defending Simon? Was it even more simple than that? Was he showing me how attracted he was to Simon? Was that supposed to be reason enough to consider why I was so uncomfortable around Simon? Was everything he'd been saying a preamble?

Alex came in before the coffee finished brewing. He gave both me and the carafe a glance, opened the refrigerator, pulled out a bottle of water, and stood there while the coffee dripped, not saying anything, doing nothing but making me nervous with his silence, and impatient with him.

"Where is this leading?" I wanted to know.

"I'm in the middle of telling you." He watched me fill my cup and waited for me to walk out, go back to the office, and sit in my chair. He sat on the edge of the couch.

"Keep in mind that he was stuck at home, dealing with nothing but disapproval, feeling incredibly lonely, and when his parents weren't badgering him, Simon had to listen to them rant about Laura's romance with Steve. He was angry at Laura. With himself. With his parents. And, with all the wisdom of a seventeen-year-old, decided that the only way out was to do something so terrible that it would wreck not only the plans his parents were making, but also the perception they and everyone else had of him. It seemed to be a more palatable humiliation."

"That's why he forged the checks?"

"It left him feeling depressed and ashamed of himself. There was a *lot* of shame attached to all of this. He'd not only disappointed his family and embarrassed them, he'd shamed himself; but I'd say the underlying feeling, what propelled him, was his anger."

I was watching Alex more than listening to him. His face had lost that pink smooth look, and the softness of a night's sleep. And when he started to speak again, as he told me more about Simon, the more hurried his words became. The timbre rose and fell, as though he were anxious, unsure of what he was saying. I'd never heard Alex sound like that.

"Remember when he said that he went off to Bennington? Well, he was just trying to get away from his parents and feeling like a screwup, and all he did was behave like an even bigger screwup. He flunked out, came back, lived at home, and went to the local community college. He lasted all of two weeks before he ran away again. Simon admits that Shady Grove may not be anyone's idea of heaven-on-earth, but it was a very pleasant sort of place to live, and it was, after all, home. The home he exiled himself from."

A discomforting thought occurred to me while Alex said this.

"What year was this?" I asked him.

"Your junior year. Isn't that what you want to know? Laura had already been to Paris with Steve. She was well on her way and having a great time. The two of you were. Simon wandered around, living by his wits, or lack thereof, first in Amherst, crashing with friends at UMass. Sleeping on dormitory floors, just as he said. Earning money delivering pizzas to some of the same kids who once envied him. Then Boston, crashing with friends at Berklee, B.U., Cambridge, for a while. He realized that he didn't know how to do anything. He worked as a busboy. A 'coffee jockey' as he called it. Telemarketing. Even did some phone sex—straight and gay. You'd be surprised how many women are into that."

I stopped him. "What you said before? Our having a great time? You're not saying that *I* had anything to do with Simon fucking up his life? Just because I didn't let him go to a wedding?"

"Do you think you did?"

"Come on, Alex—"

"New Hampshire . . . Boston. On his eighteenth birthday, he was clearing tables in a coffee shop on Brattle Street in Cambridge. That summer, he worked as a busboy on the

Cape. Provincetown, at least until he found other means of support."

"If you're trying to accuse me of—"

"It was 1986, the AIDS epidemic was quite real, and Simon was being really careful, and scared out of his mind because he's this beautiful boy, and everybody's pet. Plenty of parties, plenty of houses with soft comfortable beds to sleep in, until the end of summer and everyone's going home. Now, he hadn't seen his parents or Laura or slept in his own bed for more than a year. For all intents and purposes he was homeless. His parents were distraught. They only knew that he was alive by rumor. Some of the parents of Simon's friends would let them know the little they'd heard. Meanwhile, he kept wandering around, barely making enough money to keep from starving. This went on for about another year, when he decided to go to New York and see Laura for the first time in over a year. Maybe he thought that enough time had passed for a rapprochement. Most likely, he was just tired of running away, and was hoping he'd be able to muster a little comfort and forgiveness from his sister."

I waited for him to go on, but he didn't speak. He sat back with his arms behind his head, looking self-satisfied.

I said, "Do you want me to say that Laura was too involved with Steve to attend to Simon's problems, and to understand that Simon was coming to her for help?"

"She was too involved with more than just Steve."

It took me a moment or two to work out what Alex was getting at. "Laura was too busy with her own life, her own success to do anything to help Simon? That we were both being mean and self-absorbed? Is that what you're saying?"

"You were there. Is that what you remember?"

I was less concerned with what I remembered than looking for a clearer understanding of what Alex was doing. Was I being taken to task for being Laura's friend? Which was what I asked him.

He waved away the question with the back of his hand.

"I know Laura tried to help him, as much as she could. And Simon is well aware how deeply he hurt her. He was aware of it at the time. He'd embarrassed her in front of Steve and their friends. He was verbally abusive. He *stole* from her. And she was afraid of him." Alex sat forward, rested his arms on his knees. But even when he spoke about Laura, it seemed to me he was talking about the kid in rumpled clothes, staring at his sister's apartment door.

"And Laura had her own problems to contend with," he said. "Her parents forbade her to squander her talents playing jazz. They were both saddened and worried about her living with Steve in France. They were not reserved in their disapproval at the prospect. They said Laura was demeaning herself. They actually used the word *demeaning*, if you can imagine that. They played all of this out in front of Simon, and he'd alienated Laura so completely that it wasn't even a matter of her choosing to stay and help him. Simon had made that decision for her. And her parents, well, she must have felt that she was getting out from under her own family pressures. You'd know about that better than I. And that's where you came in: You did what Laura wanted you to do. How much thought you put into it, only you know, or knew at the time."

"Look," I said, "this was between the two of them. Brother and sister. It still is. I was never involved and don't try to get me involved in it now."

Alex shook his head. His lips went taut for an instant before he said, "You're too smart for that kind of crap, so please, shut up and listen." He adjusted a pillow behind his head and sat back. "You may not have thought what you did to Simon was cruel. You may have thought there was even something noble about it. But when he came to the city that morning, he needed to see his sister, he needed to connect with whatever was left between them, and you prevented that. And so did Laura."

"How could either of us have known that?"

Alex shrugged his shoulders.

"You really think it would have made a difference in the way things have turned out for Simon?"

"He does."

I started to speak again. Alex raised his finger to silence me.

He said, "After that weekend, thinking he'd missed Laura's wedding, Simon was more restless than ever. He simply drifted. He was fed up with all the menial work and started finding people willing to take care of him, and whenever that became too entangling, or became too tiring, he just walked out. No matter how much he tried, Simon just couldn't wrap his mind around being the son his parents expected him to be and how he embarrassed Laura and let her and everyone else down. And maybe there really was nothing much to him. Living a vagrant's life. And for all he knew, or could hope for, that was what he would be for the rest of his life. His parents died, two years apart, two other funerals he missed."

Alex looked at his watch, closed his eyes for a moment, and let out a deep sigh.

He said, "One time, he came to New York and happened to see Laura and Steve playing a gig in the Village. He didn't try talking to her, only sat at the bar and got drunk. The same thing happened a few years later in San Francisco. Meanwhile, ten years passed, and Simon went from being a beautiful boy to just another man pushing thirty, trying to survive, charming people, conning them, living on borrowed money, sleeping in borrowed beds, wearing borrowed clothes, driving borrowed cars . . . Ten more years, and he's a grown man with no prospects, and nothing to show for his life, except the same charming and conniving self, only now with more effort and fewer results, barely keeping his head above water, leaving a trail of roommates in his wake. He kept up with Laura. Read all the reviews of their American dates."

"Where *would* we be without Google."

"Even before Google. When they'd release a new CD he'd buy it. He knew the trio was based in Europe and they came to the States at least once a year, but he never got to see them after San Francisco. That was back in '92.

"Then he read that Steve had died, the trio had disbanded, and Laura had moved back to America. Then nothing more, not about the trio, or Laura. The next time he heard about his sister was from one of his old friends who he'd been keeping in touch with, at least as much as Simon kept up with anyone. His friend told him Laura had died. That's how Simon heard about it. And that Remsen was handling her affairs. From a friend. An *acquaintance*."

I was listening while I tried to imagine the two of them, Simon taking Alex into his confidence, Alex taking Simon into his; and I had to think whatever motivated Simon to open up as he did with Alex was the result of Alex opening up with Simon. Which was what I told him.

I said, "Simon must want you to know who he is."

Alex said, "He wants *you* to know. That's why he came to

see you. He was profoundly hurt when he found out what you did. You and Laura."

"How did he find out?"

"Ask him sometime."

I got up and walked out of the office. I felt like I was tumbling down a flight of stairs. I went into the waiting room. The windows were closed and the room was hot and airless. I leaned back against the wall and felt myself sweat.

Alex came out. He put his hand on my shoulder.

"You did what you did," he said.

"And all of a sudden it's supposed to *mean* something?"

"Only what you want it to."

"And what about you? What are you doing in the middle of all this?"

He pushed me down onto a chair and stood next to me, keeping his hand on my shoulder.

"You think Simon's the person who'll be glad to see you at the end of the day? Is that what this is about?" I asked.

"I don't know about that. But I wanted you to know, in Simon's words, what you're dealing with."

"You're saying you have a crush on the guy?"

"Crush is a little priggish, don't you think?"

"And I should be nice to him?"

"I'm too panicked to give a name to what I'm feeling, or what I want from you. Let's just say I've enjoyed my few days with him." He took his hand off my shoulder now. "Simon should never have lied to you about why he didn't go to Laura's funeral. The truth is, he didn't have enough money for a plane ticket. So after missing the funeral, he ran out on his roommate and used the rent money to buy a ticket to come see you. All he wants is to go back to Shady Grove, say good-bye to his sister, and try to come to terms with all of this. What he really wants, if only for a day or two, is to go home. Look, Geoffrey, all this guy's been doing most of his life is asking people for help, and yet he's bad at it and miserable about it."

"And he needs my help?" I said.

"Let's get out of here."

"I wasn't very fair to him."

"That's a long line," Alex said, "and there are a lot of people ahead of you."

I CALLED REMSEN THE FOLLOWING MORNING. HE WAS LESS THAN enthusiastic about Simon coming up there. He said as Laura's executor, I should be there while Simon was in the house. As Laura's attorney, he would prefer that I respect that condition. When I told this to Alex, he said, "So much the better. Now you have your excuse for seeing Marian again. But, I'm sure, you've already thought of that."

Ten

WE WERE IN MY CAR AND HEADING NORTH ON THE DRIVE.
I felt that I was at a disadvantage, having to watch
the road and not Simon's face when he spoke.

"Alex says I should be on my best behavior with you," he
said.

I told him to stop behaving like a child.

He said, "I see we're going to have a wonderful trip."

I said, "I agreed to help you. All you have to do is be real
with me."

"I've always found that a difficult thing to do with you."

"*Always*? Until about a month ago, the grand total of how
long we've been acquaintances came to never."

"I've always resented you for what you did."

"I'm sorry about that. But if it's any consolation, I've never
liked myself for doing it."

"And Marian? You must have seen her when you went to

my sister's place. Tell me she didn't show up when you were there and warn you about me?"

"Do you *really* think that anyone's giving you that much thought?"

"I hardly find that reassuring."

We were just over the Willis Avenue Bridge and in the Bronx, before Simon asked, "Did it bother you when Alex told you about me? You probably didn't like it."

"Why wouldn't I like it?"

"You don't have to worry about him. Your brother has a gift. He can see through walls." He said this with so much affection that I had to look at him twice: once because there was none of that acerbity in his voice, and a second time, to make sure this wasn't another part of his *routine*. It was Simon unguarded, and I was thinking how much work he must have put into his resentments and postures, the pretense.

We drove a half an hour longer and were out of the city and on the Parkway. We had music on the CD player.

Simon asked me, "Did he tell you to go easy on me?"

"*You* should go easy on you. You must be exhausted," I said. "You must exhaust yourself. After all these years." I was watching the road again, and couldn't see Simon's face when I said this.

A few minutes passed before he said, "Money and food, and how to get it. That's all I used to think about. I still do. It bothered me at first, then it became part of my life."

Another minute or so passed: "You do enough thinking about *anything* and it stands to reason you'll draw a conclusion or two." He turned down the music. "I've come to realize this country doesn't like its poor. It makes everyone feel like a failure. I mean, like the country failed in providing for all its people and can't cop to it, so we blame poor people for being poor. There are people out there who'd criminalize the poor if they could get away with it. Like it's something they choose."

"You made the choice."

"Mine was a self-inflicted injury."

"You've been at it most of your life."

"I've tried to change that. I tell myself I've tried, anyway. A few college courses here and there. And just when it looks like I might actually pick myself up and turn my life around, I lose interest or drop out or run away. I doubt that it's something you can understand, but what I've felt all these years, in absolutely the truest sense of the word, is worthless. Unworthy, if you like. Am I being direct enough for you? Enough self-awareness?"

"Why do you have to ask questions like that?"

"I did a terrible thing letting my family down like that. My sister, most of all. So why should I get a pass? Whatever else happened, or will happen, I have it coming to me."

"How will seeing your sister's house make any difference?"

"You can't *really* be this impenetrable."

"I'm sincerely curious."

Simon sat low in the seat, his eyes were closed.

He said, "Being around the things she lived with, will close it all out," as though he were talking to a simpleton. "If I can just say good-bye to her, in my way, pay my respects, maybe I'll feel like I've made amends. Maybe I just have to see for myself that my sister is dead."

"I don't understand this obsession with the past."

"Obsession is a pretty strong word."

"Then attachment. What happened, happened. And really, what you did was not so terrible."

Simon didn't answer right away. When he did, he turned his face away from me.

"There's this one time in your life, or one place, when you were the best you are ever going to be, with people whose love for you and yours for them was so absolute, that it's all you wanted. And then it's gone, and all you want is to be reunited with what it used to feel like, because you know that you'll never be able to love any other people or any other place like you do those people and that place. Laura couldn't replace the love she had for Steve. I can't replace my love for her and how it felt to be her younger brother back when we were kids. But how can I not go looking for it?"

I didn't say anything. I started thinking about Marian staying in her house after Buddy died. The scrapbook Laura saved and left behind. I was thinking what it must be like to feel that the best part of yourself is in the past. What it must be like to remember the day before it was gone. Now I understood what Marian had been telling me that afternoon when I'd driven up to see her. She wasn't talking about a time when all she was was happier than she was now, or less lonely, but a time when she felt complete— When you lose that, you wake in the morning and at night in your bed, your first thought, your last thought isn't about the irretrievable past, but the irretrievable you.

When I looked over at Simon, he was still staring out the window. We were less than an hour away from Shady Grove, the scenery must have looked familiar to him.

"This was a bad idea," he said and asked me to stop the car. "I need a cigarette."

"Just roll down the window."

"I can't stand all the wind in my face. Pull over some-where. Please."

I pulled over. Simon got out of the car and started pacing along the side of the road while he puffed on his cigarette, walked past the car, turned, and walked back.

"I don't want to see Remsen," he said, "when we get there."

"I have to stop at his office. He's got the house key. You can wait in the car."

"I don't want to see anyone."

"Who do you have in mind?"

"I just want—I'm just going to stay in the house and not go out."

"That's fine."

"Wait . . . Forget it . . . Turn around."

"I'm not going to do that."

"Take me back to the city."

"No way."

"Why should you care whether or not I go? This was a bad idea."

"Finish your cigarette and get back in the car."

Simon dropped onto the front seat and tucked his hands under his armpits; his chin rested on his chest. His mouth was turned down, not so much in a frown and not in a pout. It wasn't petulance that I was looking at. It was the look of grim defeat. The wanderer, the drifter who is neither heroic nor mythic, but just what Alex said: A man who wanted, if only for a day or two, to go home.

About a mile later Simon told me, "I don't know what I was thinking." And a mile or two later, "If anyone asks, don't tell them who I am."

"Most of the people you knew have probably moved away," I said. "And the ones who stayed won't recognize you."

"You think?"

"You'll be anonymous."

"That I'm used to."

Another mile passed. He said, "Thanks. Thanks for saying that."

IT WAS EARLY AFTERNOON WHEN I PULLED UP IN FRONT OF REMSEN'S office, went in and got the key to Laura's house, and when I came out stood for a moment under the gentle springtime sun.

It was a warm day even for the last week of April, with signs of life in the town square, crocuses and daffodils, people sitting on benches, walking down the sidewalks wearing their spring colors. One of those people was Marian, wearing an orange sweatshirt and blue jeans.

She was standing on the other side of the street, staring at me over the roof of a car, just staring with her head cocked to one side, and smiling in a way that made me think she was waiting for me to walk over to her.

I told Simon, "Wait here," crossed the street while I waved at her, cognizant of nothing but Marian standing at the corner.

"I wish I'd known you were coming back," she said.

"You would have liked if I'd called ahead?"

"I don't know what I'd like, actually."

"I think you do."

"What are you doing here, anyway?"

"I came with Simon."

"Simon? Welles?"

"He wanted to see Laura's house."

"I wish you hadn't."

"I'm glad I did."

"Please don't say things like that to me."

"I *like* saying things like that to you."

"How long are you—does Simon think he'll be here?"

I said, "I want you to know that I get it. I get it now," and maybe I should have told her that I understood the longings and fears in the lyrics in old love songs, and her emotional paralysis after Buddy died, and Laura's. And the crazy thrill of standing on this particular sidewalk talking to her about anything, even Simon Welles. But I would have felt foolish telling her that, so when she said, "I don't know what you mean," all I answered was, "I'm going to be here only for a couple days. I'd like to talk to you sometime."

"You'll only mess up my life. I don't think that's a good idea."

"Do you really believe that?"

She looked over her shoulder at the row of stores behind her, and at the few people walking by.

"We can't talk out here."

"Where do you have in mind?"

"I asked you not to try to see me again."

I smiled at her. "That's one of the things I get."

She turned around and walked away from me. I watched her until I was sure she wouldn't turn back to look, then I crossed the street to my car.

After I pulled away from the curb, Simon asked me who I'd been talking to, and when I told him, he said, "*That* was Marian? She was very happy to see you."

"How could you tell?"

"The way she was watching you, before you looked up, and the way she was grinning when you were talking to her. Weren't you *there*? Like someone had turned on a light."

"Not the most original description, but I'll take it."

On the front lawn of Laura's house was a FOR SALE sign which hadn't been there when I'd left town. Inside nothing had changed. It was just dustier.

We stood in the center of the living room. Simon looked around as though he were measuring for a new carpet, walked across to the kitchen entrance and back again, at the same time telling me, "Go sit down somewhere and take it easy. I'll clean the place up a little. Really. It's no big deal. I used to clean houses for a living."

I went upstairs and put my overnight bag in the smaller bedroom, with the twin beds, ran my hand over the soft quilted bedspread, gave the lace curtains a glance, kicked off my shoes, and lay down on the bed. I thought about Marian, seeing her on the street, hearing her voice. And was Simon right? Was she really happy to see me?

I experienced a sense of exhilaration because I knew that this was not the infatuation Alex had talked of, or the distraction. I'd seen Marian on the street, and I'd felt exactly as I'd once imagined; exactly what I wanted to feel, seeing her again. And here I was in Shady Grove, where it was now possible to see her walking down the street again. Maybe tomorrow. That was, at least for now, enough.

I started to laugh, a loud, full-bodied laugh, and kept on laughing for a moment or two longer, when the phone rang.

It was Marian calling.

She said, "I want to explain my behavior before."

"I'd say you did all right the first time."

"No. You showed up at my house, then you just drove off. Now you show up again, this time with Simon Welles of all— Where did you find him, anyway?"

"He found *me*."

"You can't do that. Coming and going like that. You've really complicated things."

"I didn't mean to."

"I don't know if I can believe that."

I wanted her to be calling from her car, parked just down the street, and if I got up and pushed back the curtain, I'd see her sitting there; in another minute, I'd be down there, leaning through the open window, asking her, "What's so awful about making each other crazy?" Which was what I told her.

"You can't just show up when you feel like it and say these things to me," she said. "You'll go back to New York in a few days, or whenever." Her words came spilling out one on top of the other without any space between them—"And then when you feel like coming back"—until she ran out of breath, paused a moment and then went on: "I asked you not to try to see me again, and here you are, trying to see me again. That makes me *so* angry. I asked you not to come back here and you did. And there's Eliot to consider."

"I'm well aware of Eliot."

"If you see me on the street, just pass me by. If we should happen to be in the same— Oh God, do you even mean half the things you say?" There was silence after that, and she clicked off.

My feelings of exhilaration had not abated.

All I wanted now was to give Simon as much time as he needed in Laura's house, or whatever else he thought he wanted from Shady Grove.

Later, when I went downstairs, stepping over the vacuum cleaner, I saw Simon standing in the kitchen door with a mop in his hand; he'd just finished washing the floor. I told him I was going out for something to eat. He said we should go shopping, and he'd cook us supper.

"I'm not in the mood to play house. There must be a restaurant somewhere. I'm buying."

I found a little place far enough from town to assure Simon that he wouldn't see anyone who might remember him; the sort of a place where it seemed wise to stick to basics. We both had pasta.

Simon looked around, as though he might be recognized. Then he said, "What you said before, about playing house, it wasn't very nice."

"No, it wasn't. And while we're talking on this lovely evening together, would it kill you to stop lying to me?"

"You are one suspicious man. I was telling the truth when I said I missed my sister."

"And missing her funeral?"

"Does it really matter how? The fact is I did."

"You could have told me the truth the first time, instead of handing me all that crap."

"You aren't the easiest person to approach. I told you the story I thought would work. If I'd told you the truth, would it have made a difference?"

"Does my brother know how devious you are?"

"Marian looks good. Like herself. She's aging well."

"I'm sure she'd be glad to know you think so."

"Do you have to be so obnoxious?"

"Was that obnoxious?"

"Where was Buddy?"

"He's not in the picture."

"Divorce?"

I shook my head.

"Buddy Ballantine *died*?" He took a good look at me, the expression on his face went from that tight smugness to a look of retreat.

"Any more questions?"

"You and Marian?"

"Marian and someone, anyway."

"Someone? As in someone from Shady Grove? Name please?"

"Does it appear to you that I want to talk about this?"

He lifted his fork to his mouth, and after he took a bite and swallowed, "You have a thing for Marian Thayer—I mean, Ballantine—and you want me to *not* to bug you with questions? Are you out of your mind?"

"Are *you*?"

"Don't think I can't find out on my own."

"Alex won't help you with this."

"I hadn't even thought of Alex." He leaned forward and lowered his voice. "It must be someone I knew, or else you'd tell me."

"Why do you care so much?"

"Who could she possibly be interested in after Buddy Ballantine?"

"Someone named Eliot."

"Eliot? Not Eliot Wooten?"

"Why not Eliot Wooten?"

Simon put down his fork and sat back.

"I just lost my appetite. That's like going from Brando to—to some guy in a clown suit coming onstage and doing tricks on a toy tricycle."

"How so?"

"Buddy Ballantine? Buddy Ballantine, even when *I* knew him, was one of the most exceptional people you'll ever come across. And Eliot— Have you met him? He's the guy all the girls in school used to say was 'nice.' I bet he's still 'nice.' Tell me I'm wrong. How could anyone do that to them—"

"What's it to *you*?"

He looked repulsed by my question. "It offends my sensibilities."

"Don't be such a drama queen," I told him.

THE FOLLOWING MORNING, WHEN I CAME DOWNSTAIRS SIMON WAS standing on a stepladder, washing the living room windows.

"I had to do something to take my mind off—" He sat on the top rung. "So?"

"So? So what?"

"Look around. The furniture, the colors, the way she placed *objets*. This is what Laura chose to live with every day."

"Yes?"

"I'm talking about the things Laura lived with," he said. "And you with a gay brother."

"Are my homophile creds suddenly coming into question?"

"*And* a psychiatrist. Your entire lineage is under question. What does it tell you? I wish I knew what she had on the walls."

I sat in one of the chairs, and while Simon went back to washing windows, I told him about my first impression of not only this room but the rest of the house: that it was where someone's grandmother would be right at home, tidy, not fussy, but in strict order.

Simon stopped his work, climbed down, and sat across the room from me. The sunlight through the living room window brought a shadow across the floor and into the corner where Simon was sitting, but the rest of the light had turned the pink walls a softer roseate color. The chair where I sat now received the heat of the sun, while moment by moment the room grew warmer. I looked up to see him watching me.

"I would have loved to see what her apartment in Paris looked like," he said, "wouldn't you? But she made herself a home here that's certainly boring if comfortable. Her way of buffering herself, wouldn't you say?"

"From the things she'd lost or the things she still wanted?"

Simon rested his elbows on his knees, and took another look around. "I don't know why she thought she had to come back here. Just because you're born in a place, doesn't mean you have to die there. She could have, or should have, stayed where she was, given herself time, gotten back to her music. She should never have given it up."

"Coming from you?"

"I'm a walking life of regret. But teaching music at the high school?"

"Don't be so quick to judge. She may have taught her students to love music the way she used to. Or still did. We can't know. Maybe it's how she wanted it."

"Then God damn her." Simon got up, walked over to the opposite corner, where the sun was brightest, and stood with his face turned to the light. "The reason I started cleaning the house, beside the fact that it was floating on a cloud of dust balls, was the hope that I'd get to know Laura, the person who lived here. Moving around the place, and all. I mean, you can't clean someone's house without getting to know them at least a little bit, right?" He laughed a dry laugh, as though the dust of Laura's life was stuck in his throat. "Maybe what I was really trying to do, scrubbing and everything, was to get it all clean and I'd find some clue to my sister, but all I found was—I feel like I'm inside a shell." He shook his head. "All it is is seeing how someone I didn't know made a bland little nest for herself. This could be anyone's home." He walked over to the stepladder, folded it, and leaned it against the wall. "I think I was looking for an agreement between what I expected to see when I came here, what I hoped I'd see, and what I'd actually discover." He looked as though he were about to cry, but he pulled himself back and said, "I didn't expect that my sister just shriveled up inside."

"You said you were looking for closure."

"I said I was looking for closure *and* to say good-bye. But who would I be saying good-bye to when Laura already said good-bye to Laura? And now I'm standing here pissed off at Laura, pissed off at myself, and a little pissed at you, too, Geoffrey. This is not what I expected." Simon looked around the room, as though he were trying to find something else that needed cleaning, or maybe he was giving Laura another chance.

All I did was think about why *I'd* come here, and that my own expectations and Simon's were as insubstantial as the dust swept from this house. I found that an intolerable concession to make.

I stood up, and started for the front door.

"It's about time we got out of here. Didn't you want to buy food and cook supper for us?"

Eleven

WE ATTENDED TO OUR ERRAND AND CAME BACK TO
unload the groceries. It was just after noon, and
Simon and I ate lunch in Laura's kitchen. He was
surprised that all the plates and cutlery were still in the cupboard. He got very quiet after this, went over to the back door,
looked outside, and just stood there. The sun was shining
through the glass, giving his silhouette a violet tint, then the
sunlight brightened and for a moment he was all but invisible.

"I used to tell myself that it didn't matter if Laura and
I never saw each other again. That I hadn't been very good
at being her brother, anyway." He kept his face to the sun.
"You have to tell yourself things like that, right?" He turned
around, pulled a chair away from the table, and sat down.
"You have to tell yourself a lot of things that aren't close to
what the truth is. But right now, I look at you and think, what
the hell did you do to stay inside my sister's head and heart
that she would ask you to take care of her after she died?"

I told him about Laura not wanting her friends to bury her twice. I said, "And I could speculate about a few more things, but I wouldn't come any closer to knowing than you. Maybe it was just an act of desperation."

Simon told me that was not the answer.

He said, "I think you're missing something." There was no tone of anger when he said this, or the sullenness I expected. "Not desperate. She had to believe you wouldn't let her down. And wouldn't you think that she'd have felt that everything else in her life had done nothing but that. The way it was ending. It could have been that you were one of the last things she could think of that didn't make her feel bad. That could still make her feel good." Simon got up and started to walk out. "I'd like to think that, and I'd like it if you thought it, too." Just as he was leaving the room, he said, "If you wouldn't mind, would you take me to the cemetery where Laura's buried?"

I told him I didn't mind at all.

The cemetery was on the other side of town. We stopped a few times, looking for a place to buy flowers, but it was too early in the season, none of the stores had any to sell, so Simon had to stand empty-handed by Laura's headstone. I waited in the car. When he came back, he told me, "They're buried side by side. Laura and Steve." He seemed bothered by this. "Why is that? Why didn't she bury him in Paris? She could have been buried with him there." He sat on the front seat, keeping the car door open and stretching his legs out onto the narrow sidewalk.

"This is all very disturbing. This business of coming back here. I can't help thinking that she was waiting for time to run out. Haven't you gotten a sense of that?"

"I'm sorry if what I told you about—"

"There's the stench of self-denial around all of this." He pulled a pack of cigarettes and a book of matches from his coat pocket. "My sister was living like a loser, as far as I'm concerned. After all the shit that she went through and then to just come here to die. It makes me sick to—" He lighted the cigarette and took a deep drag. "I don't know why you don't see it."

I sat back and stared out the windshield. Simon smoked his cigarette. Once or twice he started to say something, did nothing more than make grumbling noises, and when he finished his cigarette, flicked the butt across the sidewalk onto the grass and slammed the door.

"Could you drop me off at my old house?" he said. "And please, don't wait for me."

I let Simon out a few blocks from Main Street, in front of a large gray house set back from the sidewalk, a bigger version of the house Laura had moved into. He was standing at the edge of the front lawn when I drove away.

Maybe there were other reasons for Laura burying Steve in Shady Grove, but I liked believing that she couldn't stand to be an ocean away from him, even after death. I wanted that to be the reason.

When I drove back through town, I decided to sit on a bench in Buddy's town square. There was nowhere I wanted to go and nothing that needed to be done. I didn't know how long I'd been sitting out there, when I heard someone call my name. It was Eliot, and he was smiling at me.

"I thought it was you." He reached out and shook my hand. "What are you doing here? Did they sell Laura's house?"

When I explained that I was there with Simon, he said,

"Just like that? The two of you coming up here? Come on, let me buy you a cup of coffee."

I said I'd never had much luck with restaurant coffee.

He laughed. "Then I'll buy you a beer. The sun must be over the yardarm *somewhere.*"

We walked across the street to the Bradford House and sat at a table in the pub room, where Marian had touched my wrist and made my heart stand still. I was thinking about that, and about how it felt when I drove up to see her last month, and what she'd told me just the day before, and what Eliot would think about that. What would he say if I'd told him I was in Shady Grove because I couldn't stop thinking about his girlfriend, while he signaled the bartender, whom he knew by name, for two beers, and told me that Laura had never talked about Simon. Even after she got sick.

"That was wrong," he said. "But then I always thought she and her folks were way too hard on him from the beginning."

"I've come to agree with that."

"It's quite something, though, Simon coming to New York like that. Looking for you."

"He wasn't looking for me," I told him. "He was looking for an epiphany."

"In New York City?"

"You have your epiphanies where you can find them."

"What made him think you could help him?"

"I'm just the go-between."

"Well, it must be nice, being able to get away whenever you want."

"Simon makes his own schedule."

"I meant you."

"It wasn't like I had to turn down work."

"But still . . ." Eliot was leaning forward, his heavy shoulders hunched, his big hands clasped on the tabletop; and he was smiling again. "I bet you never thought that getting a letter in the mail would lead to you practically taking up residence in Shady Grove. I imagine you'll be glad to go back to the city." He laughed when he said this, but he didn't sound amused. It was the same tone, the same inflection I'd heard when he talked to Marian; what I saw in his face now looked so much like what I'd seen in his face then—a man afraid of losing his balance—and I realized that he hadn't made a statement at all. He was asking, looking for something. For a moment I felt as though Eliot were trying to take a peek at my phone bill, but I figured he was less insidious than that—he wanted something from me. He wanted reassurance.

Sitting there felt oppressive now, because of what I could have told him and what I decided not to say.

"Hardly residence," I said. "I'll be leaving in another day or two. And then I'll be gone."

Eliot leaned back, and unclasped his hands.

"You know, after you left," he said, "all Marian wanted to talk about was Laura. More than she had even before Laura died. But the things she said, you know, stories and some of the stuff she remembered about Laura, weren't sad at all. Marian just talked about all the *good* times they had and how much she missed her, and how glad she was to have reconnected with her when Laura moved back. Of course, not the circumstances why, but still . . . Marian seemed, I guess she seemed happier than I'd seen her in a while. At least she was smiling again."

I thought of Marian's smile, and wished I was responsible

in some way for her change in mood, but it didn't matter why, I just wanted Marian to remember Laura without tears.

All I said to Eliot was, "There are a lot of things to remember about Laura that would make her happy."

We'd finished our beers by now. I got up, paid the bartender, and told Eliot I had to be going. After we walked outside and shook hands, I watched him cross the street, and go into his hardware store.

WHEN I GOT BACK TO LAURA'S HOUSE, SIMON WAS IN THE KITCHEN cooking a supper that turned out to be quite delicious.

When I complimented him he said, "When you're a perennial houseguest, it helps if you can cook."

He didn't say much about what he'd done that day, only that everything felt far different from what he was hoping he'd feel.

After we cleaned up, I left him alone, went outside, and sat on the front steps. I was out there for only a little while when the phone rang and Simon opened the front door and said it was for me.

It was Marian.

She didn't bother saying hello: "What did you mean when you said that you get it?"

"Get it?"

"When I saw you yesterday." She sounded out of breath. "You told me that you 'got it.' Got what? Tell me what you meant."

"Not on the phone."

ॐ

ABOUT TEN MILES NORTH OF SHADY GROVE, THERE'S A COUNTY road that makes a wide arc around a low stone wall. If you like, you can sit on that wall and look at the expanse of the Hudson Valley rising to the Berkshire Mountains like an out-stretched hand and see the trail of that same county road and roads like it that cut internecine paths, enclosing pastures and farms, where the large estates and smaller plots of land spread toward you unobstructed, alert to your privilege of seeing the small sample of the landscaping talents of Buddy Ballantine, when the season is right. We were at least a month away from that season, but Marian and I stood outside her car looking at that view, seeing all there was to see.

We were there because I'd come to Marian's nursery and told her about my being with Eliot and most of our conversation. And because I wanted to see her face.

She was sitting behind her desk in the nursery office with a framed photograph of her and Buddy wearing their Wellies, leaning against the side of a backhoe, both of them looking trim and vital, Buddy's eyes looking up at the sky, Marian turned halfway toward him, her hand wrapped around his bicep, the two of them laughing. When Marian looked at me, I thought, if they ever take a picture of the two of us, that's the expression I'd want to see.

I'd pulled up the only chair available, which was old and uncomfortable. She lowered her eyes and turned her head to look out of the large window next to her, where I counted three greenhouses, as many potting sheds, and half a dozen people pushing wagons and pulling carts loaded with all kinds of plants.

"Was there really something you couldn't tell me over the phone?"

"Any excuse to see you," I answered, "but yes, there is. I've been thinking about what you said, about you and Buddy, and Laura and Steve. And I understand it now. How deeply you two loved each other, Laura loved Steve. I mean, I understand how that's possible. And why."

"Why would you give anything I say to you that much thought?"

"Don't you think you're worth thinking about?"

"You're making me blush."

"Well, that's a start, anyway."

"We've spoken to each other, what, four times? What am I supposed to think?"

"What do you *want* to think? That I'd drive over a hundred miles just to alleviate the tedium?"

"What I think is, you've made up someone you call Marian Ballantine and I'm not her, and when you find that out, you're going to be deeply disappointed."

I answered by telling her, "I broke up with Rita. The woman I was going out with."

"You shouldn't have done that." There was nothing of a reprimand in her tone, just more of the caution that seemed to rise up in all of our conversations. "Look, Geoffrey, it's sweet of you to find me attractive, but how can I not wonder why you're being so persistent? Is it a male thing?"

"And you're just someone I want to charm?"

"And get tired of. How long do you think being charming

and flirtatious will last before you get bored with that and me? And even if you don't, or not right away, in a few years, I'll be older, I'll look older—and you never know how you're going to age, how it will change what you want, who you want. Then what? You'll lose interest, and where will I be?"

"I've never looked too far back and I don't look too far ahead."

"I can't be that careless."

"How can you do *anything* if you worry about something that hasn't happened yet, that you aren't even sure will *ever* happen?"

"Aging happens."

"Differently for everyone. You don't know that I'll lose interest in you just because we're older, any more than I know that you will with me."

"*We?*" She raised the palm of her hand at me.

"Come on, Marian. You know you're curious."

"Curious."

"About this. Where it will lead. And what it will feel like."

"That wasn't a question."

"If you say so. But you are curious. Or else you wouldn't have called me yesterday. I know you are and so does Eliot. That's why he's concerned about my being in Shady Grove and the length of my stay. Which makes me think he has a better idea of what's going on than you and I do."

"Okay, so I thought about—what it would be like to see you. I didn't do anything about it. That's all it was. Wondering what if. And please leave Eliot out of this. You can't know what he knows or what he thinks he knows."

"Show me some of the places Buddy designed."

She sat forward.

"I'd like to see them."

"Haven't you heard what I said?"

"Show me some of the places."

"First of all, I have a business to run."

"Your people seem to have things under control."

"Anyway, it's too early in the year to see much of anything. You won't know what anything looks like."

"But *you* will."

WE SAT NEXT TO EACH OTHER ON THE LOW STONE WALL ALONG THE side of the county road, looking out at the expanse of Hudson Valley, not saying anything, just looking at the Berkshire Mountains, dots of yellows and greens that Marian said were the gardens and landscaping she and Buddy had done to-gether.

Marian said, "We're between seasons, really. The end of what we call winter interest, which you can still see small samples of, and the beginning of all the blossoming." There was a soft wind brushing at our faces, like it does on a quiet sea, tousling our hair, putting pink in our cheeks; and all I could think was: This day cannot move slowly enough.

We were out there for a few minutes before Marian said, "I think you need to know what you've done to me. When you came to see me at my house." She pushed her hair away from her face. "I liked it, the way you spoke to me, and the things you said. I haven't— Well, I found myself thinking about you—sometimes at the most inappropriate times." She laughed. "That didn't come out right, did it? Thinking about seeing you again." The wind picked up and her hair was all over her face; she turned away from it, lifted her head, and I saw her in profile.

She said, "When you drove away, I stood there and wanted you to ignore what I said and come back. And I was so relieved that you didn't, and so disappointed. And you never called or tried to get in touch with me—"

"As I recall, you told me not to."

"I thought about you all that night, what you said, how you described things." She got up and started pacing in front of the wall. "And the next morning I thought, what if Geoffrey doesn't listen to me and calls, or I drive into town and there he is, sitting in the diner having breakfast? Wouldn't that be just like Geoffrey? And then I thought, I have no idea what would or wouldn't be like Geoffrey. All that day, I kept thinking, what if I hadn't told you to go? And why did I?"

"Why *did* you?"

"You know how it is when you go somewhere for the first time?" She was pacing a little faster now. "You're following directions, making sure you're on the right road, passing the right road marks? And then suddenly you're sure you've made a wrong turn or passed the place you're looking for and all you feel is disorientated maybe and all alone? That's how it felt after Buddy died. That feeling of being in the wrong place. For a very long time. And I got used to that feeling, and everything was all settled. *Is* all settled. I can miss Buddy for the rest of my life and all the feelings that go with it, and tolerate what I have with Eliot, live peacefully and grow old without caring. Do you know how many times I wanted to call you or send you an e-mail? Does this sound normal? Do *I* sound normal? What do you think I meant when I said you've complicated my life? Does this sound like a normal person speaking? And now you've broken up with your girl-friend."

When Marian stopped pacing, I stepped toward her and was about to take her hand and hold it against my face. And what would she have done if I'd pressed my lips into the con-cave cup of her palm and kissed it? Just once.

"Well," she said, pulling back from me, "have you seen enough?"

"I want to get closer."

"Closer?"

"I want to see the gardens up close. And you can tell me what you remember about building them."

"I'm afraid this is as close as you get," she said, and walked to her car. "It's getting chilly and I'm tired of talking."

We were in the car, heading down the road, back the way we came, when Marian asked, "What are you going to do now?"

"Go back to New York, as soon as Simon's ready. He's trying to find his sister."

She looked at me out of the corner of her eye.

"The scrapbook she packed away," I said. "It's all that's left of her, really. He should be allowed to see it."

We drove a minute or two longer before Marian stopped the car.

"If I let him look through it," she said, "will you promise he'll give it back to me before you leave?"

WE WERE DRIVING DOWN THE BLUESTONE DRIVEWAY TO MARIAN'S house. I could see the smaller gardens, where the lilac trees were showing their buds and green shoots were pushing through the soft earth.

"Laura's things are in there," Marian said, nodding her head toward the barn. "But I want to talk to you about something, first. In the house."

She parked at the edge of the path. I followed her to the back door, through the mudroom and into the kitchen.

She asked me if I wanted coffee, walked over to the refrigerator, took out a brown bag and while she measured the grounds into the filter, I filled the well of the coffeemaker with water.

"I want to tell you why Laura asked you to be her executor," she said. "I mean, why I think she did. It's only fair."

"I'd like to hear it."

"She knew she was dying, and we were spending a lot of time together, talking about the past. One day she pulled out some of the old photographs. When I saw that one of you, I said, 'He looks kind of interesting.' Laura said she wondered whatever happened to you, and did you grow up to be anything like the person she thought you'd be. I told her if she really wanted to know, it wasn't too late to find out. Anyway, it was when she took out the photographs, and I said I thought you were attractive, and was she ever involved with you. And that's when she told me all about you. She said twenty years can change a person and not usually for the better, but she didn't think that would be the case with you. We talked like that for a while. I don't know if you can appreciate how much she remembered about you, and how much she liked you. She knew what a good friend you were. She said she'd tried a few times to get in touch with you when she and Steve came to New York to play. Later on, you know, a month or so after we talked, when Laura told me what she'd decided to do, she wanted—well, if you agreed to be her executor I had to swear that I'd meet you and find out whatever happened to her friend Geoffrey Tremont. Laura said she was *bequeathing* you to me."

"Or the memory of me," I said.

"*No.*" Marian said this with the adamance of the True Believer. "Laura decided if you said no then it answered her question straight out, because the person she remembered wouldn't have turned her down. If you'd turned out not to be the person she hoped you'd be, there was Remsen to take care of things. Or if you were married with three lovely children, a charming wife, living the American bourgeois life and couldn't be bothered, then the hell with you. But if you were who she hoped you were, wanted you to be . . ." Marian took a deep breath. "That's why I was there that first day. To meet you. For Laura."

For a moment I thought that there was a subtle manipulation occurring, and not just now but from the time Laura wrote her will, and it was the exact sort of thing that should have sent me rushing back to New York and the life I thought I was finished with. But I knew I couldn't be that far away from Marian.

"The times when I was thinking about you," she said, "I'd wonder what kinds of places does Geoffrey go to in New York? If he has expense account lunches in those midtown restaurants they write about in magazines. Does he go to the theater, cocktail parties?" She opened the cupboard, took out two coffee cups. I filled them both while Marian got out cream and sugar. We sat facing each other across the table.

"What does his apartment look like? Does he clean it himself or does someone come in? And that was all there would ever be to it. Someone to wonder about. Because I was *positive* nothing was going to happen. It was never going to go anywhere. I liked the idea of having that to carry around with me."

"Imagining your life isn't living it."

"Yes," she said. "I'm well aware of that." She lifted the cup to her mouth, but raised her eyes and looked at me over the rim, and when I looked back, she did not move her eyes away. "Do you remember standing here with me when I told you all the reasons why I couldn't leave Eliot and I said guilt was the driving force?"

"You told me you were a guilty mess."

"I also know how easily I can hurt him. That's a terrible thing. An *inhibiting* thing. You said that Eliot seemed to have a better idea of what was going on than you or I do. Why shouldn't he? Don't you think he's noticed that something's changed in me? And that it happened after you and I met?" She pointed her finger at me. "I have an obligation to him, Geoffrey. I can't discard him just on a whim."

"Is that what's going on here? A whim?"

"I'm sure you—"

"It's an opportunity."

"How can you be that certain?"

"I'm as scared as you are."

"Oh," she said, "now I feel much better."

"Simon believes that this is all about self-deprivation. Self-denial."

"What does Simon know about it?"

"I don't disagree with him."

"For that matter, what do you know?"

She stared at me a little longer than I liked, and said, "It's been ten years since I've been with Buddy. After all this time, it still feels like it happened, not *longer* ago, but further *away*. Far away from what I believed my life was going to be." She traced the tip of her finger around the rim of her cup. "For a long time, all I did was think about all the things Buddy and I had planned on doing, and how there never seemed to be any hurry to get them done. For about three or four months after he died, I didn't really do much of any—it wasn't as easy as all that."

I asked what she was talking about.

She paused a moment before she answered. "Buddy." Another moment passed. "He could be so . . . Intense. Sitting around, lying around. Thinking. All that thinking. Plans and ideas. Never saying a word. Just silence. For hours. And he expected me to—God forbid I should interrupt. It was like walking on eggs. It made me crazy. We had some very loud fights about it. So self-absorbed. And overbearing. I want you to hear me say that. In case you think I have this unrealistic idea of my marriage."

"Marriage is marriage," I said.

"A lot you know about it," Marian answered. "Ever since he died. I feel—" She shrugged her shoulders.

"Incomplete?"

Marian's back went stiff.

"Buddy had his office in the barn. I still go out there sometimes because I have this feeling—I didn't close out his business," she said, "because I like receiving mail addressed to the company, seeing Buddy's name on the envelopes. The same way I like driving his pickup, and the other things we did together after I had to do them without him. *Have* to do. They used to be reminders of the things I'd lost.

"Then they just became the things that had to get done. Mundane. Then the mundane became a part of my life, and that part became part of another part . . . I've always blamed myself. For not going with him. For a long time I wished I'd died with him. That's probably something you don't want to hear, but why shouldn't you know it." She tapped her fingernail against the side of her cup. "When I got to Buddy's cabin, I stood there, looking at him lying on that bed, and all I could think was, any second one of us is going to wake up." There was no expression in her eyes when she said this, nothing in her voice now.

"You seem so sure about everything," she said. "So sure about what you're doing here and what you want from me."

"What I'm sure of," I told her, "is we can't keep kicking this thing back and forth. I'm going to New York as soon as Simon gets Shady Grove out of his system. And you and I aren't about to get involved in some little affair, meeting in towns halfway between here and there. That's not your style nor mine. Once the last bit of business with Laura's house is finished, I'm never coming back to Shady Grove. Unless it's for you."

"Laura wanted me to like you. I *do* like you. And I don't want to. I do want to."

I rubbed my eyes with the heels of my hands. "You know, Marian, you wear a person down."

For an instant, I thought she was going to laugh—that laugh that had started everything—but she was staring at me and there was no amusement in the look on her face or in her tone of voice when she said, "What I told you before about Laura—she wanted me to meet you. For *us* to meet. She said I'd buried my heart when I buried Buddy, and the evidence of that was Eliot. She thought he was a lovely man, but what was the point if what I felt for him didn't fill my heart. She wanted me to fall in love again." Marian's voice faded at the word *love*. "And what happens—what happens to me if I do fall in love with you and you change your mind? What happens to me if anything *happens* to you?"

"That could be true of Eliot, too, you know. He could get tired of you. Something could happen to him."

"If anything ever happened to Eliot I would be very sad. But it wouldn't turn my life upside down."

I started to speak. Marian reached across the table and pressed her fingertips on my lips, but said nothing, while outside the windows, the sky was lighted with the lavender of twilight, the exquisite hour; and together we watched the remainder of our day move a little further away from us.

Twelve

MARIAN DROVE ME TO THE NURSERY, WHERE I'D LEFT MY car. Sometime during the drive, I must have asked her what she was doing that night, or maybe I apologized for needing the ride. I doubt that she volunteered that she was having dinner with Buddy's parents.

"You see," she said to me, "we're dealing with people's *lives.*"

"Lifetimes, really."

When we pulled up to my car, Marian handed Laura's scrapbook to me. "If you like, you can leave it with Remsen when you're done. It might make things simpler."

"Simplicity itself," I said back to her, and got out.

I drove in the direction of town, but I didn't want to go to Laura's house and have supper with Simon. I was in no mood to see his face on the other side of the dinner table. Instead, I kept on driving. When I saw a small restaurant just off the road, its yellow lights invitation enough, I pulled into a parking space between two other cars, and went inside.

It was a pleasant dining room, not very large, with the calming sound of dinner conversations. One of those restaurants with an eclectic menu and nothing too adventurous. I hadn't yet ordered my supper when a woman came over. She had a round face, framed by short, gray hair, and held a black beret in her hand. She said her name was Kate Callahan, that Marian had introduced us at the Bradford House, and if I was eating alone, I was welcome to join her and some of Marian's friends for supper. One more opportunity to feel close to Marian. And I accepted.

There were two other people at Kate's table, who must have arrived just before I had; they were still settling in. While Kate invited me to sit down she introduced me to Pamela and Charlie Ballantine. Charlie was Buddy's younger brother.

There was a resemblance to Buddy, at least from those photographs I'd seen. It occurred to me that Charlie was probably older now than Buddy had been when he died.

I said I was surprised that Buddy had had a sibling. "I've been thinking of him as a singular person. The way Marian speaks about him."

"There were five of us," Charlie said. His voice was a rich, relaxed tenor. "Two older than Buddy, and two younger. But Buddy was singular." Charlie had a stronger build than Buddy, like someone who'd gone out for crew in college and still did a little sculling on weekends. When he pulled his chair closer to the table, I saw the swell of his chest against his shirt.

Kate asked if my coming back to town had to do with my being Laura's executor.

I said, "Only in an indirect way," and explained with only the slightest details my mission with Simon.

Charlie said, "It's really very kind of you to do that." He wanted to know what Simon had been doing all these years, if things had worked out for him.

I said, "You're the first person who's asked me that."

He shrugged his shoulders. "I think I've always understood what it was like to be Laura Welles's brother. Probably because it wasn't much easier being the brother of Buddy Ballantine."

While Charlie floated that out there, Pamela said, "Both Laura and Buddy had a kind of star quality at a young age. It was hard not to get caught in the undertow." She looked around the table, making eye contact with everyone while she spoke, and then she sat back in her chair, and looked over at me with an expression that made me identify what I'd been observing about her: She impressed me as one of those women who young men feel comfortable speaking their secrets to, and older men their hearts.

"I'm still having a hard time with the idea of Laura moving back to Shady Grove after living in Paris," I said.

"A lot had changed for Laura." It was Pamela who said this. "Shady Grove became the *constant* in her life. Where she found stability."

"Stability."

"Laura was quite content to be Laura the high school teacher. She made it work." It was Kate who answered. "She didn't do too much talking about it, but you could see she'd come to terms with it. That she'd made peace with herself and her life."

"Not like Marian," I said.

"What makes you say that?" Pamela asked.

"Just the little I know about her. And what you said before.

Did Marian get caught in the undertow of Buddy's personality?"

"It was hard not to." Pamela was speaking to Charlie when she said this.

"Remember St. John?" Charlie said back to her. And then he turned to me. "In the Caribbean. The four of us used to rent a house there every year. High on a hilltop. Great view. The whole thing. It was always so much fun being with Buddy. With the both of them. They were hilarious together."

"We didn't like to do the tourist beaches, the places you see on postcards. We explored out-of-the-way places. Not, you know, pure beaches," Pamela explained, "just little spits of land or small keys that you had to hike to get to. Beautiful places. More difficult to get to than the tourist places."

"We all liked snorkeling," Charlie said. "And we were always looking for someplace we might not have gotten to the last time we were down there. But this one time, we went back to a beach, a bay, that we always liked to go to, not that popular—at least it hadn't been in past years when we were there. Small white beach and nice coral reefs at the end of a rock scramble."

"Lush and thick jungle that came just to the edge where the beach started. Really rustic." Pamela had taken over the narrative: "So, this one time, coming back, we're walking along the beach, lugging our stuff, with this beautiful water surrounded by this gorgeous scenery, and there are these *people*. From one of the resorts. They bring them over by boat for the day. Maybe twelve of them altogether. With a canopy, right on the beach, and of all things, designer umbrellas. And these four people were up to their waists in the water, surrounding a floating bar. Drinking. Like they were at a cocktail party.

We thought it was just ridiculous. Buddy said it was worse than ridiculous, that those people were so *alienated* from all of that beauty. That they actually were numbing themselves to the experience."

"Buddy thought of himself as a pantheist," Charlie told me. "And the sight of those people seemed disrespectful to him. And sad."

"It also made him angry," Pamela reminded Charlie. "It was all he could talk about the rest of the day. He quoted *Words*worth at us."

"He was pretty spectacular," Charlie told me.

"And spectacular people like Buddy aren't supposed to die meaningless deaths," I said. "That's why he didn't worry about ice fishing alone?"

"Buddy didn't worry about much of anything." It was Pamela who said this.

I said, "But he must have known it was a careless thing to do."

"It's where Buddy went to get away from Buddy." Kate was looking at Charlie.

"We all hated that place," Charlie said. "Not just Marian. My brothers and sisters, my parents. We couldn't wait for winter to be over and for the ice to finally melt."

"You're right, though," Pamela was speaking to me now. "It was pretty careless. And irresponsible." She looked over at Charlie, not for confirmation, at least she didn't seem like the sort of person who would look for that from her husband, but maybe, even after ten years, you still didn't speak badly about Buddy Ballantine. "*Nothing* stopped Buddy," she said.

"Not even Marian?" I asked.

"She practically lost her mind when Buddy died," Charlie

said. "Everything was tied up in their—they did *everything* together. They were the driving forces for each other. It's the difference," he said, "between doing something and being something. It's what they were. What *Marian* was. And then she wasn't."

"She had every right to fall apart the way she did. And to be angry at him," Pamela said. "Which she was."

"She thinks it was *she* who betrayed *him*," I said. "For not going up to the cabin."

This brought the conversation to an end, at least it appeared that way, for no one replied, they only made quick eye contact across the table, and stayed quiet long enough for me to think that I'd said something inappropriate, that I wasn't supposed to comment. Or it may have been that one was expected to keep the talk diagnostic rather than analytic.

"My brother's a shrink," I said. "It's just how I think about these things."

"It's not that," Charlie answered. "It's just that you might have liked the conversation a little lighter than it's been."

It was then that we ordered our supper and while we ate, the conversation turned to more pleasant subjects.

After we'd paid the check and were walking out, Charlie told me, "If you want to know more about Laura, you should talk to my parents. They were very close with her. If you want, I'll tell them you're going to drop by. I'm sure they'd like to meet you. Tomorrow, say? They're big on the cocktail hour."

ON THE NIGHT OF FEBRUARY 22, 1985, LAURA SAT IN WITH THE Mel Stevenson Trio for the first time. It was written inside a circle of what appeared to be faded red wine, on a coaster from the Village Vanguard in New York City, pasted on the front page of Laura's scrapbook, the fastidious chronology of her life after she met Steve. Reviews, concert programs, the first recording contract Laura signed, and the last, the same year Steve died; and a lot of photographs. Everything neatly dated in handwriting not unlike that on those boxes she'd left behind. A photograph of the apartment in the Marais, where Steve and Laura would live for the rest of their marriage, dated "June 15, 1986"—Simon would have approved of the décor. That same year the trio performed at the jazz festival in Montreux, played gigs in Stockholm, Copenhagen, Berlin, and other large and not-so-large cities in Europe.

They came to the States in 1990, and again in '92: Chicago and New York, the West Coast, that's when Simon must have seen the trio in San Francisco.

This was not a collection of love letters and birthday cards, no Valentine's Day poems and romantic keepsakes. It was the chronicle of ten years in the lives of two jazz musicians.

Ten years. The words filled my entire mouth, yet they filled fewer than forty pages in a scrapbook.

I was sitting in Laura's living room. Alone in the house. I preferred to be by myself without Simon or anyone else around, while I looked at the record of Laura's life. Content that there was no one there to explain my thoughts or my feelings, looking at Laura's face in photographs, the face I remembered smiling back at me.

The week of her honeymoon when she and Steve played a five-day gig in Chicago. Steve standing behind the piano in a black jacket and white shirt, hair combed back, bowing slightly. Laura at his side, her violin tucked under her arm.

Both of them circled in a narrow spotlight. Laura was twenty-two years old and exultant. It was an expression that appeared on both of their faces in all of the photographs, in photo shoots for magazines and CD sleeves, photos with friends, other jazz musicians.

Photographs of Laura when she was twenty-five, when she was thirty. There might have been changes in hairstyles and clothes, changes in venue, but there was no change in what her expression told of the thrill of being Laura Welles and what it must have been like to keep that feeling with her, to present it to an audience, and still be capable of bringing it back with her when the lights went down.

I imagined Laura and Steve rushing away from New York City trailing, not shoes and rice, but sprinklings of clef tones in their wake as they boarded the jet to make that date in Chicago.

I thought about Laura's ten years arranged in that book, like decals on an old steamer trunk pressed with faraway places; and what Charlie had said about the difference between doing something and being something.

When I closed the last page, I left the scrapbook downstairs for Simon, and went outside to walk the quiet streets of Shady Grove. I was still thinking about Laura, why she put together those pages with such meticulousness, who they were intended for. She and Steve had no children, no heirs. Was her idea of posterity the two of them looking back on their careers?

I spent the next day avoiding Simon, and the denizens of Shady Grove, until just after six in the evening, when I arrived at Walter and Eleanor Ballantine's home. I brought two bottles of a pretty good Burgundy I'd found in a local liquor store.

It was a large house on the corner of a street of large houses. Theirs was three stories, painted sage green, with yellow shutters, an enclosed porch, set back from the sidewalk on a wide lawn. Walter—once we shook hands he insisted that all formalities were finished—had thick white hair, wore a pink polo shirt, gray cotton pants, and worn leather moccasins. Eleanor was tall and slim, with dark brown hair tied in a knot and just enough gray to stave off pretense, above a long, straight neck. They must have both been in their seventies.

It was a first impression, I knew, but Eleanor seemed the kind of woman the word *demeanor* was intended for. It was the clothes she wore, a pair of black slacks and tapered white blouse, and the way she walked, back straight as though she might once have been a dancer, or else she still kept to her aerobics.

Walter moved like a slow truck, heavy body, thick arms, speaking as he walked us into the enclosed porch, with high windows, a view of the creek on the other side of the lawn, and chairs that were deep and forgiving—this was also an apt description of Walter and Eleanor, although it wasn't something I immediately realized; that came later in the evening.

Walter waited for me to get settled in my chair before he offered me a cocktail. "We have just about everything," he said.

"What do you two usually drink?" I asked.

"Wine," Eleanor answered, "so what you brought is just right, but if you prefer something else, scotch or vodka . . ."

"This seems the perfect night for wine," I told her.

Walter said, "What you brought is better than what I was about to open, so I'd like to pour one of those."

I said, "I'd be honored."

Walter uncorked and poured one of the Burgundies. "I hope Charlie didn't give you the idea Eleanor and I are a couple of lushes. We just think every day deserves its proper send-off." He made easy eye contact when he spoke, with me and with Eleanor, while Eleanor prodded the plate of cheese and bread in my direction, and made sure I served myself.

Walter was an architect, now semi-retired—Charlie was his partner—and Eleanor had been a high school physics teacher until she retired eight years ago.

While we drank our first glass, we talked about New York City, what part of town did I live in . . . And what sort of work did I do . . . Walter and Eleanor liked to drive down a few times every year and spend a week going to the theater and concerts, seeing the museums and galleries. They talked about their favorite restaurants, and asked me about mine, and the conversation never moved too far from these topics until Walter refilled our glasses, and Eleanor said that Charlie had told them why I was in Shady Grove, that both she and Walter thought it was a good idea that Simon had come back to see his sister's house. But that was all they said about it. Then, in a tone so warm it made me think she was going to tell me that they'd made up the guest room for me, Eleanor asked, "Now, what would you like to know about Laura? Charlie seemed to think you wanted to talk to us about her."

"I did," I said. "I do. And I was pretty sure I knew what I wanted you to tell me. But that's changed."

"In what way?" Eleanor asked.

I told them about looking through Laura's scrapbook, that I'd found it troubling.

"But I don't think you really want to talk to me about that," I said. "Or if I have any business having that conversation with you."

Walter and Eleanor looked at each other.

"There were several things about Laura that were troubling," Walter said. He leaned forward, just a little. "Laura didn't come back to Shady Grove because she missed her hometown. She wasn't a small town girl at heart who wanted to go back home."

"Both of her parents had died," Eleanor told me, "so it wasn't family she was coming back for, either. She just couldn't stand being in Paris without Steve. And not only Paris, *any*where in Europe. We thought it was just a temporary move. That Laura would stay here for a year or two. Just to get her legs under her, and then she'd get involved in her music again."

Walter said, "She could have put another group together in Europe, or in America, or joined one. She had the chances."

"But what she wanted, *needed*, actually," Eleanor said, "was to stay as far away from that part of her life as she could."

"She lost her taste for it," Walter said. "No, not her taste." He turned to Eleanor.

"Her passion."

"Her passion," Walter agreed.

"It was the life she believed in," Walter said. "And one day, Steve's walking down the street and drops dead. Forty-five years old."

"And just like that. Gone." Eleanor snapped her fingers. "Laura was only thirty-two."

"There wasn't much left for her to be passionate about," I said. "Considering— That was a huge decision she made marrying Steve. Anyone that confident when they're that young usually ends up miserable, divorced, or disenchanted. But Laura *knew*, and she was *right*. It makes sense," I said, "doesn't it? That she wouldn't want anything more to do with that?"

"And yet," Eleanor said, "if she hadn't gotten sick, she might have gone back to performing. She talked about doing it."

I thought for a moment before I decided to tell them, "She told Marian that she wished she could fall in love the way she'd been in love with Steve. Just once more. She said she just wanted to feel that way again."

"*Marian* told you that?" Eleanor asked.

I said, "That's right." When they didn't say anything, I said, "Did I say something out of line?"

Walter shook his head. "Nothing like that. It's just—"

"Did Marian have an answer?" Eleanor asked. "For Laura, I mean."

"Marian said she wished she had Laura's courage."

There was another quick glance over at Walter before Eleanor said, "We knew that Marian talked with you, but she never indicated that it was with such—"

"Candor," Walter said.

"If we seem taken aback," Eleanor told me, "it's because Marian is not that forthright with most people."

"Did she just come out and tell you that?" Walter wanted to know.

"She couldn't have just blurted out something like that," Eleanor added.

"What we're saying," Walter explained, "is that we assume it was part of a longer conversation. And that she must have been quite at ease talking to you."

"Look," I said, "you're Buddy's parents and Marian's in-laws, and I'm not all that comfortable talking about this."

"We're comfortable talking to you," Walter said. "So please. For one thing, we'd like to know how you got Marian to talk about Laura so honestly. And about herself. All she told us was that she met you and you seemed to know what you were doing."

"She's more than just a daughter-in-law to us," Eleanor said. "She's like our own daughter. She always was. And when we lost Buddy it brought us even closer together. It's been ten years and she's still so unhappy. And that's very upsetting."

"What I told you before," Walter said, "that there were some things that troubled us about Laura, we feel the same about Marian. They were like, well, two peas in a pod, as far as their sorrows were concerned. And that probably wasn't very good for either of them."

"Like they'd found a kindred spirit in each other." Eleanor got up and walked across the room to close the window. "Laura should never have come back, and Marian should never have stayed. It was the worst thing. For both of them. Of course, Geoffrey, there's all kinds of death. Laura in her little house. And Marian out there in the country all alone. That's no way to live." She came back to the couch.

Walter started to uncork the second bottle of wine, but Eleanor stopped him and smiled.

"If you're going to open that one," she said, "Geoffrey's going to have to stay for supper."

I said I'd like that.

"Don't be so sure." Eleanor said, "Walter does most of the cooking and we can't guarantee anything better than just all right."

Walter got up. "That second bottle of wine can only make dinner better," he said and left the room.

WE DIDN'T SIT IN THE DINING ROOM, BUT AT THE SMALL TABLE where we'd had our wine and cheese. Eleanor put out place mats, with linen napkins, yellow and white plates, and what looked like their good silverware.

Supper was more than just all right, although Walter said, "In New York City you call for some kind of exotic takeout. In Shady Grove you have to settle for defrosted leftovers."

I told him I'd take the defrosted leftovers.

Eleanor said my good manners did not go unappreciated and any and all compliments, true or politic, were welcome.

A little while later, Walter told me, "You're not a very judgmental person, are you, Geoffrey?"

"Because I like our supper?"

"Because with all you've seen and heard," Eleanor said, "you don't seem terribly critical."

"If you're talking about how Laura or, for that matter, Marian chose to live their lives, I find it hard enough to imagine those lives let alone criticize them."

"I can certainly understand that."

Walter said, "I don't know what Charlie and the others told you about that first year after we lost Buddy."

"My God," Eleanor said looking first at me, then at Walter, "we all walked around like we were in trances."

We were all quiet for a moment or two after she said that until Walter asked me, "Do you know Eliot?" Which seemed an odd segue.

"I've met him," I said.

"One of the kindest people you'll ever know," Eleanor said. "I'm not the only person who'll tell you that."

"One of the most generous," Walter said.

"I can see that," I said.

"It's doubtful Marian would have gotten through that first month—that first *year*," Eleanor said, "without him. Now, this was before Laura moved back. And Marian felt that she couldn't impose herself on her friends, or us, to come out there and help her. Which wasn't the case of course."

"Marian has a way of seeing things that challenges explanation," Walter added. "Eliot's been married once, and divorced, but he's been in love with Marian since high school. Hasn't he?"

Eleanor nodded her head. "But that's not why he did what he did for her. There was no agenda."

"No," I said, "Eliot doesn't impress me as someone who'd have an agenda."

"And that would have been fine, for a short while," Walter told me, "but . . . whatever you've heard about Buddy was not an exaggeration. And it's understandable that Marian would have found Eliot the least—"

"Threatening." The word seemed to break out of Eleanor's mouth, then in a gentler tone, she repeated, "threatening. To her love of Buddy and his memory. *Her* memories. The Marian you've met, Geoffrey, is not the Marian who was married to our son."

Walter said, "The two of them together were incandescent," and I recalled the first time I heard Marian's laugh.

Walter shifted his body, and the movement beneath his shirt was more muscle than fat. "We thought Eliot was just helping her get past the loneliness while she came to terms with what happened to Buddy. But the two of them staying together like this and for so long. It's just not healthy."

"And then Laura—Marian and Laura—just reinforced each other's grief." Eleanor smoothed her napkin and fitted it along the edge of her plate. "If it was only for a year, maybe, then it was just a normal time of mourning, but after that, it's the way you're living your life."

I said, "And when Laura died, I suspect Marian's sadness only grew deeper and more intractable."

"I just don't think Marian ever saw her way out." Eleanor was looking at Walter.

Walter put his hand on my shoulder. "And now, you've come along." He held his hand there a moment longer, before he picked up the plates and walked out of the room.

I started to speak. Eleanor lifted her hand to stop me, got up to turn on a few lights, looked past me in the direction of the kitchen, said, "You don't mind if I leave you alone for a minute," and walked out.

I sat there thinking about the expressions on the faces in the photograph Marian kept at her nursery; and the faces in Laura's scrapbook; the way couples know each other's conversations; and the things they keep framed on the wall, sealed in a book, and when that can't ever be enough.

I heard Walter and Eleanor talking in quick, muted voices as they came back to the porch. Walter was carrying a tray with coffee and a setup. After he and Eleanor sat down and while Walter poured, Eleanor leaned forward and put her hand on top of mine. "In the ten years since Buddy's death, the two children who weren't already married got married. Charlie, as you know, stayed here in Shady Grove, and our other son and both daughters have moved away. They all have their own children, we have grandchildren. And all Marian's done in those ten years is grow ten years older."

"Coming here every week for dinner . . ." Walter said.

"Keeping herself and, to a lesser degree, the rest of the family in a state of grieving," Eleanor put in.

Walter spread out his hands and turned them palms up. "Robert Frost said he could state what he knew about life in three words: 'It goes on.' Marian has got to allow her life to go on."

"It can't stay like this," Eleanor said. "It's driving the whole family crazy. And that includes Marian. It's time she had a real relationship instead of—"

"I'm either missing something," I said, "or I'm just dull." I was speaking to Eleanor, but it was Walter who answered.

"Dull is not the word that springs to mind."

"Do you think Marian's ever been as candid with Eliot about anything as she's been with you? So, if you want to—what, Walter?"

"See where it might lead?"

"Where it might lead," Eleanor repeated, "we're all for that."

"There's Eliot to consider."

Walter asked me, "When are you expected back in New York?"

"Thinking of locking Marian and me in a closet?" I asked back.

Eleanor said, "As if."

"I'm sure we'll think of something." Walter was speaking to Eleanor. Then he raised his coffee cup and said, "Here's to the time when we have more in common than the death of our friend."

✿

WHEN I GOT BACK TO LAURA'S HOUSE, SIMON WAS SITTING ON THE sofa. The scrapbook was next to him. He looked up at me with an expression I'd grown used to.

"I think I've seen enough," he said. "I'm ready to leave."

"I'll put you on a bus," I told him. "I'm ready to stay."

Thirteen

THE FOLLOWING MORNING, I PUT SIMON ON THE EARLY morning bus out of Lenox, Massachusetts, but not before I slipped a hundred dollars into his hand.

"The fifty you asked for the last time," I told him. "And fifty more because I feel like it."

When the bus pulled away, I got back in my car and drove northwest, heading to the town of Minnota, New York, in the Adirondack Mountains, where Buddy had his cabin.

Walter had offered to come with me, but all I wanted were directions. I preferred seeing the place all alone, on my own. A little more than two hours after I left Simon, I found the gravel driveway. It was at least half a mile long, bisecting the deep woods, then opening to a large field where a yellow clapboard house was nestled just off-center, with a long, wide lake at the end of a small clearing, and several yards away an inviting little guesthouse of cedar shakes. There was no sign of the ramshackle cabin Buddy had left behind, or one that even resembled it.

If Walter's directions hadn't been so exact, I might have thought I'd made a wrong turn along the way. And then I thought about the ten years that had passed, with only Marian standing still.

I left my car at the side of the driveway, called out "hello" a couple of times, but no one appeared from inside the house or out.

Although it was late April, there was a chill in the air, the sky was overcast and pale, the wind was quick against my face.

I called out again, again no one appeared, and I walked up a narrow dirt path, passing the lake where Buddy loved to fish. A wooden dock extended about fifteen feet over the water, and farther out, three or four hundred feet from where I stood, was a small island with a gazebo.

I tried imagining Buddy walking to the frozen lake on a frigid morning and back to his cabin when the sun set on the winter afternoon. What he might have seen in the woods. What he heard within the heave of the ice and on the wind. Or did he see, did he hear, only his isolation? If this was Buddy's respite from being Buddy, was Marian part of what he was escaping? Did Marian ever wonder if she was?

I was walking back to the driveway when I saw the car pull up; then a man was coming toward me. He might have been forty or even younger, his hair was thin on top, his face suntanned, at least what was visible behind his dark red beard. He wore overalls and a gray rain slicker. He looked like a seasoned boatswain.

"Insurance salesman or Jehovah's Witness?" he asked as he approached.

"Tough choice," I answered.

"Then I'll assume you're lost."

"Not the way you mean."

"Lost is lost, isn't it?" he said.

"I'm falling in love with the widow of the man who used to own this place. I wanted to see it for myself." I was as surprised by my honesty as he seemed to be. He smiled and made a "hmm" sound without moving his lips, kept showing me the smile while he said, "Well, take your time," pushed his hands into his pockets, and told me, "I'm Aubrey Stein, by the way. This is my place now."

I introduced myself, and Aubrey asked, "Did you just get here, or have you already had your look around?"

"Just pulled up. You've made a lot of changes, haven't you?"

"You sound disappointed."

"This place is fixed so firmly in the minds of the people who told me about it, it's been fixed the same way in mine. That's all."

"Sorry, but I had to do something with it."

"I'm sure this is a big improvement. The house, the gazebo. All of it."

"Do you mind if I ask what you *thought* you'd find?"

"The woman I mentioned? Her husband died up here, alone, in the cabin that was here. I guess you tore it down."

He looked in the direction of the guesthouse. "It was over there. I kept the original floors. Beautiful pine. Not that that's any help or consolation."

"What did you do with the stove?"

"You came with an inventory?"

"Another person's memories."

"I had it repaired and gave it away. All the old lumber, too. Does that matter to her?"

"She doesn't know I'm here."

The expression on his face made me think that this amused him.

"Look around," he said. "Take your time."

"I won't be long. I think I have the general idea."

The sun was out now. Aubrey said it was feeling downright tropical, opened his coat, and walked toward the lake.

"I'm sure you've driven a long way," he said over his shoulder, "and I don't have that many visitors this time of year, so why don't you stay a while. It's nice enough, we can sit out by the water."

We grabbed a couple of folding chairs, set them up on the dock, took off our coats, and sat low to get the full warmth of the sun.

I said, "Buddy, the man who used to own this place, liked to come up here to ice fish."

"This is a dreadful place in winter."

"I'm beginning to think that's why he liked it."

Aubrey made a low sound with his voice before he said, "I close it up at the end of October and don't come back till spring. Even now it's almost too early."

I considered his suntan. "You obviously head south."

"Africa."

"Africa?"

"Go to South America and turn east?" He was grinning, and I grinned back at him. "I teach school in Namibia."

"That's a long way to go to teach school."

"They need teachers. I volunteer."

I looked over the property again and said, "This is not where I'd expect a volunteer to live in his off-time."

"Back in the nineties, I was riding high on the Bubble."

"And you read the entrails and cashed out."

"In retrospect, it looks like prescience, doesn't it? Although the people I worked with thought that I lacked vision and ambition. But I think a person has to ask himself: How much is enough? I had enough and I walked away."

"I think it's also a question of how much do you need."

"Not such an easy thing to answer."

"So I've only recently discovered," I said.

The sunlight settled on the surface of the lake. Two hawks circled above us, their shadows following along the ground. Somewhere in the woods the cawing of crows came like the rush of disaster, and the mad hammering of a woodpecker, then silence all around us and the empty sky.

Aubrey got up and walked to the end of the dock. He sat on the edge, his feet hanging over the side.

"A few months after I left my job, I found this place. Or it found me, if that doesn't sound too precious."

"Then Africa found you."

He looked over his shoulder at me, as though he wasn't sure if I was being snide or serious, pulled his knees up, and leaned back on his elbows.

"I researched various foundations that were about helping people, found one that did volunteer work in Namibia, and I signed on. I've been doing it for the past seven years. But, if I'm not being too nosy," he said, "what else do you do besides look for the broken heart of the woman you're falling in love with?"

"Right now that's a full-time job."

I assumed that Aubrey knew an equivocation when he heard one, and even if I'd had any idea what the past few days came to, even if I'd been able to come to any conclusion, I doubted that I could have expressed what I was thinking, and if I could, the only person I would have talked to was Alex, but I was sure he'd soon be occupied with Simon and what Simon had to tell him, and that was all right with me.

Aubrey had no other questions, and I had nothing more to say. If I'd closed my eyes, I would have seen Marian sitting in that small office at her nursery, Buddy's photograph behind her, because Buddy was always close by, looking over her shoulder. I would have told her about this day and offered her my explanation and she would tell me what she thought, and once more, time could not move slowly enough.

Aubrey said, "I don't think you found what you came for."

"I'll just have to look somewhere else."

I SPENT THE NIGHT ALONE IN LAURA'S HOUSE. I DREAMT THAT I WAS trying to rescue a sinking sailboat from Buddy's lake.

Fourteen

NOT TOO EARLY THE NEXT THE MORNING, I SAT IN LAURA'S living room with a cup of coffee. Outside a light rain misted the windows. I was thinking that it wasn't only other people's lives I was interfering with, but my own, and I was not in the least comfortable with this, or settled about what I might do. I was thinking that I'd go back to Manhattan and leave Marian behind. I was thinking that was what Alex meant when we talked that night in the cab and he told me that I'd chosen a woman so unavailable it allowed me not to act, that both she, and my feelings for her, were disposable. Then I was thinking about going upstairs, making this a lazy, desultory morning and doing nothing at all.

A little after twelve noon, long after my coffee cup was empty, I was still hanging around the house, and it was still raining. The doorbell rang. It was Eliot, wearing a baseball cap, holding an open umbrella, looking like the high school kid with the crush on Marian Thayer, but when I looked at his face there was only a man with deep lines around his mouth and tightness in his eyes.

He didn't wait for me to ask him to come in, he leaned his umbrella against the hallway closet, and said the last time he was here I'd asked him if he was a musician, and did I remember.

I told him, no, I didn't.

"I wonder why you asked me that?"

I invited him to sit down.

"It was an odd thing to ask someone." He walked into the living room, sat in one of the chairs, and said, "I never thought I'd see the inside of this place again," in a low, vacant tone.

"I bet you never thought you'd see me again, either."

Eliot didn't acknowledge this. He leaned forward, rested his arms on his knees, and clasped his hands together. "If I talk to you about Marian," he said, "will I be making a jack-ass of myself?"

"What do you think we need to talk about?"

Eliot looked away from me, then he looked past me and around the room as though he were in the wrong house. He looked back at me, but now his cheeks were pale and his mouth open. The expressions on his face did not come to rest until I said, "I think you should know that I drove up to Buddy's cabin yesterday, and I've been wondering if Marian thought he went there to get away from her. If she ever talked to you about that."

Now the color returned and his lips began to move.

"That's way too deep for me," he said. "But why is it so important to know the reason why? What's that accomplish?" His voice was high-pitched now. "Whatever she's done is probably the way she wants it."

"I don't think that's what I'm asking."

"Why would you want to go up to the cabin, anyway?"

"I went to see the Ballantines," I said. "And they thought I should go up and see the place for myself."

"You do get around." There was nothing unpleasant in the way he said this.

"There was an entire year *before* Laura," he said. "After Buddy died. After the funeral. After everyone went home." He walked over to the window. Slow rivulets of water lined the outside of the windowpane. "I'd heard she wasn't doing very well. She wouldn't let anyone see her." Eliot still hadn't turned around. "You know, when I ran into her friends. So I went out there. She was having a bad time of it. Not taking care of herself, not eating. Nothing you'd call a meal, anyway. You could see that as far as she was concerned, her life—I made a point of getting out there after work to fix her supper, sit with her to make sure she'd eat, also it didn't hurt for her to have some company. For her to have someone there with her. She didn't seem to mind. After, I don't know, a couple of months maybe, she was ready to pay some attention to the nursery, which got her away from the house for a few hours. We started meeting for lunch in town. I was still going out to the house to make sure she was all right. We'd talk. That's the way things stayed for the rest of the year."

"You kept her alive," I said.

"That's not how I see it." He walked over to the stairs, and sat on the middle step.

"And the next year," I said, "Laura moved back to Shady Grove."

"She had nowhere else to go, so she came back to her home-town. It was her own idea. Marian may have agreed with it, but it was only till Laura got herself—you can—*anyone* can understand, losing their husbands like they did, that they comforted each other in ways no one else could. If anyone kept anyone alive, it was the two of them."

"You're not just the caretaker."

"Oh, I know. But with someone like Marian . . ."

It was the way he said this that reminded me of how his voice sounded when he was around Marian, the caution and constriction. And what did that feel like, ten years of catch-throat when he spoke to her, when he spoke about her?

As I sat there watching Eliot, I was remembering Marian's face, the lilt in her voice when she said: "You need to know what you've done to me." I was no longer paying attention to Eliot, until he stood up, walked over to the door, and picked up his umbrella. "She's doing what she wants," he said. There was a plaintive quality to his voice now. He stepped outside and looked over his shoulder. "Or she wouldn't be doing it." While I listened to the soft madness of the rain.

I DROVE OVER TO SEE ELEANOR AND WALTER LATER THAT AFTER-noon. I knew they were expecting to hear me talk about my day at Buddy's cabin, but I needed to talk to them about Eliot.

We sat in the den, the fire in the fireplace taking the chill out of this damp day; tea and a plate of gingerbread on the coffee table, music playing. I was pretty sure it was Chopin.

While Eleanor poured the tea and Walter put another log on the fire, I told them, "Eliot just gave me a brief tour of the unexamined life. I think there are things to recommend it."

Walter asked, "Do you feel like telling us about it?"

I said there really wasn't much to tell, except that it made me wonder what I was doing in the middle of all this.

"As well you should," Eleanor said.

"Eliot has a point: Marian's an adult, who's made an adult decision, and just because there may be an attraction between the two of us, and the three of us here might think she should be doing things differently, doesn't mean she needs to be wrenched away from her life. Or for that matter, me from mine." I managed not to sound strident when I said this, but I could feel the muscles in my throat tighten. "Eliot knows a hell of a lot more about Marian than I do. Maybe it's better to leave the two of them alone."

"As I recall," Walter said, "you asked Marian what she wants. And she told you she lacked the courage to fall in love again."

"That was before I talked to Eliot. He told me to back off, in his way. I don't think it would be fair to him not to."

"No," Eleanor agreed, "it wouldn't be fair."

"He's not the heavy in this," I said.

"More the innocent bystander," Eleanor said. "If Buddy hadn't . . ." She pulled her sweater around her shoulders. "It determined their relationship. Marian's and Eliot's. It *defined* it."

"Which explains why nothing gets examined too closely," I said.

Eleanor shook her head. "Of course, that doesn't make Eliot a passive player in this."

"I'd say he took the initiative. He went out there and took care of her. That was a gutsy thing to do."

"Marian stayed out at the house," Walter said, "because she chose to. We wanted her to stay with us here in town, and she wouldn't. And she wouldn't let us stay with her out there."

Eleanor reached over and put her hand on top of Walter's. "We went out to the house and tried to see her. Several times. And Charlie and Pamela went out. Marian wouldn't even come to the door. Didn't answer her phone. She cut herself off from everyone in the family."

"And her friends," Walter said.

"She thought everyone held her responsible." Eleanor turned to Walter. "That somehow, she hadn't taken care of Buddy."

"She said she couldn't face anyone," Walter said. "Eventually we talked this all out, but my God, that was a miserable time."

"Eliot didn't tell me about that part of it," I said.

"He probably doesn't know about it. As you've observed, Eliot doesn't look any further than he can see."

"Is that what you meant by Buddy's death defining their relationship?"

"It's all that she and Eliot have in common. Her loss and Eliot's ability not to interfere with how she chooses to cope with it," Eleanor answered. "Not cope, *sustain* it, is the better word."

It wasn't impatience that I saw after she said this, that would have shown a rudeness I was certain Eleanor didn't possess. It seemed that she wanted something from me.

I leaned over, poured tea into our cups, giving myself more time for a better read of Eleanor's expression; it may have been that they were expecting more insight from me than I could give, more depth. Eleanor didn't say anything, neither did Walter, they only sipped the tea I'd just poured. Walter sliced a corner of gingerbread. The music played in the background.

I thought about my last afternoon with Rita and the certainty I'd felt that day and about how compelling Marian was.

What I said was, "If Marian loved Eliot, nothing we say would matter." I got up and walked over to the fire. "Buddy's cabin is gone. That's why you wanted me to go there."

"If we'd simply told you," Walter answered, "it wouldn't have been the same." He didn't say anything else, neither did Eleanor.

It took me a moment. "It's all in the past," I said. "It's all about the past. *They're* all about the past. Eliot's in love with a girl he hasn't known since high school. The boy Marian fell in love with and married was her childhood sweetheart, and he's been dead longer than they'd been married." I may have been shouting. I knew I was speaking louder than I preferred. "It has to come down to not only who you love, but who loves you in return." I lowered my voice now. "Marian deserves another chance. They both do."

"And so do you, Geoffrey." It was Eleanor who said this. "You like to stand back and look at things from a safe distance, examine them, analyze them, don't you? I think the time has come for you to move in closer." When I didn't answer, she turned first to Walter, then to me. "You're going to have to take us at our word. We've been living this a long time."

"I've been living what I'm living a long time, too."

Eleanor said, "I can't believe you've never been in love."

"Not the way we've been talking about it."

"Then, Geoffrey," she said, "I'd say your time has come."

"I'd say that idea scares the hell out of me." I stepped away from the fire. "What if I'm wrong?"

"About Marian?" Walter asked.

"You have to understand, I've never been one for permanent relationships."

"You make it sound like you've *never* been involved with anyone," Walter said.

"Of course I have. They always end up feeling clingy and stifling. And I'm always a little more than relieved when things end. I can't remember not being this way and I've been completely at ease with it, or was. And I don't want to go back to that. What I'm afraid of is, we'll pursue this, Marian and I, and I'll get that old feeling and be scared away. I can't do that to her."

"I doubt that you'll be scared off," Walter said.

I was about to tell him that I didn't share his optimism, but now I was thinking about what he'd said earlier, about Marian rejecting her friends and family. I didn't know which startled me more, the question I wanted to ask or what I expected the answer to be.

I took another step back. "Why did she let Eliot come in?"

THE FOLLOWING MORNING, I DROVE OVER TO MARIAN'S NURSERY. It was Saturday and there were more than few customers walking the aisles of flowers and plants, loading their vans and hatchbacks.

Marian was sitting in her office, and when she saw me her mouth opened, her lips started to move, but I didn't give her a chance.

"We have to talk," I told her.

PART II

Geoffrey

Fifteen

MARIAN LIKED WHEN BUDDY WENT UP TO THE CABIN. Deep in winter, last summer's work finished, next spring's assignments far away. Late on a weekday afternoon, early on a Friday morning, Marian looked forward to these few days by herself. She was never troubled by this, or by the thought of Buddy staying out on that icy lake all day, sleeping in the cold; although why he or anyone else could find pleasure in that . . . but this had nothing to do with Buddy wanting to go away, and all to do with her antipathy for those ten acres Buddy had been so determined to own, and the days there doing nothing but being cold, sitting with Buddy, fishing and freezing—or skating with Pamela and Charlie, or the three of them skiing through the woods while Buddy fished, making the best of her time up there.

The icy nights of winter, wrapped in a sleeping bag inside their tent, were the worst. Cooking their meals on an open campfire. Reading by Coleman lanterns. Sleeping on those awful mattresses before they built the cabin, and the same horrid mattresses after the cabin was built.

There are certain places you take a dislike to, the way it is with certain people. They were there on a Friday morning in October, sitting close to the campfire, drinking hot coffee, the sun rising through the trees, Marian wrapping her sleeping bag around herself like a serape, Buddy dressed in jeans and hooded sweatshirt, sitting cross-legged on the ground, staring straight ahead with an expression that Marian described as his just-come-down-from-the-mountain-look.

He asked her how she would feel about his making an offer on the place. Marian wanted to know what was wrong with the arrangement the way it was. Buddy said the owner, Ike Barlow, was going to sell it, and Buddy didn't want to lose it. He hadn't told this to Barlow but he was pretty sure Barlow already knew how he felt. Assuming he'd ask a fair price, how would Marian feel about buying it?

Marian told Buddy she didn't mean to be an underminer but she hated this place. She moved closer, put her arms around him, rested her chin on top of his shoulder, and asked why he couldn't just buy a red sports cars like other men having a midlife crisis.

Buddy said because he was years away from a midlife crisis. And Marian told him not as many as he'd like to believe.

They sat side by side until they finished their coffee, then Marian got up to take her morning hike. Buddy stayed sitting, his legs crossed, smiling up at the sky.

On the other side of the undergrowth of bushes and trees, between the edge of the woods and the edge of the water, a narrow path circled the entire perimeter of the lake. Marian walked that path, as she did most mornings when she was up there.

Kicking through the dried leaves, listening to the crinkle-crunch beneath her feet, she wasn't thinking about her conversation with Buddy, she wasn't concerned about it, or surprised—she would have been if he'd wanted to buy a red sports car—and the only thing that was surprising about his wanting to make an offer was that he hadn't talked to her about it before.

Marian wasn't concerned about a thing.

Halfway around the lake, she veered off and walked deeper into the woods, where the leaves were damp with dew and glistened gold in the sunlight, and the sunlight brightened shy grass shoots and turned the mosses on the rocks pale and fragile shades of green. She watched the light change the colors in the ground and in the trees, and the way these colors changed the light; but it was the sweet mulch scent of leaf mold—an awful name for such a beautiful aroma—that made her pause. She knelt and lifted a handful to her nose, as though she might breathe in the living parts that grow gardens and strengthen the soil. She started to laugh, not at what she was doing, but at what she was feeling. To have arrived at this day in early October, after the past seven months, the endless spring rains, the worries that she and Buddy would never get started on their work. The demands of a ridiculous summer. The worries that once work started they would never catch up.

There are no problems, Marian, only opportunities. That's what Buddy had told her, last April, when the month seemed to be washing away.

They were upstairs in the office Buddy had built in the barn. It was raining, as it always seemed to be. They were sitting next to each other at Buddy's drafting table, studying their latest design, or what there was of it. It might have been the Tyrells' estate because Marian said she wanted to use lots of blues and yellows; the Tyrells impressed her as blue and yellow sort of people. Hydrangea and coreopsis, and later in the season, delphinium. Buddy wanted to use boxwoods to break up the garden rooms. Marian thought beeches would create a more dramatic entrance. And where, Marian wanted to know, would they build the pond—why had the Tyrells insisted on that pond?

Sometimes, it was Marian who made the first draft, sketching out a stand of trees, shaping a path; placement and shape. Sometimes, Buddy chose the flora, which colors and where, density and size; and always it was the two of them, like time and season, color and shape. Blank spaces washed with light and shadow. Buddy and Marian, side by side at the drafting table.

That rainy afternoon, when Marian got up and paced across the wood floor, her boots making a loud and rapid clicking sound, Buddy stayed in the old swivel chair they'd found when they bought their house, wearing a yellow rain slicker. Marian told him she was worried. Would they have enough time to meet their spring schedule? Were two crews enough, or did they need a third? They should have already been breaking ground over at the Dodson place, and what about the Millers'? It was making her crazy, this do-nothing.

Buddy told her nothing lasts forever, not even the rain, and spread a fresh piece of paper across the drafting table, tapping his pencil against it, to assure her there was plenty to do, and did she want to get back to work or wear out a hole in the floor, which wasn't good enough for Marian. Why couldn't he just say she was right, that there was nothing to be gained sitting around like this, that the weather really sucked and doing nothing day after day was a waste of time, and money lost? Why did it always have to be his take, his attitude?

But he was right, Buddy told her. It said so right here in the paper. The rain will end on . . .

Marian walked as far away from Buddy as she could in that small office. She said these people weren't going to wait around just for the privilege of having Buddy Ballantine landscape their property. She wished he would at least *pretend* to feel a sense of urgency. Buddy said now she was asking *too* much, and laughed at her, before he bent his head over the paper and his pencil began to work—you start with a line, he liked to say.

Marian went back to her desk, sat at her computer, bringing up one model then another, building gardens, tearing them down. Manipulating colors and shades, shapes and shadows.

The rain passed. The annoyances dissolved with apologies and a hug. Buddy spun around in his chair, and when it came full circle, he got up, walked over to Marian, pushed his hands through her hair, and kissed her neck. Marian told Buddy he'd never be truly happy until he learned to worry.

If it wasn't the Tyrells, it was the Millers, who were in love with lilacs and clematis, and where did Marian suggest they plant the barberry? Or the Rothmans, over in Hillsdale, with their five acres and all that morning sunlight.

When a curious client asked, and many often did, who thought of what, Marian or Buddy? the answer in truth was: We did. Marian was never surprised at how much she enjoyed saying this.

⚭

BUT NOW IT WAS OCTOBER. SWEET AUTUMN. THEIR TIME TO MAKE plans for the rest of the year. Marian loved the anticipation, loved looking forward to the expanse of weeks and months coming at them without haste or hurry, the way the new season approached when the change was startling because it had been happening all along. This was what she was thinking about walking through the woods.

A little farther along, the earth was soft beneath her, the land opened, and the contours of the ground seemed to sweep her forward like a soft hand in the small of her back.

How many things can you be sure of? That's what Buddy used to ask her, sometimes when they held each other at night, sometimes when they were doing nothing more than sitting around the campfire. Buddy wanted to know what they both could rely on. What they both could trust. Marian never asked Buddy what prompted the question. Buddy did not say these things simply to fill the silence. There was nothing rhetorical about it. She didn't always answer. Sometimes all she answered was: each other. Or maybe she just thought it and hadn't said anything at all—that was how she remembered it walking through the woods, following the shoreline; because that's what Buddy had been speaking of earlier that October morning.

Marian could be sure of Buddy striking the campsite while she was gone. The tent would be folded and the sleeping bags rolled up, placed in the back of the pickup. The fire would be doused, and Buddy would be sitting just where Marian had left him, as though he'd never moved, as though he'd packed the gear by an act of levitation.

Marian would ask what he was doing. Buddy would answer that he was thinking. If she asked what he was thinking about,

Buddy might say he'd been thinking about the work left on the Harrington place, and show her a design he'd made in a bare spot on the ground; or maybe it was about one of the places they were going to start on next year. He might tell her he was wondering what *she* was thinking about while she was walking, and Marian would tell him. Or Buddy might shrug his shoulders and say he was was thinking of nothing of any importance. Nothing at all.

Sometimes they'd pick up the conversation they'd left more than an hour before, without dropping the thought. It was no different that morning, when Marian came back from her hike.

Buddy told her, patting the ground so Marian would sit next to him, that what it was really all about was not pushing back. Pushing back against nature, which was what they did at their house, in their work. So why not have a place where nature pushes against them? No clearing away the trees, or planting or designing. He asked her to think of a kite moving about without resistance. It was a wonderful feeling. Sometimes.

All Marian could say was that it was always winter up here. So what's to push back against? Besides snow?

Buddy told her he had it from reliable sources that the Adirondacks actually experienced the standard four seasons.

Not that Marian ever noticed. All it ever was to her was cold and colder, and perhaps he'd explain to her sometime, Mr. Ballantine, just how sitting on the ice all day doing nothing, and sleeping in a tent in subzero weather was nature pushing back? He said he would tell her some snowy night by the fire, and anyway, Barlow was only *thinking* about it, so there was nothing to decide until there was something to decide. And if that time came and Marian was still against it, Buddy would let it go.

Just because *she* didn't like it here? No, Marian told him, she'd never do that to him.

THE LAST TIME BUDDY WENT UP TO THE CABIN WASN'T MUCH DIF-ferent from any of the other times. This just happened to be early on a Wednesday morning, driving the yellow pickup away from the house. And he decided to go alone.

He told Marian it was hard to round up a posse in the middle of the week, and when she said he could always wait for the weekend, Buddy told her, no, he preferred it this way.

He was smiling when he said it, and when he hugged her, Marian could feel the smile on his face. When they kissed good-bye, Buddy said her lower lip should be reclassified as contraband. That was the last thing Marian would hear Buddy say.

MARIAN WAS STILL ALERT TO THAT QUICK APPREHENSION WHEN Buddy left. There was always the anticipation three days after, four days, when he was due back. It was never tinged with anxiety or fear. She even enjoyed the fatigue she'd feel at the end of the day, being able to indulge in it, which she could not always do with Buddy around.

You don't worry about someone who knows how to read the ice. That's what Buddy had told Marian, and why shouldn't she believe him? Even when he was snowed-in for a day and late coming home, Marian would remind herself that he'd been doing this for most of his life.

She used to see him lots of times, ice fishing, when they were teenagers. That was when she fell in love with him.

Marian would watch Buddy out at the pond in Peery Park, where she used to go ice-skating with Laura and their friends on Saturday mornings. She'd see Buddy out there fishing through the ice with his friend Alan; sometimes Alan's father was there, sometimes three or four other boys. Marian knew who Buddy was, everyone knew Buddy Ballantine. He was only fifteen and already a senior in high school. He always seemed to be in the center of a crowd, joking and laughing in the hallway and cafeteria. Light brown hair hanging an inch or two over his forehead. Lean body, firm, narrow face, favoring his mother more than his father. Always having a good time.

But the day Marian fell in love with Buddy was the day she saw him sitting all alone out there on a small folding chair in the middle of the frozen pond wearing a black cap and a fleece jacket. Marian and her friends skated past him, Buddy didn't look at them, he just kept staring at the hole in the ice, solemn expression on his face like a lost boy, which may have been why Marian decided to speak, just loud enough for him to hear.

She asked if he was ever afraid the ice would crack and he'd fall in. He said a person just has to know how to read the ice, and wasn't that what she did before she started skating? She asked him if he ever got bored sitting out in the cold, and then she started to skate away. Buddy said whenever that happened he would think about the randomness of fishing. The way sometimes the fish took the bait and sometimes they swam away. It was more than accidental, there was causation to consider, because anything can happen at anytime. Like Marian stopping to talk to him that day, after all the other times she'd been out there.

When Marian pointed out that Buddy could have talked to her instead, Buddy looked amused, it was in his eyes. He said but it didn't happen that way, did it? That's why it was random.

Marian may not have understood or fully appreciated what Buddy was telling her, but she'd never heard anyone her age speak this way, and while Buddy looked down to check his fishing line, and Marian's friends were yelling for her to come on and skate with them, Marian didn't want to leave. She told her friends to go on without her, as she skated nervous ellipses behind Buddy and told him that, whether or not he knew it, people said he was the smartest boy in school, and now she saw why. And Marian, Buddy said, was the girl who never stopped moving. Anytime he saw her she was on the move. Rushing through the halls to class, or out the door after school. He'd even seen her a few times running on the outside track.

Marian stopped short and whipped around. What Buddy said made her feel self-conscious and she might have left then, but he held up his thermos and invited her to sit with him on one of the benches and have some hot chocolate.

The next time Marian saw Buddy, they talked about miracles.

It was about a week later, after school. Marian saw Buddy walking home alone. When she caught up with him, she said she'd been thinking about what he'd told her about randomness and all the possibilities of things happening, and maybe that's why people believed in miracles. Buddy told her that was one of the most intelligent things he'd ever heard, and for the second time Marian felt self-conscious around him; but she lifted her chin, looked directly at him, and asked why he sounded so surprised. Did he think she was just some girl jock or something? He said of course not, and then he asked if she believed in God, because to believe in miracles you'd have to believe in people's conception of God, and he just didn't believe that.

They were walking down Marian's street, and when they stopped at her house, Buddy asked if she'd ever read Tennyson's "Flower in the Crannied Wall."

Marian said she wasn't sure if she believed in God or miracles, and no she'd never read the poem.

That Friday night, Marian and Buddy sat in the enclosed porch in the Ballantines' house and read Tennyson.

They talked about most of the things two teenagers talk about and Marian noticed how eager Buddy was to listen to her. It made her feel that the things she said were important. Had she been a little older, she might have realized that contained in Buddy's eagerness to talk with her was his loneliness.

It was that same night when Buddy told her, confided in her, why the Tennyson poem was so important to him. He said if there was a God, that whatever *it* was, because you certainly couldn't ascribe a male or female pronoun to it, it was something so complex and magnificent that humans couldn't possibly be able to comprehend it; and to try to codify it was just to diminish that magnificence. What Tennyson was saying—and it was something Buddy believed—that magnificence and complexity was possessed by a tiny flower in a wall, and to understand *that* was to understand the meaning and purpose of God and humans and Nature. There had to be something a person could do to bring him or herself closer to that phenomenon.

Marian didn't, or couldn't, fully appreciate what Buddy was talking about, not with any more depth than that possessed by a fifteen-year-old. When Marian was an adult and remembered what Buddy had said to her that Friday night, she was more impressed, but by then she was no longer surprised by anything Buddy said.

The year before they got married, Buddy already had his master's degree and was starting his landscaping business. Marian had just graduated from college. Buddy told her that most of his life he'd felt like a freak, not just when he was in high school being the youngest kid in the class all the time, but always. When he was a little kid, and in college and graduate school, he felt as though he were standing on the inside of a window, seeing and hearing what was going on outside but not being a part of anything other than what was happening inside his mind and his imagination. He told Marian that he'd become proficient at hiding this from everyone, and hiding all of the things that he knew and thought from his teachers and his friends and even his family, and the boy Marian used to see standing with the crowd, having such a good time, was just a pose to make him appear less of an outsider, to cover for his feelings of being, not so much an impostor but a stranger. For a time, he wanted to believe this was just one of the consequences of his intelligence; but what he felt most often was fear. He was afraid that if he talked about this, people would think he was crazy. He was afraid that what he was experiencing was a type of psychosis and he doubted his sanity. But what he never doubted was how he felt about Marian. Marian made him feel normal, integrated in the community and in life. He said she kept him grounded. That she emboldened him, and it started that night when they read Tennyson, and did she remember their conversation?

Marian wanted to laugh because she found it such a relief to hear Buddy say this. She may have kept him grounded, she said, but he emboldened her to *leave* the ground.

Neither of them was unaware of the burden and the promise of that responsibility; of what they were confiding to and conferring on each other. A collaboration that would have felt daunting but for their excitement and certainty.

WHEN BUDDY WENT FISHING, IT WAS MARIAN'S OWN TIME WITHOUT annotation: "Just going out to the barn . . ." She pushed Buddy's voice out of her head, at times like an old song that won't go away, at times the reminder of all the things they were, when the whole is greater than the sum of the parts—something else Buddy would say. A time without mediation or Buddy's commentary, anticipated solely because of its impermanence, and enjoyed because of the privacy it allowed.

In the middle of a January morning there are intimations of summer. Inside catalogs, on Web sites. You only have to know where to look.

Spirea.

Bee balm.

Astilbe.

Phlox.

The names read like an evocation of summer.

Evocation. Another word Buddy would use.

In the middle of a January afternoon, sipping her coffee, sitting with a book, the days coming a little earlier, staying a little longer. The sunlight shining over her shoulder, Marian was home.

Place a vase just so on the table and create vignettes of contrasts and complements, and it is no longer a room, it's a home. The way you space the heliopsis and the tall grasses, the lady's mantle and the hosta. Then it's no longer a clearing or a backyard, it's a garden.

A FEW MONTHS AFTER BUDDY CLOSED ON THE PROPERTY, HE STARTED to build the cabin, when he had the time. Sometimes Marian went up there and helped him. It wasn't much of an improvement over the tent, except for the solid walls and floor. There were mice everywhere. The first time Pamela and Charlie stayed there, they suggested that Buddy do something before the mice got into the food or built nests in one of the mattresses. Buddy said unless people were up, there was really no food around for mice to get into, and the cabin was too cold for them to want to nest inside; besides, mice couldn't do that much damage. It was the *idea* of them, Pamela said, and Buddy should put out some poison.

Buddy looked uncomfortable when she said this. He said he'd thought about that but then remembered a poem about a man who wakes up early one morning and sees a poisoned mouse lying on the floor, not quite dead, and he imagines the mouse asking him, "What have I done that you wouldn't have?" Pamela reminded Buddy that he didn't show this sort of sentimentality toward fish, and Buddy reminded her that he drew the line at cold-blooded animals.

WHENEVER BUDDY WENT AWAY, THE FIRST NIGHTS WERE THE LONE-liest. By herself in their bed, Marian was keen to the sounds of the house, to the cold part of the sheets. She missed Buddy's body heat, the way he moved in his sleep, the way he was slow to wake up, always seeming a little surprised at where he was, as though he were still inside a dream, what he referred to as the "Morphean crease."

MARIAN WAS STILL A JUNIOR IN HIGH SCHOOL WHEN BUDDY WAS A freshman at UMass in Amherst, far enough away from Shady Grove for dormitory living, close enough to come home any weekend and for Marian to visit him. It was Buddy's idea that they should date other people while they were separated. How else would they ever be sure of each other, and who wanted to be married for five years and realize it was the mistake of a lifetime? There was a caveat: They never had to say when they went on a first date, or with whom; only if there was a second date with the same person did they have to tell the other one—Marian remembered the long and serious discussions they had all that summer, and how dangerous it felt, which might have been one of Buddy's reasons for doing it. They did not come to a quick agreement, and while Marian went along with it, she found it disturbing and unnecessary, almost like a game Buddy had devised, a challenge they each had to master.

Marian never heard about any second dates. Buddy heard about seven.

ON THE MORNING OF THE SECOND DAY, MARIAN WAS STILL NOT ready for Buddy to come home. It was her day. Her time. She'd walk out to the front of the house, and along the five acres where she and Buddy had finished the most recent gardens, making sure the burlap was secure around the boxwoods and evergreens, that the deer hadn't broken through the fencing or leaped over it. At the end of those gardens was the woodland park she and Buddy had just begun work on and was at least two years from completion; but for the moment, she stayed inside with nothing to think about, nothing to concern her.

You build a garden from the ground up and the top down. You render designs and plant for the future. There were places Marian and Buddy designed and built and never saw in full growth, except in photographs and magazines. You build a garden and wait.

THE DIFFERENCE BETWEEN TALENT AND BRILLIANCE IS THE DIFFERence between sight and vision.

This wasn't something Marian considered until she and Buddy had been married and working together for a year. She told Buddy that she could feel him thinking sometimes, feel him struggling with his thoughts. The deliberation. She said it made her feel excluded from his life.

This was what prompted Buddy to tell her that she made him feel normal, what they meant when they talked about the promise of their responsibility to each other. The way they would sit together in the spring scheduling their work, it didn't have to be in the barn, they could be outside walking their property, or on their way home from a party. Marian would tell Buddy that she knew what he was thinking. Buddy would say he could sense Marian's thoughts.

If they had a problem with an inconvenient slope at the end of a property, or difficult access for a pond, Marian would say she had a good idea where Buddy's plan had gone wrong and how to get it right. Then they were talking at once, as one.

Coming back from dinner, and it would be the same talk about some other place, or different talk about the same place.

There were a few times when they talked about how they each completed the other, not only in their work, but in their lives—it distinguishes doing something from being something, as Charlie would say. Marian did not say, perhaps she wasn't aware, that it was the intensity of who she and Buddy were that she often found terrifying.

They had their best conversations in the car.

One night, driving back from a dinner, or maybe it was from a movie, Marian asked Buddy if there were ever times when he felt as though the two of them were sharing the same burden.

Buddy didn't ask her what burden she was talking about, all he asked was if Marian worried about it.

Marian said at times it was overwhelming, and she cherished that feeling.

⌘

IT WASN'T MARIAN'S IDEA THAT THEY SPEND TIME AWAY FROM EACH other, or Buddy's. They talked about it a few times; kept coming back to it. Just another collaboration.

Marian was the first to go away, there was nothing forced or contrived about it.

Three years into their marriage, toward the end of February. She and two friends spent a week in Bermuda, sailing, swimming, riding bicycles. She was happy to be with other women after spending most of the year in the company of men.

She didn't like sleeping without Buddy in an unfamiliar bed, waking up to no other sound than her own breathing. Yet, she liked this kind of loneliness, it was reassuring and did not make her feel like the wife-in-exile, the way her friends said they felt. Marian wasn't escaping from children, or trying to block out a job she didn't love, but she was leaving something behind: The slow narration inside her head, telling Buddy—no, *hearing* herself talking to him. Listening for his . . . opinions? His approval? Did she need his affirmation, his bearing witness to her experience? Or was there more to it? Was it the integration of their personalities? Like astrological twins.

There was always something missing and something to be missed when they were apart. As though there were nothing substantive to what either of them did without the other being there; the tree falling with no one there to hear it. Marian felt nothing oppressive about this, or subordinating. She didn't resent it and didn't resist it. She was twenty-five years old and not afraid of her life.

When she returned from Bermuda, lying together upstairs, her head on Buddy's shoulder, she spoke in a low voice, in the low light, telling Buddy about her vacation, listening to him tell her all about the things he'd done and seen while she was gone.

They told their stories, made deeper for the sharing, and always a little more real.

ICE FISHING IN THE ADIRONDACKS FOLLOWED THE NEXT YEAR. FISHing on Barlow's property came two years after that, not without Marian's argument. She remembered driving up the rutted logging road, before the snows came. Bouncing in the truck, past the junk trees, the rotted-out trunks and stumps. The clearing and the lake looking scrubby and rank. The lake itself nothing more than unremarkable. Even the birds sounded harsh and shrill.

She told Buddy the place was awful. Not just awful, *ugly*. There had to be other lakes where Buddy could go to get away, if not in Shady Grove, at least closer to the comforts of home. Buddy said conveniences had nothing to do with it, and neither did aesthetics. It was because of its inconvenience. It was about the rusticity. He went there *because* it was so unappealing.

Buddy said it was possible to have too many precious things in your life, and people and places that you love so much it was necessary to go somewhere that you didn't have to maintain, that you didn't care so much about.

Marian told him he had a perversity of thinking that was maddening.

❧

MARIAN STOPPED GOING TO THE CABIN THE WINTER AFTER IT WAS built. She'd been telling Buddy all along that she would stop once he didn't need her help with it. Buddy asked her to go up there a few times after that, but she never went, he never insisted, or was hurt by her refusal. Besides, it was he who said there was no reason to discuss it again, that it was not a big deal. For the next seven years, which was as long as Buddy owned the place, they never felt the need to justify this decision. It was important to Marian that she remember this. Seven years and nothing ever happened to him. It was important that she remind herself of that, and that Buddy knew how she felt. It was important for her to remember the mornings when she watched the yellow truck go up the driveway and felt herself lighten with the absence of Buddy's lassitude.

And it was important to remember that it wasn't always winter and it wasn't always about sitting out in the cold, or flying down to Bermuda. There was summer.

It was summer that Marian loved most. Waiting through three seasons. Then she and Buddy were outside with their crews until dark, checking that the completion of older projects was not being rushed, that the new ones were starting on time. Cutting down trees, digging the soil, sculpting the land, watching their work taking shape. What Buddy called pushing against nature. Marian was moving again.

Summer, the shortest season. The one they savored in spite of all the work, and because of it.

There were weekend parties, music playing, loud, playful chatter rising from their back deck and the front porch with the verdant, spicy fragrances. Killer croquet matches and volleyball games that were not to be trifled with. Marian in the middle of the action, Buddy working the grill, filling plates with one hand, lifting a beer to his lips with the other. And dancing—Marian needed to remember how much Buddy loved to dance, slow, holding her in his arms, and fast, head thrown back, legs stomping, hands clapping.

There were the melt-away Sunday mornings when they came up for air, spread their blanket on their lawn, just the two of them naked under the hot sun. Listening to the hum of the earth. Listening to nothing at all. Buddy's hands on her body, hers on his. Feeling the certainty of their flesh.

That last summer, they needed three crews to keep up with the work. All idleness was gone. It should have been the time of irrevocable pleasure. It was less than that. What in past years had been their season of excitement, of restoration, was now their summer of discontent.

Their impatience with each other, with their crew, was like a fingernail scraping against glass. The flora looked shabbier than last year's and Marian sent back more than she accepted—she began looking forward to the times when she drove out to her supplier to complain, just for an excuse to yell at someone.

Couldn't Buddy see, she would ask, how poorly the jobs were going? The men were working too slowly, their attitude seemed listless. Couldn't they get anything right, damn it? And why was it always *him*, he would answer back, who had to speak to them? Why was it her, Marian wanted to know, who had to *tell* him? Was she the only one who *noticed*?

There were the long silences. In the morning. Across the table at supper. When she tried to tell her concerns to Buddy, Marian could not speak to the expression on his face.

Something was lacking, Marian thought. Something was being overlooked. By Buddy, by her.

When Buddy did speak to her, Marian sensed it was not what he was really thinking. What she was thinking, she was not able to say.

She would look at Buddy in the sunlight, his thin face thinner, his eyes set deeper. She was not sure if what she saw was weariness or indifference.

At night when they were in bed, holding each other, moonlight coming through the window, it seemed like old times. Almost. Or when they made love, it would begin to feel as though they were getting back to the way things were, back to themselves. Then Marian would feel that tug, the shapeless sense of emotional lethargy, and just like that they were out of synch with each other. Buddy felt it, too. He said he'd never felt this separate from Marian before. He said maybe they were simply preoccupied.

Marian said it frightened her.

This was the way June ended. Nothing changed in early July.

Sometimes, Marian woke up in the middle of the night and Buddy would be gone. More than a few times, she heard him walking the floor downstairs. One time, she went looking for him and found him standing outside, naked, staring up at the stars.

Marian told him he was behaving like a man with a secret. Buddy said he had no secrets from her. He said he didn't know what was wrong. She didn't want to live like this, Marian told him. And what were they going to do about it? Buddy said they'd have to live with it, for now. That became the theme of their summer.

By the end of July, Marian and Buddy had grown so inured to the dismal way they felt that they stopped talking about it.

Not that they denied its presence; more that they defied it, or tried to, the way you wait out nasty weather. That there was no longer a thrill to their work, or sneaking away for a day off, was not an aberration but a way of life.

Then, one morning in the middle of August, while Marian stood alone by a stone wall watching the work in progress at the Lyntons' place in Millbrook, listening to the soft, sifting sound of shovels breaking the earth, about to get in her car and leave, she saw Buddy coming through the new clearing about fifty feet from her. He was sipping coffee from a paper cup, stopped to speak with one of the workers over by a pile of felled trees, walked farther along, poured what remained in the cup into a stack of dead branches, crushed the cup and put it in his pocket. When he saw Marian he walked toward her. His face had the ripe suntan of late summer, and there was animation in his expression that had been absent for the past two months. Marian should have enjoyed seeing this. All she felt was apprehension.

Buddy must have seen that and expected her to walk away, because he waved and called out for her to wait a minute, and when he reached her, he put his arm around her waist and held her close. She leaned into him so she could feel the warmth of his body and his breath. She inhaled the familiar scent of his sweat, closed her eyes, and when she felt Buddy's head move she raised her face to his. He whispered that he didn't know about her, but *he* wouldn't mind if the two of them could find an unspoiled jungle somewhere, rent a tree house, and live on coconuts.

Marian told him that coconuts can get annoying, could they make it a four-star tree house with room service? That, Buddy said, was precisely what he had in mind. Marian wanted him to please tell her just what the *hell* was going on.

Buddy said maybe it had to do with the two of them running dry on their work. Running dry on their lives. The way they were living.

They sat on the stone wall, in the shade of a maple tree, away from the crew.

Buddy still had his arm around Marian's waist. He said he thought he had it figured out. That it wasn't landscaping that they loved as much as doing landscaping with each other.

All this time? That's what he'd been thinking about? Because all Marian had been thinking about, all that she'd been feeling, anyway, was a deep sense of estrangement, like one of those horrid, unhappy couples, and she hated it, so if this was what Buddy thought was the problem, they'd better get busy fixing it.

Buddy said he wasn't joking about the tree house, four stars or not. He asked if it would be such a crazy idea to close up shop and go away for a while. Was money an object? Did Marian think next summer would be too soon?

Marian said they still had a few projects under contract and money was always an object. They could go away the summer after next, then they'd be sure to have more than enough for a year, at least, probably longer. And when their money ran out?

Buddy said they'd come home and pick up where they left off. Unless a newer, younger genius had taken his place, Shady Grove passed them by, and no one wanted a Buddy Ballantine design anymore.

In that case, Marian said, they would start over. From scratch. She raised her arms to the sky and let out a shout. She told Buddy it was about time they'd gotten around to saying what they needed. She felt as though she and Buddy were—

what's centrifugal force? As though they were no longer being compelled toward Shady Grove, but spinning away, out of its orbit. It made her feel giddy. She grabbed Buddy's arm and squeezed it, pressed her cheek against his bicep.

Buddy said he was thinking they could start out in the Caribbean, the Virgin Islands, and make their way south, all the way to Peru, Brazil, Argentina . . . And when they got tired of that . . .

Africa.

Or Asia.

Or the Mediterranean.

Anywhere that interested them. After all, Buddy pointed out, Marian was still the girl who couldn't stop moving, wasn't she?

All the places they might see, not as tourists but as travelers. . . . All that time to look forward to . . . All the possibilities . . .

THEY WOULD LEAVE SHADY GROVE BEHIND. THERE WERE TIMES when it felt like a surrender; although Marian insisted that they were not giving up or giving in, but giving over because it wasn't enough to feel discontented and to recognize it, but to reject it. Sometimes it felt like defiance, and sometimes it felt like a confession of faith.

They talked about feeling a sense of release, not only from the past month, but from what they'd been doing together for the past couple of years. It wasn't that they'd been working too hard, but they'd been too single-minded for too long. And for what purpose? It wasn't about making a lot of money.

It had never been about the money but about the joy they derived from doing their work. Now it was about its absence. Buddy used the word *absence*. Marian used the word *loss*.

If pleasure from their work had been lost they would have to find it elsewhere and carry it with them, if not back to Shady Grove then to some other place they hadn't yet considered, that they would discover along the way.

Marian wanted to know how Buddy felt about never moving back to Shady Grove, about not *wanting* to pick up where they left off. What if they came back only long enough to sell everything and move away and start over? What if they only came back to see his family?

That was all right with Buddy. There were other houses, other towns. Other ways to live. He said you can't travel the world, even a small part of it, and not expect it to change you, and a year away from Shady Grove would no doubt change them. And wouldn't Shady Grove have also changed, if only their perception of it because of what had changed in them? Isn't that the way it happens? Is that what they wanted?

Shady Grove had always meant home, now Marian thought how exciting it was to get away. She told Buddy that she loved the feeling she had when she thought about leaving. She said she wasn't afraid to start over. She said it felt like floating. Floating words. Floating plans. One more summer floating in the future. Because life is the act of motion. Of moving. That was what Marian told Buddy the summer morning when they sat on the stone wall in the shade of the maple tree, Buddy's arm around her waist. She didn't tell him if life is an act of motion, stasis is its antithesis; although it would occur to her long after this conversation that she'd been telling him just that every time she told him how much she hated the cabin;

that Buddy sitting alone out there in winter was Buddy sitting with death, or defying it, defying his mortality, and denying it—Marian didn't believe in premonitions or her own pre-science, neither did she doubt her feelings—but these were not the things she and Buddy talked about that last summer. These were not the things either of them thought about while they made their plans.

MARIAN WOKE EARLY AND WENT CROSS-COUNTRY SKIING THAT morning by herself, something she liked to do when Buddy was gone. In the afternoon, she met Pamela and a couple of her friends for lunch in Great Barrington. All through the day, she was aware of the remaining time, the uninterrupted hours before the sound of Buddy's truck came down the drive-way, the snap of the door hinges, her awareness of giving back this piece of her day, her sense of relinquishing herself, when Buddy came back needing a shave and a shower. The inside of his yellow pickup would smell like a man who'd been alone in the Adirondacks for three days, but that would fade away in a short time. Marian neither anticipated any of this nor took it for granted. It was what she knew.

Buddy's return was also her return to Buddy. They started calling it their reentry. It was Marian who named it, one eve-ning, the second or third time Buddy had been to the lake. She asked if he ever felt that he needed time to regroup after he got back; that he might not want her to be there, because there were a few times when she felt that way after she re-turned. There were times when she felt this way when Buddy returned.

Buddy said that his three-hour drive allowed him that time, and didn't Marian have enough time to decompress? A little while later, Buddy said yes, when he first walked in the house, he felt as though he was being pulled out of his— reverie was a silly word for it, but some sort of privacy was being breached.

Marian wanted to know if it felt like a jolt. A shock to the system? Buddy thought those were strong words for it, but there was a distinct moment of adjustment, or readjustment. She said sometimes she liked it when Buddy wasn't home when she came back, she liked coming back to an empty house. For a slow reentry. And would he prefer that she not be home?

Not ever. He said he wanted Marian to be there always; but after that night, whenever they took time off from each other, they called from the road on their way back home.

ON THE FOURTH DAY WHEN BUDDY HADN'T PHONED, MARIAN called Charlie. They drove up to the cabin early that same morning.

Sixteen

ARIAN STOOD IN FRONT OF THE OFFICE WINDOW. HER HEAD was down, the tip of her chin touched the top of her collar. She raised her eyes toward the photograph of Buddy and her leaning against a backhoe and laughing.

"Sometime I'll tell what we thought was so funny," she said, in a way that made me look forward to that time.

She was still looking at the photograph while she said, "I'm not sure how I feel about your going up to his cabin. Not that I have any hold on the place, but I would have liked if you'd asked me, or if Walt and Ellie had. Or told me."

"If I'd told you, what would you have said?"

"I don't know. What did you expect to find?"

"I just wanted to see the place for myself."

Marian came around to the front of her desk. I'd been sitting in that uncomfortable wooden chair since I'd arrived, and only now did I get up. I was close enough to take her in my arms, which I was finding difficult not to do, and tell her that I understood what it meant to be married to Buddy.

Marian said, "And now if you don't mind . . ."

"Let's get away from here," I told her. "Find some place where no one will recognize us. I'll buy you lunch, and we'll speak of nothing of any relevance."

"Aren't you bored with me by now?" She was smiling when she said this.

We took Marian's car and drove away from town, on one of the county roads I was now familiar with.

We stopped at a store that sold prepared food. I bought a couple of sandwiches, two small bags of potato chips, and sodas. Marian drove another few miles until we came to a dirt road and followed it to a narrow wooden bridge by a waterfall. She stopped the car, lowered the windows, and cut the engine; although there was a cool breeze blowing, we kept the windows down so we could hear the sound of water rushing against the rocks.

I watched Marian as she looked out the car window.

I said, "Every time I'm with you you appear different to me. Not like you're a different person, or because of the clothes you're wearing or anything like that. It's looking into your face and recognizing your different expressions. I won't say I *understand* them, but I know them, and the changes in your voice when you speak. The way you sit straight up when you're unhappy with what we're talking about, sit low when there's more that you want to say."

"I don't like when you say things like that." She shook her head. "I *do* like it. And I have no idea what you think you're doing, and if you told me, I wouldn't believe you." She turned to me. "Why won't you go away, please." A moment later she said, "Only I'd probably miss you if you did, and if you came back, I'd only want you to go away again. So please don't say things like that to me."

"So much for irrelevance."

"You didn't really expect that, did you? Anyway, I wanted to show you this place. Buddy and I used to come here to get away from everything. This is where we convinced ourselves that"—she let out a soft breath—"that we could have whatever we wanted. Down there, sitting on those stones." She looked over at me and said, "God, but we took our marriage seriously. *Ourselves. So* seriously. Very intense. Very high maintenance. That's what we wanted to get away from, really. We were too young to state it like that. But that's what it was about."

"When you care about something and someone," I said, "the way you two did—"

"It was work. *We* were hard work, and incredibly self-involved. I mean the both of us, as a couple. I was beginning to understand that, our last year together, and my opinion hasn't changed. It was the nature of our marriage. Maybe we'd have grown out of it, I don't know." She turned to me. "I don't miss that part of it. I should say, I've *stopped* missing it. With all the other things I've felt since Buddy died and all the things I've missed, I've also felt released from the intensity. His intensity. Maybe that's why I'm—I'm afraid if we got involved, you and I, it would be the same thing. And I really don't know if I want to do that again."

The sun was shining directly into our eyes, so we tilted the seats back, our faces parallel to each other, as though we were lying together on a couch, or in bed.

"When you described your relationship with your girl-friend, remember? After you left, I thought about how easy you made it sound. How light and easy it was for the both of you. I envied that. I wanted that. To skim across the emotional surface without all that monitoring, without the fear, I suppose it's fear, that you're cheating on the depth of it. Not feeling it deeply enough."

"Also the fear of losing the person you love."

"You made it sound very inviting. Inviting," she said, "and fun."

"That wasn't my intention."

"You can't help it. It's what you do for a living, isn't it. Making things sound inviting and fun."

I thought she was making a joke.

"I'm quite serious," she said. "You make it sound very appealing. I wouldn't mind a relationship like that."

"You already have one."

"Then why isn't it fun?" Marian rested her hand on top of mine. "Do you miss her? Do you miss your girlfriend?"

I said I didn't.

"Didn't it make you sad? To break up with her?"

"I didn't feel anything. It was like it never happened. After three years and I don't think either of us felt much remorse. But I was terrified and exhilarated, and I felt like I was upside down. What I'd done was contrary to most everything I've ever done leading up to that day, and yet it felt right. Incontrovertible. And, at the same time, I had no clue as to what was going to happen to me or what I expected to happen. All I thought was: What the hell have you done? And all I felt was liberated."

Our heads were close enough for me to smell Marian's hair, feel the warmth of her body.

"I was on my way to my apartment to tell my brother, but I never got the chance. Instead, I get to tell you, which only seems right, since my breaking up with Rita had little to do with her, and everything to do with you."

"Don't."

"After I left Shady Grove," I said, "the *first* time, all the things that had been important to me felt superficial and unsatisfying. I knew what was lacking—what *I* lacked. It wasn't a *relationship* I was leaving when Rita and I broke up. There was no relationship to leave. We were just two people who happened to get along a little more than just well enough, and spent time together with absolutely nothing at risk, nothing to regret. In the end, there was no heartbreak. It wasn't even Rita who I'd broken up with. You might say I'd broken up with the way I was going about my life and all the things that had held my little world together. I could no longer tolerate what *you* say you find so appealing."

She sat up, took our sandwiches out of the bag, and told me to stop talking and eat.

We ate in the car, and listened to the rush of water, and by the time we finished, the inside of the car was hot from the sun and our bodies. Marian opened the door, brushed stray bread crumbs off her lap, stepped outside, and walked over to the side of the bridge, She stood with her back against the railing and called to me: "It's really nice over here." I was already out of the car.

"We both knew that we were attracted to each other that first time," I told her. "And we both knew how inconvenient that was. But I liked the idea of being attracted to you. Now it's more than just the idea."

"And it's still inconvenient," she said.

"It's the feeling that matters."

"There's a lot about me you wouldn't like."

"That's not going to work. Saying things to try and keep me back on my heels."

"So what?"

I enjoyed hearing the sound of resignation in her voice,

and I laughed, not only because of that, but because all the things we'd ever started out talking about always led back to this conversation and it never seemed inappropriate; just as nothing else between us ever seemed inappropriate. I turned to look at her. I just wanted to see her standing next me.

She unbuttoned her coat and let it fall open.

"You must have felt *something* for her," she said. "For Rita."

"Or else my telling you it's the feeling that matters can't be trusted?"

"I'm just curious."

"I liked Rita very much, but there wasn't any passion. We never argued, never disagreed, not about anything important. In fact, there was nothing of any real importance to anything. Don't you think that's odd?"

"Unsatisfying, really."

"It made me angry. That's mostly what I was feeling after I walked away from her. Not angry at Rita, definitely not Rita. I *liked* Rita. But I was angry at those three years. It was a waste of time."

"Only if there was something else you thought you should have been doing."

"Then it was even more of a waste of time because I never gave it that much thought."

"Then you were in the right relationship. For that time."

"Just like you and Eliot." I stood close to her and spoke in my most professional voice, the one that made things sound so damned inviting: "Skimming the emotional surface is fun only if you both want the same thing."

"Ahh, the perfect world," she said. "And you're welcome to it."

Marian might not have been able to keep me on my heels,

but she did have the ability to make me have a clearer read on what she was telling me. At that moment I felt, and not for the first time with her, that slight shifts were taking place between us, between what I thought was happening and what she was going to tell me was happening.

"I wouldn't mind being sad about something besides Laura and Buddy," she said, and gave the waterfall a passing glance. "And now I have to get back to work." She did not sound enthusiastic. "But I want to see you again before you leave town."

MARIAN DROVE US BACK TO THE NURSERY. CARS CROWDED THE parking lot, all the place could tolerate; customers were scurrying past the large wooden tables of perennials and annuals; some were pulling little wagons loaded with pots and soil; others walked in slow, contained strides, as though they were in a botanical garden on this early afternoon. A couple of men were in serious discussion with one of Marian's people as they approached the arbor. Two women wearing red bandannas were struggling with a spruce that was too big for them. The constant and busy hum of locomotion was everywhere. While a few more cars pulled in and jockeyed for space, I couldn't help but think of the awakening of bees from dormant hives and butterflies from cocoons, early and eager to join the season.

We walked to my car at the front of the lot. Marian put her hands in her pockets and kicked at the gravel with the tip of her shoe.

She said, "Listen, Geoffrey: I love living in that house. I love seeing photographs of Buddy on the walls and the gardens we built. I love that it reminds me of him, who he was and how he thought. His confidence, his arrogance. For a long time I thought it was his arrogance that killed him, and mine that allowed it. I wish I could have sat out there with him and waited for the fish to bite and heard the poetry of randomness. Most of all, I wish I hadn't been so stubborn about going up to the damn place." She took a breath and let out a shallow sigh. "Now I'm in a relationship with someone who is so goddamned reliable and predictable that I can look at my watch and tell you where he is and where he'll be two hours from now and the day after tomorrow. I like that. No surprises. Nothing unexpected. This is what I want. Wanted. *Want.* I've had enough of all that other stuff. I know a little about passion, and you aren't missing anything." She tilted her head and frowned at me. "And that's so much B.S., how can you stand it?" She straightened up and walked away. "I'll call you," she said over her shoulder. "We'll talk. Okay?" A throwaway line, cuing her exit.

THE FOLLOWING AFTERNOON, I WAS SITTING OUTSIDE ON LAURA'S front steps wondering how long ago it had been since I'd broken up with Rita. How long since I'd come to Shady Grove, or read a newspaper, or heard any news about the world.

Time had lost its application, and that was all right with me. I enjoyed this lack of context, and might have continued enjoying it for the rest of the afternoon, except for Eliot walking up the sidewalk, baseball cap on his head, a button-down oxford blue shirt open at the collar, hands in his pockets. He was smiling at me, taking a moment before he approached the house.

I said hello and smiled back at him.

He said he was just taking a break from work, and thought he'd stop by and say hello to Simon. When I told him Simon had gone back to New York, Eliot said, "Oh," his voice soft and hollow. He sat on the bottom step, took off his cap, and scratched the top of his head. He didn't say anything, but I recognized the look on his face; it was the same one I'd been seeing every time we met, on the street after I first got to town when he came here the other day and stood on this same porch, an umbrella in his hand. I might have been willing to assure him, again, that I'd be gone in another day, and didn't plan on coming back, if I hadn't been listening for Marian's phone call, wanting her to give me a reason not to go. I turned my head to look into the house, when I turned back, I was thinking, what else can I say, what can I tell him that's more to the point than words of assurance? Only, I didn't want to tell Eliot anything.

Eliot was staring behind my head like one of those dolls made of balsa wood and rice paper—the cut of his clothes, the angle of his body. If I'd tapped his shoulder he'd have crumbled backward, if a wind came up he'd have blown away. I was thinking that the right words from me, or the wrong ones, and he would break apart and scatter, but I was protecting him, monitoring what I said whenever I was with him, never unaware that I was a threat to him and his happiness. And I hesitated before I spoke, girding myself, taking a slow ten count to consider what I was going to say, hoping that Eliot would hear it for what it was, for what I wanted it to be.

"It must be very lonely for you," was what I said.

Eliot stared at me. "I don't know what you mean."

"I guess I meant that as a question."

234 / JAMIE M. SAUL

"I'm not any lonelier than, well, you for instance. Aren't there times when you feel like not being by yourself."

"Is that what you think I mean by lonely?"

Eliot stood up, brushed off his pants, and walked away.

I went back into the house. I wasn't there for long when Eliot walked into the living room and sat on the arm of a chair.

"I've always liked this room," he said.

"You didn't come back to tell me that," I answered.

"I saw your car parked outside Marian's office yesterday and her car was gone. I don't mean to sound like a jackass, but is there something going on that I should know about?"

"I'm as confused as you," I said, which was not the answer he deserved, but I was thinking about the afternoon when Marian said she was sure I wouldn't tell anyone about our conversation if she asked me not to. Well, maybe she hadn't asked me, but I wanted to remember it that way. I told Eliot, "You're going to have to talk to Marian. And whatever you're thinking, that's *not* it."

"We used to have some nice evenings here, Marian and Laura and me," he said. "We went way back, the three of us. Nice talk. Old friends."

Did he go all the way back to Saturday mornings skating the pond in the park? Did he happen to look up one Saturday morning and see Marian skating those tight circles? Did Eliot watch Marian fall in love with Buddy?

"Were you one of the kids who skated at Peery Park?" I asked.

Eliot just stared at me for a moment, then walked to the door, with his head down, as though he needed to watch each step.

Seventeen

T HE BACKYARD OUTSIDE LAURA'S KITCHEN DOOR WAS NOT SO much in disrepair as in need of a spring cleanup. The wood trellis was overgrown with wisteria. Weeds had crawled up between the bricks in the patio. The three metal rocking chairs had been tilted over and small pockets of puddles from the recent rain filled the indents and crevices, adding to the rust. There were four empty birdfeeders—two hanging from trees, two others on thin metal poles—and a small collection of terra-cotta flowerpots that held only moist soil were lined up under a tree like poor relations. I turned one of the chairs upright, cleaned it with a damp towel, and sat out there in reasonable comfort.

There are times when the thing you least want to do is the thing that most needs doing. I needed to wait. Wait for Marian to make a decision, wait for Eliot to act, and all I could do was choose where to do my waiting: here in Shady Grove or back in Manhattan and the pleasures of being home.

Or was my waiting for Eliot and Marian nothing more than the convenience of my own passivity? When was I going to declare what I was feeling? When was I going to tell Eliot— *what* was I going to tell him? What was I supposed to say? That Laura had bequeathed me to Marian?

It was a tight triangle, Marian, Eliot, and me; and Marian and Eliot and Buddy; and Marian, Buddy, and me. There seemed to be a need for a specific kind of arithmetic to arrive at the sum of all this.

I don't think of myself as having much insight into the human heart and psyche, but I knew that the dispassion that Marian and I had been living with were the same things, although mine was cultivated and hers was studied. Buddy had sought to escape the obligations of the heart, at least temporarily, and perhaps he'd found it: Going to the cabin was his way of taking his heart slumming because of that high maintenance Marian spoke about. The confidence that allowed him to leave was the confidence of knowing what he was coming home to, that it was constant. Otherwise, it wouldn't have been slumming, but a way of life that was careless and pointless, with nothing to give it substance and shape.

However long it took me to reach this conclusion was just as long as it took Eliot to realize he wasn't finished with me. I was still sitting in the backyard when he walked out the kitchen door, straightened one of the chairs, and told me, "When I got back to the store I felt— restless I guess best describes it, like I'd forgotten something. Like I'd left something behind. I couldn't concentrate on a damn thing. And this is Saturday."

"*Saturday?*"

"My busiest day this time of year. You know, all the weekenders . . . I've got to be on my toes." Eliot wasn't shouting, but there was agitation in his voice.

He walked over to one of the birdfeeders. Looked into it, walked to the other birdfeeder, looked into that one while he flicked his finger against the side, watched the dried seeds fall to the ground, and said, "I haven't thought about Peery Park—I didn't go there all that much back then. I'm not much of a winter person, skating and all that. This is my time of year, or just about. I play a little tennis, a little basketball after work. Pretty soon the evenings get warm enough so you can start sitting outside again. I start looking forward to that. Winter's not for me." He shook his head. "The best skater out there was Simon. Did anyone tell you that? I don't mean just *ice*-skating. He was an excellent hockey player. Can you believe it? Buddy wasn't much of an athlete, though. At least he didn't go out much for sports." Eliot looked over toward the kitchen door. "This has turned into a sad little place. I'll be glad when they sell it." He sounded so bitter I thought he was going to spit on the ground. He walked across the patio, and sat down again. "Someone should buy this place, clean it up, paint it." He rocked back in the chair. "Laura once asked me, it seems not too long ago, she asked if I was happy. I said, 'What's happy?' That kind of thing was more important to her than to me. I don't have any complaints. Isn't that happy enough? She wanted to know if I ever thought about leaving Marian. She didn't say *leave*, I forget the exact word, but didn't I want to meet someone who just knocked me out? Didn't I think I *deserved* to be crazy in love with someone, just once in my life?" He laughed a soft, breathy laugh. "Maybe because she knew she was dying she was thinking about these things." He let out that laugh again. "She said I should sell my store and use the money to go somewhere that I've always wanted to see. That I should put some distance between myself and Shady Grove. I said I'd never given much thought to moving away from Shady Grove. That this is my hometown, and I felt attached to it. Isn't that why she came back? To be home, right? And why Marian stayed after Buddy—I don't think there's anything wrong with that. It gives a person a solid feeling when he stays in his hometown. Her hometown."

My cell phone rang just then. It was Alex. I took the call inside.

Alex said he was calling to tell me not to worry.

"Okay. I won't worry."

"If you call and get my voice mail or bounce-back on my e-mail. Don't be alarmed."

"I won't worry," I assured him.

"I'll be out of town for a few days—more like a week. That's why. I'm going to the Bahamas. Tonight."

I assumed this had to do with Simon.

"Twin beds?"

"Don't be vulgar."

"How about ecstatic?"

"Don't read too much into it."

"Only volumes."

He told me I was very funny, and oh, yeah, how were things going and was I ever coming back to the city?

"I've got Eliot with me right now."

"The boyfriend? What's he want?"

"It's been verbal sleight of hand for the most part."

"How's that?"

"Misdirection."

"Call him on it."

"He's performing it on himself."

"Then keep your mouth shut is my best advice."

When I went outside, Eliot was still sitting in the metal chair, looking up at the sky.

Before I sat down, he started talking.

"It was great that Laura could ask you to be her executor."

"She was my friend, she asked for my help, and I helped her."

Eliot stood up. "I don't think it matters what the reasons are, we care about the people we care about and when they need our help . . ." He walked over to me, patted me on the back, went up the steps and into the house. A moment later I heard the front door close.

I could only wonder what fresh thoughts might disturb his concentration on his busy day.

It wasn't as calming back there or as comfortable since Eliot had come and gone; although I did enjoy thinking that Alex was on his way to the Bahamas, and if I was surprised that he was going with Simon, it was more because my brother was taking off an entire week so soon after his previous vacation, but it wasn't very long before I was back to thinking of all the things that were not at the moment giving me much enjoyment. I was wondering what I wanted from Marian. From myself. And why this was so important to me. Or was it only the feeling that mattered? Was that the attraction?

Or was it the peril? Of being consumed by the strength of your own emotions? Or empowered by someone else's? Was that what Buddy was escaping when he went off to fish? Was that what compelled Eliot to appear outside Marian's door when she refused to see anyone else? Was that the message in the music Laura left behind? Or was it, as Alex told me, nothing more than interlocking neuroses? Could I reduce my attraction to Marian and the drama of her life to a neurotic reaction?

Whatever Marian thought we needed to talk about must not have been too important. She didn't call that afternoon or that night.

The following morning I took myself for a walk. I just wanted to get out of the house, I didn't care where I walked. Since that damn letter from Remsen arrived I felt as though I'd been trying to crack the code of unarticulated intentions, circumspection, and it was a nuisance and frustrating. Except for the Ballantines, no one had yet offered me a definitive conclusion about what they thought, what they wanted from me.

I walked down the sidewalk, staring at the dreary, dun-colored street, the same dreary light hanging in the sky, obscuring the horizon, like the conversations I'd had with Eliot, with Marian, full of reticence, hesitant and halting, determination indistinguishable from desire. It wasn't only Marian and Eliot; I was just as complicit.

When I reached the corner, I turned around, walked in the direction of town, and across the town square to Eliot's hardware store.

Eighteen

IT WAS A BRIGHT, CLEAN STORE, WITH WIDE AISLES, SMELLING OF cleansers and paints. There were quite a few customers, some looking lost in the aisles of pumps and piping, others looking content with their boxes of lawn and leaf bags.

I didn't see Eliot, but there were several salesmen in bright red vests and crisp white shirts, most of them talking to customers. One was stocking a shelf of lightbulbs, and when he looked up I asked him if Eliot was around. He pointed to the office door at the back of the store.

Eliot was sitting at his desk reading a spreadsheet. He didn't wear a red vest or white shirt, but he was now wearing a striped tie with his oxford blue shirt. When he saw me, he didn't glare, but he didn't have a congenial expression on his face, either. I closed the door, and sat in the chair across from him.

"I don't think you were finished talking to me," I said.

He rested his elbows on the desk, and rubbed his eyes with the tips of two fingers. When he looked at me again, the expression on his face wasn't any more congenial than before. He folded the spreadsheet, lining up the corners, pressing it flat, and placing it inside the top drawer. "Inventory," he said.

"I think you came by yesterday to talk about Marian," I told him.

"I have nothing to say about Marian."

"And I think you also wanted to talk about yourself."

Eliot got up and walked around the desk, sat on the front corner farthest from me.

He said, "You know what equilibrium is?"

"Equilibrium."

He leaned back, inverted his hands, and braced himself with his palms, getting still farther away from me. "You came to Shady Grove and you didn't know anyone, of course you couldn't. You didn't even know why you were here, I bet. But hell, Geoffrey." He moved his weight to the right, then to the left, resting on his hip, but only for a moment before he sat forward and, apparently unable to get comfortable, stood up and walked back behind his desk. He didn't sit down, he just stood behind his chair, and having, it now appeared, found the proper buffer, told me, "I made her tomato soup. When I went to see Marian. From a can. It wasn't quite a month after Buddy died. She looked like someone from a shipwreck. Her *life* was like a shipwreck. She was . . . How could you know that? You couldn't know that. Or what she was like back then." His voice was flat. It granted no absolution. "I didn't make her talk to me. I didn't ask her questions. Whenever I saw her she said whatever she wanted, or nothing at all." He smiled an anemic smile. "I certainly didn't ask about her *feelings*. I think they're very private things, feelings. I respect that. It's the same thing now. With Laura. It's just the way I am, the way Marian is." He said this as though the information were just a matter of the facts before us, found, perhaps, on the spreadsheet he'd just put away.

"It's how you keep your equilibrium."

"Ten years."

I wanted to walk out. Walk out on why I'd come to see Eliot. Walk out on telling what I wanted him to know; leave him unchallenged and unenlightened about my five days in Shady Grove. If Marian had more to say to him, then that was between the two of them. If she kept quiet, well, didn't Eliot just tell me that's how they are? It would have been convenient to leave Eliot alone with his myth intact, and mine intact as well: my myth of trust, the trust in my silence. But that would have been no different than what I'd done to Simon when I'd kept him away from Laura's wedding, the secrecy of that day was not unlike my secrecy now, my reluctance to tell Eliot what I wanted him to know.

I'd never doubted the integrity of Laura's confidence in me; but what we had done to her brother was nothing but an ungenerous act, a conspiracy in deception and cruelty.

Was I keeping silent because I thought Marian expected me to? An extension of Laura's confidence in me? Just another act of cruelty? An adherence to an adolescent's ethic? Was this my attachment to the past? Where I thought I'd find the best part of myself? Tricking an eighteen-year-old kid out of his sister's wedding? Treating Eliot to my own sleight of hand? My act of misdirection?

What would have happened if I'd broken Laura's confidence that afternoon? Who would have been harmed, except

Simon, who was harmed already? And now, if I broke Marian's confidence, what would I be doing except urging a conversation she'd been avoiding for ten years?

I came there thinking that Eliot and I were in love with the same woman. But we weren't. She wasn't the same woman. And I would have to tell him who I was in love with.

I told him, without inflection, making sure the narrative sounded as objective and impersonal as possible, about the things Marian and I had said the day I'd come to empty Laura's house, and the afternoon when I drove up, and Marian described her gardens to me and we talked until it grew dark about her loneliness and sadness. And the time Marian took me to the overlook and we sat together on the stone wall and talked about the madness of love and its dangers. And when I came to Marian's nursery and she told me all about Buddy and their gardens and how the two of them had lived together and how he died, and how empty she felt without him. And about our impromptu lunch on the wooden bridge by the waterfall.

Eliot never interrupted. By the time I finished, I was standing across the room, my back to him, looking at the alley outside the window. I didn't want to look at him or see the expression on his face. But I heard the sound of his breathing.

I was watching a little girl trying to teach her puppy to sit on command. Every time she pushed down on the puppy's rump, he leapt forward and licked her nose. I watched her for another minute until she gave up and carried her puppy out to the sidewalk.

When I turned around, I saw a tightening around Eliot's jaw, other than that, he showed nothing. I'd said as much as I was going to say. He had the facts now. What was he going to do with them?

Eliot was holding a ballpoint pen in his hand, clicking the top over and over again. His throat made a sound, like the inversion of Marian's laugh, and for a moment I wished I hadn't said anything. I felt as though I'd just stolen what purpose he'd claimed; and why didn't he grab me by the shirt and clock me, which I wasn't too sure I didn't want him to do, or would have done in his place. I could have even argued it was what I deserved.

"Well, you certainly gave me something to think about, didn't you?" Eliot let go of the pen, and watched it drop on top of his desk. "I guess she needed to tell you these things." He did not sound unhappy when he said this. "It's not like—" He picked up that ballpoint and started clicking the top again, over and over. He said, "I think it's a good thing that she can talk to you the way she does. I mean, it's like with Laura— now that she doesn't have her to talk to and you being Laura's old friend . . ." There was a discomfort that appeared in his expression that was equally discomforting to witness.

I might have told Eliot that it was my intention to make him uncomfortable; that I knew I was being manipulative, and that I wanted to coax him toward the conclusion of his relationship with Marian, and this was the way I thought I could do that. Alex would have recognized at once what I was doing. He would have said that I was practicing without a license.

A few more clicks and Eliot dropped the pen on the desk and this time pushed it out of his way.

"Necessity isn't need," I told him.

"What's that supposed to mean?"

"It's something I just thought of."

"You do the things that need to be done." He unbuttoned

his collar and relaxed his tie, leaned his elbow on the desk, rested his chin in the cup of his hand, and lowered his eyes. "But you can't look at things— You can't— I don't know where this is going or what you want." Eliot had not looked up while he said this, or when he said, "So just drop it." Now he lifted his head, pushed his chair back from the desk, and when he started to stand I thought he was getting ready to kick me out, but he sat back down and said, "She just came out and started talking to you about Buddy."

"I told you, we talked about a lot of things."

"Hell, skating at the park? That was a long time ago."

"It was *all* a long time ago."

"I don't know where you get these things."

I was watching him, but I was thinking about Buddy's down-from-the-mountain look, as Marian had called it. And how Buddy would have found clarity in quoting Tennyson, right then, or Wordsworth or Frost. Then I recoiled from that and for having thought it, for I was doing what most everyone else did, watching Eliot through Buddy's eyes. It always came back to Buddy. Like the town you have to drive through to get to wherever you're going.

"I don't think anyone ever considered what it must have been like for her to be in that house by herself." There was no expression of revelation when Eliot said this, but something had changed. There was a tone of animus when he said, "They took her at her word, I guess. She was going to die alone, just like Buddy. I didn't want to let that happen."

The room felt hot and airless with the masculine smell of sweat and stress. Eliot got up to open the window, and asked me if I'd mind hitting the switch for the ceiling fan. "It isn't like ten years is—like there's a shelf life to all of this." He walked the length of the room, opened the door, and looked into the store for a moment. It was still busy out there, and he kept watching for another moment or two longer before he closed the door, leaned against it, and crossed his arms over his chest. "Marian told you they were going to leave Shady Grove and not come back? She and Buddy?"

I lowered my eyes in affirmation.

Eliot unfolded his arms, raised himself up, his body heaving forward just a little bit.

"She's not going to let herself die like Buddy," I told him.

"Is that what you think?"

He moved away from the door and came forward until he was standing in front of me, staring down. "Let me ask you something. How do I know that this isn't just for your own amusement, or to build up your self-esteem? How do I know that's not what you do?"

I didn't bother with an answer. I only looked back at him.

"I won't lie and say I never wanted her to talk to me like that," Eliot said, "or how she talked to Laura." He took a few steps away and sat on the edge of his desk. "Marian wanted you to know. And it occurs to me, just now, that she must have given a lot of thought to talking to you."

Eliot didn't say anything else for a moment—pausing the way a musician might, holding a beat longer than you expect. You might think it's an affectation, or the preparation for the diminished note to follow, but sometimes it's the moment preceding the crescendo. He started to speak and stopped. Started again and again stopped, and put out his hands, palms up.

"And now that I'm over my initial reaction to what you've been saying, I have the impression that you're just trying to help. But, to be honest, I have nothing to say to you." There was no longer the timidity, the man afraid of losing his balance, in his voice. I wanted to think our conversation was supposed to bring us both to this moment. Eliot was standing up and telling me, "I'd like you to leave."

He put his hand on my shoulder and showed me the door.

I WALKED ALONG MAIN STREET, WHERE THE SHOPS WERE EMPTYING and business had slowed, and down narrow sidewalks, past quiet lawns at afternoon, on my way to Laura's house.

I began to consider what Eliot and I had talked about today, what we'd been talking about all along, actually, when I remembered the question I'd left behind with the Ballantines: Why had Marian let Eliot in?

THE FOLLOWING MORNING, I WAS DOWNSTAIRS MAKING COFFEE, thinking about the automatic espresso machine in the kitchen in my apartment, the patisserie around the corner with the warm chocolate brioches, and how simple my life used to be, when Marian called. Maybe I thought about this just before her phone call, maybe right after.

Marian didn't bother with hello: "What did you tell Eliot?" Her voice was soft with sleep, and silky. I hoped she was still in bed. "Did you tell him what we've talked about?"

"Is that what he said?"

"Something very weird. As soon as the weather gets warm, he wants us to play tennis together."

"That's not so weird."

"I don't play tennis."

"Can we continue this face-to-face?" I said. "And not in Laura's house."

MARIAN WAS WAITING ON THE BACK DECK, THE KITCHEN DOOR WAS open behind her. She was grinning at me and as I came closer, she put her hands inside the pouch of her sweatshirt and said, "Well, we're face-to-face." She sounded amused.

"Eliot's not intimidated," I told her.

She nodded toward the kitchen, and we walked inside.

"Do I know what you're talking about?" she asked.

"The reason he was able to help you when no one else could is because he's not intimidated by Buddy. And everyone else is, Charlie, his parents, you. But not Eliot."

"Eliot told you that?" She pulled a chair away from the kitchen table.

"There's this assumption everyone has," I said, "that Eliot wants to be like Buddy."

She went over to the counter, started to bring the coffeepot to the table, and stopped.

"Whose assumption is that?" she asked.

"That he *should* want to be like him? You don't need me to tell you. But it's not only incorrect, it's wrong and unfair."

Marian put the pot of coffee on the table and told me to help myself.

"You're explaining Eliot to *me*?"

"If you think about it, everyone's still seeking Buddy's approval. And that doesn't mean anything to Eliot."

"And my feelings about Buddy?"

"But all the things that you, that everyone, love about Buddy and admire, don't matter to Eliot. He doesn't want to be like Buddy any more than Buddy would have wanted to be like him."

"Of course he doesn't."

"But don't you think people act like they expect him to? Except that deep thinking and introspection don't impress him. All it gets you is a lonely death. Which he believes he's saved you from?"

"He said *saved*?"

"He doesn't want you to die alone like Buddy."

"I don't believe— That doesn't sound like Eliot speaking, it sounds like you."

"Eliot also made a point of telling me that Simon was a better ice-skater than Buddy, and Buddy wasn't a very good athlete. "

"That would explain the tennis."

"It's his way of saying he wants a more intimate relation-ship."

"He told you that? He said he wants a more intimate—"

"My guess is, he thinks it's something he *should* want. Maybe because he can't talk to you about the things you and I talk about."

"Then you *did* tell him what we talk about."

"I told him *about* the things we talk about."

"That's the same as telling him." She didn't sound angry when she said this, or disapproving. She said, "I'm a little bothered that you— I mean, they're personal."

"Someone had to tell him what's been happening. And wouldn't you think he'd want to share something with you that you never shared with Buddy, never did together?"

When she said, "Now you see what kind of person he is, and why I told you that I can't hurt him." Marian sounded exasperated. "And neither can you. I know you won't let that happen."

"Is that what we're talking about?"

"Isn't that why you're telling me all of this?"

"And so I can understand what's going on between the two of us."

"You don't need help with that."

"Is *that* what we're talking about?"

She reached across the table and took my hand. "We have other things to talk about."

I thought about what I wanted those other things to be, while Marian asked me to go outside with her.

It was warmer now than when I'd arrived. We walked to the woodland gardens that she and Buddy had built, and down the white pebble path that she and Buddy had designed, past the benches and flower beds that she and Buddy had planned and placed, the groves of trees that she and Buddy had selected and planted; not that it had taken me until today to feel how imposing Buddy's presence could be. Hadn't I felt it yesterday with Eliot?

I said, "I can't talk to you here. The gardens, the house. Buddy pervades every conversation, every consideration. It wears me down."

"Wears you down?"

"I never knew Buddy and he's everywhere." I shook my head. "It's worse than that. It's the two of you. Marian and Buddy."

"He was my husband. We were a couple."

"I know . . . I know . . . And I can't talk with the two of

you around, and you're both always around. Like specters. I can't compete with ghosts."

"Is that what you think I'm asking you to do?"

"You keep the two of them around. Buddy and Marian. In the gardens, the house."

"But this is where I live."

"Yes."

Marian walked away from me, not fast, as though she were doing nothing more than extending our stroll. She turned around and said, "You're saying that you want me to leave?" There was a note of incredulity in her voice. "Leave my home? What if I told you you had to leave New York?"

I came closer to her. "What if you did? I'd have to take it seriously. If it was an impediment."

"An impediment from what—from doing what?"

"Do I really have to tell you?"

"Yes," she said. "You do."

"From being more than a clown on a trick tricycle."

"How's that?"

"Buddy's a tough act to follow, and I'm not as confident as you seem to think I am."

"Oh, I think you are."

I told her, "I can't talk about it here."

"Then where can you talk about it?"

I hesitated for a moment. I could have told her that whatever she was looking for, whatever she wanted from me, was more than I could deliver. But when I spoke, I was looking only at her eyes: "Somewhere you have never traveled."

She smiled. "The nearest airport is Albany."

"And I left my passport in my apartment. I'd settle for some town nearby that you've never been to before."

"No such place exists."

"Then Barcelona."

We stopped next to a dark green bench, but we didn't sit.

"I'll give Eliot this," I said, "he manages to block it out. Compartmentalize. Separate you from Buddy."

"He doesn't think about it. And once you stop thinking about things, who know where that leads?"

We started walking again.

"Geoffrey, I won't deny that we're attracted to each other—"

"I'd say we've moved beyond euphemisms. Wouldn't you agree?"

"You're asking me to run off with you?"

"You once said you wouldn't mind being sad about something besides Buddy and Laura. You can either be sad about breaking Eliot's heart, or my leaving for New York without you."

"Is that an ultimatum?"

"Marian, I really can't talk here."

When we came to the edge of the path, Marian said, "I think I've figured out what *your* impediment is."

"I have one?"

"New York City. The ex-girlfriend you hold up to me and say, 'See? I can let go of someone.' Your apartment, where I suspect you maintain a quite organized, compartmentalized life, and which I suspect you are so very attached to. And if I told you right now, okay, I'll break up with Eliot, close the house, and fly off to Barcelona or wherever with you, but you'll have to give up your place in the city, I bet you'd turn white and head for the nearest exit. This feeling of having to compete, this *euphemism* you mentioned is—I don't have to tell you what it is." She walked a little farther while she said, "I want to show you something."

I stayed with her, and when she got to her car, she opened the door and said, "Get in."

"Where are we going?"

"Since you've got ghosts on the brain, I'm taking you to a haunted house."

"Aren't you going to blindfold me first?"

"Maybe later." She started to laugh. "If only this *was* about sex. We could go away for a few days and get it out of our systems."

I was more than a little impressed with her associative thinking.

"That would depend on the sex, wouldn't it?" I said.

"Great sex, of course."

"And what's great sex?"

"Sex with a person you enjoy having sex with."

There wasn't much I could say to that.

After a few more miles, Marian told me, "We're going to Lenox. If you want to know. The Fitzgerald house."

A moment or two later Marian said: "If it's still there."

"Haunted?"

"In the late eighteen-nineties, a family named Fitzgerald lived there, father, mother, two children. He was a clock-maker. One day they vanished. The entire family. Gone. The house was still furnished, food in the pantry, but no Fitzgeralds. They were never heard from again. About a year later, the house was sold, and the new owners began to hear strange sounds. Footsteps on the bedroom ceiling late at night, like someone pacing across the attic floor. Once each day, at various times, they could hear a clock chiming, as if from a room in the other part of the house. Four times, once for each member of the Fitzgerald family."

"Ask not for whom the bell tolls . . ."

Marian looked at me out of the corner of her eye. "People said some nights you could see the shape of a man walking behind a curtained window, other times, when the house was known to be empty, lights going on in the upstairs room. No one ever owned it longer than a year before selling the place. By the time I was in high school, the house was abandoned. A lot of the kids during senior year would dare each other to go inside alone for five minutes. I was never one of them. Not that I believed the stories, not really, but you know, there's always that twinge of 'what if it really is haunted?' And I did want to see for myself, but I was embarrassed to admit that to anyone, or tell anyone, let alone go there. It seemed like such a silly thing to do. But the place intrigued me. It still does. And I've never gone there. Until today. With *you*, Geoffrey."

We drove down a paved road. There weren't many houses around, and the ones that were there were set back from the street, large and looking neither prosperous nor in disrepair, just old and settled. Down a few more streets, where prosperity seemed even further removed, and a few minutes more Marian turned onto a cul-de-sac where the road was cracked and the few houses there looked grim and neglected, some with boarded-up windows.

Alone at the far end of the street was an old, broken-down palace of a place. If I'd known anything about architecture I could have identified the style and era, but all I saw was a big house on a patch of land overgrown with weeds.

Marian pulled up to the curb, paused long enough to give

me a look of mild trepidation, then we got out of the car and walked up to the front porch, which was crooked, the stairs broken and weather-beaten, the front door, or what remained of it, hanging off rusted hinges. The glass in the four front windows was missing. Marian peeked through an open space into the dark house, went over to the entrance, and whispered to me, "Are you coming in?"

"I'm always up for silly things," I told her.

She made a shivering gesture while she grinned at me and pushed the door aside with just the tip of her shoe. The floorboards creaked under our feet as we stepped across the threshold.

We stood close together inside the foyer, facing a dark hallway. The air was colder inside and damp. A little bit like a tomb. Like necrosis.

To our right was a staircase leading to the second floor, with all the steps collapsed onto each other, the banister unattached from the few balusters that remained. Shafts of sunlight broke through the holes in the ceiling where the joists were missing, there was mildew along the floor, and the boards were warped. I could see names scrawled and scratched on the walls, with dates next to them—high school seniors, proving their mettle.

Marian said, "Want to look for ghosts?" Her voice echoed as voices do in an empty room. She took a step forward and I followed while our shadows preceded us. As we walked farther along the hallway, quick scurrying sounds, like small animals running across the bare floor, retreated from our footsteps, and there came a flutter of wings.

At the end of the hall were just more empty rooms. A dilapidated living room, a dining room without any ceiling above it, and the kitchen, minus the appliances, old rotted pieces of linoleum and a bird's nest in the corner above the place where there had once been a back door. All indications that people had ever lived here, even the faintest patina of residency, were absent.

I said, "Nice little place you've chosen for our talk."

Marian frowned at me.

"I don't know," she said. "I was hoping for something spookier."

"Like the crazy old caretaker warning us to keep away from the master's bedroom."

"Or Jack Nicholson chasing us around with an ax."

"For all we know," I told her, "the only reason no one wants to live here is high property taxes."

"I'd prefer the crazy caretaker."

"Always a crowd pleaser."

We were in the living room now. Marian looked around the floor for a place to sit. I took out my handkerchief and cleared two large circles for us.

"More comfortable talking here?" I sat on the floor and leaned back against the wall. "Before, when you said you were embarrassed to tell anyone that you wanted to come here, you meant Buddy. He was a lot of things, but silly wasn't one of them?"

"I really hate an empty house." Marian pulled the hood of her sweatshirt over her head, and sat next to me. She said, "Sometimes I wonder what you do in the city. And the kind of people you know. Are they all in the media? Do you socialize a lot?"

"You mean the life I'm so attached to."

"I'm trying to tell you something, Geoffrey."

"I'm trying to tell *you* something. Remember what I said yesterday, about skimming across the emotional surface not being fun? Well, this is fun."

"Sitting on the dusty old floor in a cold, empty house."

"Sitting on a dusty old floor with *you*."

When I looked over at her, Marian was resting her back against the wall, as though this were the most comfortable place we might ever want. I was thinking, if this was about sex and we were tucked away in a hotel room in a town where no one recognized us, we could not have been any more intimate than we were right now. And for the second time in as many days I felt that time belonged only to the two of us.

"When I told you we had to talk"—Marian was now looking over at me—"it had nothing to do with Eliot. I was thinking that you wanted me to reassess the past ten years, explain them, or that I had to apologize for them."

"What did I say to make you think that?"

"But it wasn't you that I needed to explain it to. It was Buddy. Since I first met you, I've been wondering, what would Buddy think about the way I talk to you? Would he approve of how I feel about you, and what I tell you? I've never thought about that with Eliot, not that that's news to you. But I do with you." She got up and walked to the end of the room where the hallway began and the short shadows of noon appeared across the floor.

"I care about what Buddy would think," she said. "That's why I'm—" She walked out of the room.

As I sat there alone, I was remembering when Marian sent back my handkerchief, and the aroma of her laundry soap. That same aroma was in the air now, in the wake of her leaving. It made me want to touch the back of her neck with my lips, breathe in the scent on her skin, feel her body press against me. Because any act of intimacy between us made sense and had everything to do with what she was talking about.

A moment later, I heard the click-clack of Marian's shoes as she walked down the hall, farther away the sound of a door closing, then her slow approach back to where I was sitting.

"I can tell you this," she said, and walked over to me. "I have to ask myself what does it mean that we can talk to each other like this about all the things we talk about? What does it mean that we can be here like this today, and act silly in front of each other?"

"I want to spend the rest of the day with you," I said. "Here in this house, or anywhere you choose. I want to dream about you tonight. What would Buddy think of that?"

"You know what? I don't know if, after all this time, Buddy would even know me. Who I am. He'd still be thirty-two years old. What would we have in common except the past?" She tilted her head back until it was resting against the wall, raised her face, and stared at the ceiling. "When you said that you felt Buddy and Marian all around you? Buddy and Marian are dead. I've been afraid to accept that. Even think it. And I hear your voice in my doubts." She closed her eyes when she said, "I blamed you for putting the thought in my head. But you didn't put it there." She took a deep breath and let out a sigh, while a breeze heaved across the room, joists creaked and beams stretched. As though the entire house had sighed. "I was just thinking. When I was walking down the hall before, there were once people living here, hanging up their clothes, girls' sweaters and boys' shoes. New and shining. It made me think about what they tell you, the things you find in other people's closets, or don't tell you, about who lived here. Or the things people discard and forget about. Not pictures and things like that, but just the things they keep and use every day."

Like fishing tackle and a faulty gas stove.

"And what they leave behind when they go." Her eyes were still closed. "What do you leave behind when you go? Or do you ever leave anything behind?"

I told Marian about those early mornings when Rita would steal away, or when I would, taking only what we came with. And the night when Rita threatened to start leaving her clothes in the dark corners of my closet, and wouldn't that make me feel the worst kind of claustrophobia. I told Marian that I would feel a terrible absence if she were to steal away, that now, if I were to anticipate driving back to the city alone at the end of this day, if she were to tell me that what she wanted was for me to leave so she could go back to her house and her memories, that feeling her absence would be a permanent way of life, and that would be impossible to accept.

She moved her shoulders, just a slight shrug, as though it had nothing to do with what she was thinking, opened her eyes, and stared straight ahead at the mottled wall.

She told me, "I'm sitting here wanting to make a case for— for not changing anything about how I live, or about myself, because of all the things we've said, of all the ways I've told you— Geoffrey, there's a part of me that firmly believes if I were to really fall in love, it would negate the love I have for Buddy, make it less legitimate. That's always been my worry. One of them. I don't know if I'm courageous enough to take that chance." She moved her shoulders again. "And at the same time, all I want right now is to have the rest of the day to ourselves." She turned to me. "Because, as you can see, there are no ghosts."

IT WAS NO LONGER IMPORTANT TO FIND PLACES MARIAN HAD NEVER been to, only that we spend time together, in the car for a while until we stopped along the way and walked close together in whatever little town we came to.

We sat at the counter in a tiny shop and ate sandwiches wrapped in wax paper, strolled down narrow sidewalks eating chocolate cake out of a paper bag. There was nothing hurried about the day. The afternoon had the feel of a holiday. In a moment the music of a calliope would swell, the aromas of cotton candy and French fries would sweeten the air.

I was thinking about all the other times I'd waited to feel the touch of Marian's hand, or the feel of her hair against my face, on the cold floor of an abandoned house, in a brisk wind by a stone wall when I stopped myself from pressing my lips into the palm of her hand.

What was stopping me now? Stopping us? What had always stopped us? The restraint of a self-styled decorum? This was not about decorum, and not about restraint. It was about constraint, deeper than a semantical distinction. If there was a specter around us, it wasn't Buddy alone, but Eliot, who carried his own pocketful of constraints, and the drag of those constraints was the string tugging at Marian and me. Not that I thought this was Eliot's intent. More the consequence of personality, and psyche.

There was no calliope playing. The air held only the stale smells of small town exhaust. The only thing waiting for us was our imminent return to Shady Grove. The afternoon had lost its feeling of a holiday.

I might have slowed down and walked a few steps behind. Maybe all I did was pull my shoulder away from hers.

Marian turned her head and glared at me.

"What just happened?"

"What just happened?"

"In your eyes. Around your mouth."

"What just happened?"

"Geoffrey."

If I'd been more reckless, I would have assumed that Marian's question was an expression of an insight into each other that informed our attraction. I would have believed that such a thing was possible. That what she'd just asked me was as much an act of empathy as perception; not at all a matter of chance, or caprice. A declaration. If I'd been willing to believe this, I would not have answered her with my silence. I would not have hedged. But my silence held.

Whatever Marian had sensed, the change in my footsteps, the expression on my face, she grabbed me by the lapels of my sports coat, pulled me to a stop and said, "Tell me what just happened."

For a moment, I wanted to tell her to forget all about it. Only there was just the right kind of sunlight on her face, I could smell the chocolate on her breath, and there was her laugh, which I'd somehow prompted and which could never be denied—not that I felt steady enough to determine what I was seeing in her face, or hearing. I couldn't rely on myself to know what I heard in *her* step.

"What is it?"

"I'm tired of imagining the things I want to do with you. It isn't enough just to want you."

"Then tell me," she said, "what you imagine."

WE WERE LEANING AGAINST MARIAN'S CAR. SHE SAID, "I KNOW I can trust you, Geoffrey. Now I want you to trust *me*." She smoothed the front of my coat with the palm of her hand. "I want you to go back to New York, and I'll call you in a few days. You can wait a few days, can't you?"

Nineteen

THIS WAS THE WAY MARIAN TOLD IT. THE WAY IT WAS TOLD to her:

Whatever else Eliot was feeling when I walked out of his office, it wasn't envy for my talking with Marian the way I had. All that talking was too much talking for Eliot.

What Eliot was thinking about was Buddy and Marian planning on leaving Shady Grove. Moving away from home.

He didn't know why he was thinking about this. Maybe it was because I knew about it and he didn't, although he was sure his feelings had nothing to do with me and nothing to do with Buddy, either. It had to do with Marian and him. They never made plans. They'd never gone away on a vacation together. Why was that?

Alone in his office, Eliot thought about the first time he got Marian to leave her house and meet him in town. It was for breakfast at the diner. He remembered the solemnity of that morning, the intensity of her sorrow. He didn't mind it. He was glad to be in her company, watching the way she sat, the way the expressions changed on her face, the hand gestures when she spoke. It was just as he'd remembered from years ago. It was like sitting with a memory. He never told her how much he liked that, or how much he liked being in her presence.

He thought about the afternoon when he came by to move the boxes out of Laura's house and say a quick hello to her old college friend who had come up from the city. He remembered thinking that this was all he needed to know going into that March afternoon. Then he pulled up to the curb and saw that Marian had been crying. It was the sight of her crying, the return of tears he'd tried to wish away that disturbed him. It was troubling to see it and it didn't matter to him what she'd been talking about that made her cry. What mattered was hurrying to change the subject. Make the coin disappear. He realized it was a mistake letting Marian go to Laura's by herself that day; that he should have gotten there before I arrived. He believed that at the time and he was certain of it now.

He didn't remember when it had occurred to him that Marian had been crying in front of someone she'd met only a few minutes before. It must have been after I came back to Shady Grove and he saw me sitting in the town square and came over to ask me— He couldn't remember what he wanted to ask me, and whatever I'd said did not satisfy him.

Was Marian going to leave him? That's what he wanted to know.

His face was hot. The office seemed small and airless. It was about time he expanded, knocked a few walls down, raised the ceiling.

When he tried to work, all he managed to do was pick up the phone and start to call Marian at the nursery, put down the phone, start to call her house, put down the phone again. He didn't know what he would say to her. He wondered if he was supposed to want something more than their relationship. He couldn't think what that might be. Hadn't he behaved the way she wanted him to behave? Given her what he assumed she wanted from him?

Eliot sat for quite a while and wondered what it was he wanted from Marian. He had never asked himself that question before, and he didn't know why he was asking himself now.

After ten years with Marian he was wondering why they never talked of love?

But what bothered Eliot most was why, all of a sudden, was he even thinking this? Why, when he thought of being with Marian tonight or tomorrow or next week, didn't it seem as satisfying as it had just the other day, and when had satisfaction become important?

When had it become true that it was no longer enough just to be with her?

Eliot sat at his desk, head down, until he heard movements outside his door and realized it was getting near closing time. The phone rang. It wasn't Marian's voice he heard, but one of the guys. Was he up for some basketball tonight?

Later that evening, he was out at the high school shooting hoops with his friends, the six partners of the Bradford House.

Pounding the ball on the hardwood floor. The physicality of playing a game, uncomplicated, absolute and clear. Move. React. He felt like he was flying.

After the game, when he and his friends went over to the pub at the Bradford, they sat around the big table in the corner—the usual crowd was there at the bar watching a hockey game on the TV. The talk was about nothing of any consequence, the way it always was, what Eliot looked forward to, what he depended on had he given it any further thought, except he wasn't there to give further thought to anything more complex than the beer they drank and the jokes they told. As uncomplicated as sports radio and no more profound.

He was feeling lightheaded and it wasn't the beer, but this sense of escape, and if he didn't know from what he was escaping, well that was the point. As long as he sat there, Eliot felt as though he'd come back home and was unconnected to and unconcerned with all the considerations that puzzled him.

The respite, the *spell*, lasted until they all walked outside and Eliot got into his car. He didn't drive off, only watched his friends as they pulled away, going to their wives, their girlfriends. Eliot did not want the night to end, he did not want to be alone.

He wanted to call up Marian, and without any explanation tell her, "I don't feel like being by myself . . ." But he'd never called her spontaneously, or made an unannounced visit. Maybe he could change that tonight. Marian would meet him at the pub, or come to his house or invite him to hers. She would understand what he was asking.

He sat looking out at the empty sidewalk, and when he got out of the car, he left his coat on the front seat and started to walk. He didn't notice the chilly air, the quick breeze, only that he needed to move, the solitary man, hands in his pockets, staring at the tops of his shoes.

Eliot couldn't express, even to himself, what he was thinking. He once told Marian—apropos of something she'd forgotten—that he didn't understand why people thought it so important to learn foreign languages; but now he felt as though

Marian and I had been speaking a language foreign to him, and that he needed another language to understand what was happening to him, or else what did all the talk come to?

He wondered what this feeling of loneliness was about. Why tonight?

These were paralyzing questions, without resolution, and Eliot was unable, not unwilling, to push them aside. He had to stop walking and brace himself against a tree. He felt the entire day cascading over him. All those words. He could feel their weight, their volume, pressing down on him, and what he felt was so ridiculous, what he was thinking so improbable, that he started to laugh, not with amusement, nor pleasure. He was laughing at the absurdity of what he was thinking. That he and Marian never made plans.

He and his ex-wife used to make plans, he thought. They took vacations together—Marian could have told him that you can't make plans with the past. There is no future to a memory—but Marian and Eliot never left Shady Grove.

Eliot wanted to take back that day when he saw Marian standing with me. He wanted to take back that afternoon. But what did he want to have back? What was he so afraid of losing?

It had never been clear to him before, and he had never given it any consideration, not beyond its chronology, but he and Marian had just one year to themselves, that first year after Buddy died. Then Laura came back. It was Laura, he thought, who was able to distract Marian from her sadness. Who understood Marian's sorrow and her mind. It was Laura, Eliot realized, who compensated for what he lacked. He was just the boyfriend.

Twenty

O N THE MORNING THAT I LEFT TOWN, MARIAN CALLED Eliot and told him just enough to bring him to her house. A few hours later, looking weary and rumpled and dark under the eyes, Eliot told her, "I think we should go away. Isn't that what couples do when they have to work things out? Go away?" He'd started talking as soon as he walked into the living room.

Marian wasn't sure if she was surprised that Eliot had joined the term *work things out* with the word *couple,* or distressed by it. It gave her an anxious feeling. She wanted to talk him down, talk him away from the idea that there was something worth working out, or that for the past ten years they'd behaved anything like a couple.

Eliot still hadn't sat down. He leaned the back of his legs against the side of a chair, pushed his hair away from his face.

"I don't mean we have to go off to some faraway place

and talk things out," he made little quote marks in the air. "I mean so we can be alone together and see what's what." He said this in one quick breath, as though he was anxious to get it out of the way. "I think it's important that we find things we can do together. You never needed me to tell your troubles to, anyway." He lowered his voice. "I know that. And I know I can't replace Laura in that way. And I don't want to." He took a breath and sat down. "But it doesn't mean that we can't—we can— There's a feeling you get just by being out on the courts. Doing. It's liberating. Playing tennis . . . Golf . . . I know it doesn't sound like much."

She smiled at him. "What do you want to liberate me from?"

"A year wasn't much time. If you know what I'm—I mean, Laura, well, she did so much to help you, but it was always the two of you and the three of us. We never really had a chance."

A chance at what, Marian wondered. Sports? Running five miles together every morning? Entering intramurals?

"Maybe we get to have a do-over," Eliot told her. "Do things together. And other stuff," he said. "If Laura hadn't come back, I don't know if I could have ever been the person you wanted to confide in. Or did what she did for you. I don't think I can do it. I'm not sure I want to." He shrugged his shoulders. "But I don't have to do that now, do I."

Eliot stood up. He walked over to the window, a stream of light, ocher-colored and rippling, appeared to struggle for purchase on the wall. He stood where the color faded into the corner.

"There's nothing to stop us from finding the things we can share and—well *share* them."

"It's what you've been offering all along," Marian said. She did not sound ungrateful.

"Don't you ever think that we were—that there was an interruption? I just wanted to get you out of your—I thought in time, we'd have taken up—gone bike—"

"Joined a club? Played golf?"

"And gotten away from all this second-guessing. That's all it's ever been. Second-guessing everything. And now, we have a second chance." He walked back to the chair and sat down. "But hey, you're the one who called *me*."

"I want to know what you think about what Geoffrey told you."

Eliot didn't tell Marian what he thought. He told her what he'd done, the evening of basketball and beer. What he called "uncomplicated living."

Then Eliot told her what he'd been thinking about last Sunday in his office when I was there and after I'd gone; and what he'd been thinking when he was home by himself; and how unsatisfying that time alone had been.

Eliot was on his second cup of coffee when he'd finished talking.

Marian could see that he was trying to get at something, trying to show her that his ruminations these past two days had led him to his conclusion, as skewed as she might think it was.

She couldn't pin down when or how often, but it was early on after Eliot started coming by that he talked to her this same way. She was in no shape at the time to focus on what he said, and what attention she did show him was a pose; but the sound of his voice had been so rich with joy that she would pull herself toward whatever he was saying, a ball game, a place he wanted to go with her, talking about what he now called things they could share.

"We never had a chance," she said. "Because I never *gave* you a chance."

"There was too much happening, that's all." He looked over at her. "With Laura—not just her—and everything else." There was a stiffness around his mouth, his lips were pressed together. It was an expression not unfamiliar to Marian. It was the look of constraint when Eliot had gone as far as he cared to go.

She was not surprised to hear him say, "I don't know why we have to get bogged down in all this soul-searching," or how impatient he now sounded. "What's important— All I know is there's something really exciting when you're out there smacking a ball around, working up a sweat. It's like the outside world doesn't matter. Doesn't exist."

"You mean the inside world."

"Inside. Outside. What's the difference? When I said we should play tennis together, or any sport, it's because I think you'd like it. I think you'd like—well there's a purity about it. And what's wrong with wanting to experience that with you?"

Marian pressed her hands flat against the arms of her chair, as though she might have been able to tamp down her words, at least long enough to give herself an extra beat to think, an added measure to stop herself from saying what she needed to say. It was Eliot who spoke instead.

"It's like all the things that brought you down all day just disappear. All the bad thoughts."

If there had ever been a collaboration between the two of them, if they had ever acted like the couple Eliot now wanted them be, it was all the times Marian allowed their conversation to follow Eliot's lead, when the conclusion was imminent, not because there had been resolution, but only because Eliot had reached the limits of his emotional vocabulary. Marian had permitted it—perhaps they were less collaborators than conspirators. She'd been no more eager for deconstruction than Eliot—she'd accepted the contours, the parameters, of his temperament. There was nothing revelatory about this or her motives. She'd needed Eliot's uncomplicated living. She'd acquiesced to it.

"If I tell you that you're remembering Buddy's girl when you talk of bicycles and baseballs, would you know what I mean? It's that girl who you're speaking to when you tell me these things." She was careful to keep her voice soft. "Who you've been speaking to all the time." If they'd had the kind of relationship that allowed it, Marian would have taken Eliot's face in her hands As it was, she leaned forward and rested her elbows on her knees and let her hands hang at her sides.

"You're asking me to be that girl with you," she said. "To be a kid. It's what you think I want." She frowned at him. "It's what you think I need, and what I think you mean by purity."

"You're not this woman, the one you are right now, when you're with Geoffrey, are you? You're not like this." Eliot looked down at her hand. "I've never wanted you to be anyone but who you are."

"Who do you think that is?"

"I don't know how to answer that."

It wasn't disappointment that Marian felt. Her expectations of Eliot had always been so slight that he never had a chance to let her down. It was sympathy for Eliot and the limitations of the relationship he seemed prepared to accept.

At first, Marian felt a chill at the back of her neck, as though she'd just swallowed a mouthful of cold water, and then resentment for his simplicity of thought.

"It's like in a fable, a myth." Marian got up, walked a small circle, and stood behind her chair. She watched Eliot's face, knowing that she wanted to see more than he could show, and she wanted to be angry at him, but she was never angry at Eliot, she never disapproved of him. Her feelings were just as flat-line as they always were. And what she had to do was lead Eliot to his unavoidable conclusion.

It was her unavoidable conclusion as well. What was the fable she told herself, the myth? That love can stay alive in photographs hanging on a kitchen wall, behind the wheel of an old truck, in its faded logo?

When she looked over at Eliot, she did not see his high school face, although if she'd ever thought to identify what his expression contained it was their adolescence, an expression she was so accustomed to seeing in his face—the face that appeared all those years ago outside her door.

"It's an awful lot like being children who won't take responsibility for themselves," Marian was now saying. "That's what Laura and I were like, holding on to all our memories, our pasts."

"That's not what I ever asked you to do."

"You didn't have to ask. It's what we did. The three of us."

Eliot leaned his head back, looked up at the ceiling, and said nothing.

All those times, staring out of a window at the end of another day, driving alone, it came upon her, so recognizable that she didn't need a name for it. When she wanted to make an accounting to herself. Long after Buddy had died. The nights when she was unable to make it all the way home. She'd pull off the road and weep; call Eliot from her car and ask him to meet her at the pub, or could she come by his place. He asked no questions and gave no counsel. He would tell her, "Just don't think about it." Not a balm but an anesthetic. It's what she depended on.

"I think all I've ever been good at is being a kid with someone." Eliot managed to say this without sounding disapproving of her. "I wasn't very good at being a husband. I wanted to do better at being your boyfriend."

"If you're looking to redeem yourself—"

"Do you think—"

"You've been very good at being a boyfriend," she said. "It isn't easy for two people to do what they want to do. You and I did. It's how we wanted it. But it was also about compliance. At times."

Eliot lowered his head. "There are lots of times I feel like I'm still trying to convince you of—I don't know, of *me*, I guess. My good qualities. It's hard work."

"You mean *I'm* hard work."

Eliot didn't reply. He got up and went outside. Marian could see him from the window, arms across his chest. She poured herself a cup of coffee, and when she looked again, Eliot had turned his back to the house, and she did not mind sitting alone. She would have liked to stop thinking about the things she was going to say, all those elastic thoughts, the elaborated sentences pushing the conversation, bringing Eliot to the resolve that would liberate them from each other.

"I don't know how to do this, what we're doing now." Eliot was standing in the doorway. "I don't even know what it's supposed to mean. But it could be—" He walked inside and closed the door; sweet, warm air rushed into the room. "It could be that people have expected you to do certain things a certain way." He shook his head at this. "I mean like people in town, your friends, they all expected you to be like a specific kind of person, and maybe no one took into consideration what you wanted to be."

"Just where did this insight come from?"

When Eliot smiled at her, Marian thought about the density of personality that one life weighs against another, and she wasn't thinking only about Buddy. When Eliot said, "I think that's what you were talking about before? What you meant about doing what we want?" Marian thought, there's still time for the right words. A sentence or two and we can go back to how it used to be.

"If what we've been doing," Eliot said, "the way we've been going along isn't for us anymore, then we'll just have to come up with something else."

Marian said, "Tell me again what you want us to do together."

Eliot said, "I don't want to tell you anything right now. I just want us to go ahead and do it." He shook his head. "That's not what I mean. I want us to be one of those couples that just goes out and has fun when they're together. Be*cause* they're together."

"No," Marian said. "Tell me."

Eliot told her again about all the fun they would have.

Repetition enhanced Eliot's narration until the simple act of pedaling a bike, rising early and walking a trail possessed of its own majesty—not dissimilar to the morning walks around Buddy's lake—no more exertive than stepping from one smooth stone to another in a narrow stream, compelling Marian by the strength of her own concession, taking her neither forward nor back but around, to the top of the circle, the ten-year circuit; and perhaps this had been what she needed.

What if she'd been wrong about Eliot? What if everything else had been noise and clutter, and what he offered was the thing that had been missing? If Eliot had stopped talking that might have been enough. Marian knew how to dull her heart. But Eliot would not stop talking, his gestures became more expansive, his voice grew louder; and the more expansive and loud, the more constrictive it felt to Marian, as though she'd stepped inside a diorama.

Marian had waited. She'd been fair. She no longer believed this was about choosing one man over another. It had become a matter of how she chose to conduct her life.

Eliot had stopped speaking, and was grinning at her. Marian felt as though she were wading through that grin, trying to reach what she wanted to say.

"I don't know if I can stand still anymore."

Eliot's grin vanished. He said, "I thought I was saying the opposite." He walked behind Marian, and put his arms around her shoulders. It was the first time he had touched her since he got there. Whatever he was thinking never made it past his mouth. He held her a moment longer before he stepped back.

Marian did not reach for his hand. She didn't want Eliot to say another word, she didn't want him to make an argument for himself, or to argue his way back into her heart. But there was something that needed to be said at this moment, *for* this moment. Marian was not the one to speak.

"Do you want to break up?" Eliot's voice was not loud. Had he been farther away Marian would have thought he was talking to himself.

"Oh, Eliot . . ." Marian answered.

"Yeah. That was a stupid question. It's what we're doing, isn't it?" His voice was louder now. "I don't know if all it is, is being like a child," he said, "or what's so wrong with that if it is. I just wish someone wanted what I want."

THEY WERE STANDING OUTSIDE WHERE THE BACK STEPS MET THE edge of the stone path.

Eliot kept his hands at his side, his face was lifted toward the sky as though he were checking for rain. Their duet was at an end, in need of, if not a crescendo, a coda. It was Marian who provided one, after Eliot asked, "What about Geoffrey?"

"A month from now," she said, "I could be sitting here all alone."

Twenty-one

As I drove back to the city, I thought about my last conversation with Marian. The following morning, after sleeping in my own bed, on my own pillow, and a joyous morning with coffee and eggs while I stood outside on my terrace looking at the park and the truncated progressions of my fellow humans, I was still thinking about it.

Marian and I were on our way back to town to get my car. I suppose we were both thinking about the next few days. I anticipated lonely ones for myself.

Marian said, "I always imagined that one day, I'm talking about after Buddy died, that I'd get used to his being gone and that would be it. I'd be alone and that was how it would be. And even with Eliot, I knew the time would come when being together wouldn't be what either of us needed, and a part of me was looking forward to not being involved with anyone. A single woman. I liked the idea. I still like the idea. Kind of."

"Does this have something to do with trusting you for the next few days?"

"Don't you think it's possible that the time comes when you've had enough depth of emotion for one lifetime? That it's all right to just glide along in a relationship of convenience? I might have been reaching that point. And then I met you. I feel safe with you, Geoffrey. I'm going to break up with Eliot and it's going to hurt me to do it, and hurt Eliot. And I never thought I could do that. I certainly never wanted to. I wish I could say what will happen next." She turned her face toward me. "I haven't had a lot of time to get used to all of this. According to my daybook it's been all of six days since you've been in town." She turned back to the road. "It's been about two months since Laura died. To say that my life has been upended of late—I can't say *how* I'll feel a week from now but whatever I do, I have to do it with you back in New York."

We drove on for another minute or so.

"It can wear you out just *thinking* about being with another person," she said. "I can't dismiss the idea of living some Emily Dickinson–like existence. Her house isn't too far from here. Do you know that? Just me and a couple of neutered cats, in a small cottage all to ourselves somewhere. Actually, Laura and I discussed that. Living solitary lives. It does have its appeal."

"Are you trying to tell me something?"

"What would I be trying to tell you?"

"Neutered cats?"

"Don't you like cats?" She turned to me and grinned.

"There's enough chastity going around."

Marian slowed the car.

"Is that what we're talking about?" she said.

"It's what we're talking about now," I told her.

"Sex?"

"There's more than one kind of chastity. You know that's what you're going to think about after I leave."

"Having sex with you?"

"Wondering if the heat's going to die down once we're away from each other," I said, which made her laugh. Not the dreamy laugh, but she sounded committed to it.

"I like that you can be glib about this," she said. "And I like that you can take it seriously."

"Because you have no idea what's going to happen next. You can't say *what* you're going to do."

"Can you? Can you say what you're going to do?"

IF ALEX HAD BEEN IN TOWN, I WOULD HAVE BEEN ON THE PHONE with him by now. I might have coaxed him away from his office, and neither of us would have shut up; but I wasn't about to call him and interrupt his Bahamian vacation, even if I'd known where he was staying. Instead, a strict silence settled in, and restiveness. All there was left to do was wait for Marian to call. All I could do was choose how I waited, and I couldn't sit still, I didn't want to hang around the apartment, and there was nowhere that I wanted to go.

I would have liked knowing that Marian was feeling the same restlessness, and what she was doing right now, and what she was thinking. And what if I was right about our cooling down once we were apart? What if she changed her mind about me? Or I changed mine about her? There was always that chance and the chance of never knowing what it was like when we kissed, or to wake up in bed and feel the soft warmth our bodies made together. What a shame that would be for both of us. Unlike Marian, I had no problem with applying the first person plural to the two of us; but if we backed away from that and each other, it wasn't as though our emotions were transferable, that we could carry them over to anyone else. We had altered the part of ourselves that had resisted this, not an unpleasurable admission, and in no minor way were Marian and I dependent on each other; not in the way that she and Buddy had been. This was not about the whole being greater than the sum of the parts, or building gardens—after all, there comes a time when you have to leave the garden. Buddy wasn't mistaken about that. We were not in our twenties and starting out together, or in our thirties favoring the prospects, or reeling from the wreckage. After forty you'd better be prepared to recognize what your true needs are, and locate the better parts of yourself and who around you can best identify them. If Marian hadn't come to realize this, there was no way we would be together, and that would leave us each with little more than that solitary life she and Laura had found so damn inviting.

And there was nothing I preferred doing that morning other than thinking about Marian and all those possibilities. I wanted to spend the day doing just that—quite insane—except the world and New York City have a way of rushing in uninvited.

Unpacking clothes. Sending out laundry and dry cleaning. Phone calls to answer, not from Marian. E-mails that needed replies. And a week's worth of mail to sort through. The triumph of the quotidian over the sublime.

Early in the afternoon I did receive an e-mail from Marian asking me not to send her any e-mails.

Half an hour later Marian sent another: "H. Bogart to

I. Bergman: 'The problems of three little people don't amount to a hill of beans in this crazy world.' Me to You: 'I've decided the entire world is nothing but bean hills.'" With the request not to reply.

A few minutes later: "Five dozen geraniums just arrived at the nursery today. Even this is more commitment than I'm willing to make at the moment."

A few minutes after that: "Not the ubiquitous American geraniums, but the lovely cranesbill, a beautiful, leggy shade plant that brightens even the dark corners."

When I checked a little later, after paying some bills and sorting a lot of junk mail: "I need to mourn for this alone without interference or interruption . . . I don't quite . . . I don't want to know what you're thinking . . . I'm embarrassing myself . . ." Then nothing; and an hour later nothing still.

I had to get out, walk around, breathe in the city air, pretend that I was back to normal.

It was a warm May afternoon. The kind of weather that dissuades you from believing in both caprice and misfortune, and permits you to feel the part of yourself that never ages, that adheres to the conceit that all you'll ever believe in and cherish is everlasting and immutable. Wordsworth's intimations of immortality; until the intellectual collapses on the psychic, and the street is just the street again.

THE DAY AFTER MARIAN ASKED ME TO LEAVE SHADY GROVE, BEFORE I went back to the city, I drove over to the nursery to say good-bye. We were standing in the parking lot outside her office. Marian was leaning against my car door.

"What if *you're* the ghost," she said. "The ghost of Geoffrey Tremont circa nineteen eighty-six?"

"Have I ever given you the impression that I'm not the person you think I am?"

"That's not exactly what I mean."

"Afraid that you'll wake up in the middle of the night screaming, 'What the hell have I done?'"

"You have to admit there's the possibility."

"I admit all possibilities."

Marian looked over her shoulder in the direction of her greenhouses, or beyond them. I couldn't see her eyes, while she said, "I could never forgive you if you've ever tried to deceive me, Geoffrey." Her voice was pitched deeper than I was accustomed to. "I have no room in my heart for that."

I thought I was past the slippery feelings. I'd been certain that Marian no more believed that I had or ever would mislead her than she believed she would deceive me, but I could not dismiss the jangling nerves that always accompanied my being around her, that lack of a splendid confidence.

Marian was looking at me again. "If you weren't leaving I'd be the one who'd have to. It's very tempting to run away from all this." The smile on her face was tepid. "It's too much, don't you think? Too high-alert."

"Then it's not such a bad idea if we do cool down for a few days."

"I wish you wouldn't say that."

"What word do you prefer?"

She said, "I wish we stopped turning everything we say inside out. Turning each other inside out. Please. It's scary and troubling and I don't like it." She took a few steps away from the car. "And I don't care if I sound cranky. I'm *really* not looking forward to the next couple of days. To *anything*, right now." She turned on the balls of her feet and walked away. She didn't appear to be in a hurry, kicking at the stones in the dirt, stopping for a moment, staring at the ground. When she lifted her head, the wind blew her hair away from her face. She looked around, her eyes not resting on any particular spot, then she stared at me as though she might have been seeing a room for the last time.

I was thinking: I better remember this.

If I never saw Marian after today, this was all I'd have and it would have to be enough and it never would replace what I was feeling at the moment—not unlike living alone in an old house with nothing but clippings in a scrapbook.

I was thinking: She watched her husband drive away for only a few seconds before she made herself busy, she didn't wait to see him to the top of the driveway, and she's wondered ever since what was so important that she gave up those few extra seconds.

Marian came toward me. "Can I go inside now?"

WHEN I GOT BACK FROM MY WALK IT WAS ALREADY DUSK. THERE were no e-mails, no phone messages, and none the rest of that night. In the morning, when I still hadn't heard from Marian and couldn't stand waiting, I went out to run errands that didn't need my attention, came back in the early afternoon, and there was still nothing from Marian.

But I did send an e-mail to Alex in the Bahamas, more out of concern than curiosity, and he e-mailed: "I'm sending Simon back to California and if he can get his shit together, then we'll see. I'm not ready to set up house with anyone but I'm having more fun than I've had in a long time and am really quite happy at the moment." He did get around to asking me how I was doing, and when I replied, he said I should remain hopeful.

The following morning, after a not-too-restful sleep, and after the delivery of my clean clothes, I started packing my travel bag. I didn't know why. If there was no turning back and no going forward, perhaps there was just going.

I thought about the first time I'd visited Shady Grove and the sweet melancholia that had replaced my emotional stasis. That feeling of stasis didn't seem as troubling as the emotional limbo where I now found myself, and where I might be stranded.

It had been three days since I'd left Marian with her thoughts and doubts, with time to make her choice, whatever that would be. I was thinking the hell with it, I'll call her or send her an e-mail, tell her time had expired, and what's it going to be? Or I could just leave—"You said not to get in touch, so I didn't get in touch . . ." Welcome to the eighth grade. Pack up and get away.

I packed for a tropical vacation, unpacked and repacked clothes for somewhere farther north, then Asia, then a European trip. I was in the same room where I'd first read the letter from Laura's attorney, where I'd listened to all the songs of love that Laura had left for me. It was where I thought about falling in love and going mad.

When I finished, and had no idea what I'd packed, I sat on the floor, rested my head against the soft, fat part of the bag, and started to laugh. I fell asleep waiting for Marian to call.

In the middle of a dream, the phone rang and Marian's voice woke me.

"I went up to Albany to renew my passport. The man said it could take up to a month."

"The man said?"

"I said I couldn't wait that long, and told him how we met and what a pain in the ass you are, and how you've completely screwed up my life."

"And to a total stranger."

"He said any man who's that persistent—"

"And he uses words like *persistent*."

"'Determined.' He said a man that determined won't want to wait for the federal bureaucracy to get around to my passport request, so he promised to put a rush on it."

"And in Albany of all places."

"So what do you think we should do in the next four weeks? And keep it domestic."

"Who *is* this?"

"The voice of your impending demise."

IT DIDN'T TAKE A MONTH TO GET THE PASSPORT, ONLY ABOUT TEN days, not counting the weekend. In that time, Marian arranged for her staff to run the nursery, and did all the other things a person does before leaving town for an undetermined amount of time.

I untangled myself from a small web of obligations, rescheduled what I could reschedule, and postponed what I couldn't. Everyone was most understanding when I explained why; although I doubt I did as good a job as Marian did with her passport.

Marian and I agreed that we should see Walter and Eleanor before we left. I wasn't sure how Marian would announce our plans, or if she'd even decided to, but I was looking forward to seeing the Ballantines again.

As soon as I walked into the house, Walter shook my hand and squeezed my shoulder, said a robust hello, let out a quick laugh, held onto my hand a moment longer, and led me to the enclosed porch. Marian was already there, sitting in one of the soft chairs.

Eleanor came toward me and we hugged.

"Marian's told us," she said, "at least a little bit. But Walter and I want to know everything." She and Walter sat next to each other on the sofa, and even before Marian or I said another word, they were leaning toward us—it seemed like the entire room was leaning toward us.

"We're just going away." Marian's face was flushed.

"Just like that?" Walter asked.

Eleanor had to ask a second time before Marian began to tell the tale of our past few days.

It was obvious that Walter and Eleanor were enjoying the story, the way they interrupted every few sentences with a rush of questions, and even interrupted each other. If I hadn't been so charmed by their exuberance I might have been alert to the tone in Marian's voice, the absence of enthusiasm when she said, "I mean, don't you think your excitement is a little over the top?" and the tension.

"Anything *but*," Walter said.

Marian started to stand, stopped, and sat down again.

"If nothing else," she said, "I think this is disrespectful."

"To what?" Eleanor asked. "And to whom?"

"She's talking about Buddy," I answered.

"I should say not," Walter said.

"It feels a little like dancing on his grave." Now Marian did get up and walk away from us. "We're going away for a few weeks," she said, looking only at me. "It's not like we're . . ."

"Why not act like you're . . . ?" Eleanor said.

"I haven't even had sufficient time to absorb leaving Eliot," Marian told her. "I think we're all just a little too—*festive.*"

"He was our son. We love him, too," Walter said. "And we also love you. We've waited a long time for you to—" he looked over at Eleanor.

"To find someone."

Marian turned to me. "Say something. And please don't be understanding."

"Eleanor's right."

"I can't help it. I know it's crazy." Marian started to cry. "It's like you're going to for*get* him. It's just not fair."

"Not fair?" Walter said.

"I mean, it's like you're sending me off, without asking for an explanation, or an apology."

"You don't need to explain anything to us," Eleanor said. "Or apologize."

"And sometime from now," Marian told her, "you're going to say, 'How could she do that to our son? Going away like that?'"

"We've been waiting for you to do this, and exactly this way."

I went over to Marian, gave her my handkerchief, and put my arms around her. She laid her head on my shoulder, and leaned into my embrace.

"It's you and me now," I whispered.

"I know that, but do *they* know that?"

"They know it."

"I thought this was a good idea," she said. "I really did want to go with you, and I really meant all the things I've said, but right now"—she raised her head toward Walter and Eleanor—"all I want is to say I'm sorry. To the two of you." Now she raised her eyes to me. "And to Buddy. Tell me you're able to understand that?"

Marian held onto me for another moment, said, "It's like a second funeral." She walked over to the chair where she'd been sitting, and sat down.

"You're asking if it's all right if you leave Buddy" Eleanor began.

"It's all right," Walter finished for her. "It's time."

"And it's that place. That *place*," Marian said. "That fucking place. It's there. It's *always* going to be there."

"That was a long time ago," Eleanor told her.

It may have been a long time ago, but Buddy's cabin was still crowding Marian's interior landscape, her emotional landscape. That's what I would have told her, if we'd been alone.

Walter said, "It's been long enough."

Marian leaned her head back and, letting out her breath, said, "I need to know that it really is all right with the two of you. I don't mean just for now. I mean, if I move away from here and you don't see me."

"Because all means of travel and communication will leave with you?" Walter answered.

I sat on the arm of Marian's chair, put my hand on her shoulder. She put her hand over mine.

"Travel," Marian repeated. "That's another thing . . ."

Walter sat forward. "It's time you got away from Shady Grove."

"While I have a complete meltdown," Marian said.

"It's not going away that worries you, is it?" Walter said.

Marian smiled at him. "It's what comes after. It's turning me into jelly."

I thought it was time for me to say something. "More to the point, neither of us knows what comes after." I was looking at Marian, but speaking to the Ballantines. "Where we'll be living for one thing. I'm selling my apartment."

"And I'm selling the nursery," Marian said. "And the house."

"Then a meltdown is perfectly appropriate." There was a tone of solace in Eleanor's voice. "But only for a little while."

There would have been a time, and not long ago, when I would have recoiled from the familial presence in the room, and found it cloying. That afternoon, I was drawn to it, delighted to be a part of it: when Walter shook my hand and Eleanor gave me another hug and kissed me, when she said how she was proud of Marian, and how happy.

For this was an act of expiation. Marian breathing out, not only the remnants of her sadness, but her years with Eliot; and for a moment longer the levity remained, and then the laughter stopped and the smiles dissolved. Marian uncoiled her legs and sat low in her chair. Walter and Eleanor sank into the corners of the couch.

If this had been about extracting Buddy from the room it wasn't any longer. It was now about Eliot and our realization, if not in concert, certainly in consort, that another human being, another life, was involved.

Walter and Eleanor would be reminded of this night whenever they saw Eliot on a checkout line, or anytime they needed to go into his hardware store.

"And it would be so sad," Eleanor said, "if seeing us reminds Eliot of Marian."

Then no one spoke a word, and we stayed quiet for a little while to acknowledge Eliot and his abandonment. Until Marian cleared her throat, said, "I know Eliot well enough to know that he's going to be all right. He'll be fine." And I felt all of my doubts sailing away.

I WAS NOT GOING TO SPEND THE NIGHT WITH MARIAN IN HER HOUSE and sleep in her bed. We drove north for about an hour, and stayed at an inn off of a state road, one of those old Victorian houses.

Our room was on the top floor. Flowered wallpaper, four-poster bed, thick mattress on which Marian and I lay together, her head resting on my shoulder. I inhaled the fragrance of her hair with unabashed pleasure, recalling those clandestine moments when a breeze brought the suggestion of a scent. When I imagined the taste of her mouth on mine. Tonight, I felt the tug of Marian's flesh when she moved, the texture of her skin and its deep warmth. When she put my hand to her lips, I remembered the afternoons when I wanted nothing more than that.

The window was raised, and the breeze had that new warmth that lets you know spring has arrived at last.

Marian said, "Tell me what you're thinking about right now."

"That I've been wanting to be like this with you since the day we met."

"How could you want something like that? No one can be that sure."

"That's what I was thinking."

"Now? Or when me met?"

"Have you any idea what you're talking about?"

She pulled me closer to her and breathed, "I would like to forget everything that ever happened to either of us before tonight." She rolled to the far side of the bed. "You weren't supposed to be like this."

"How was I supposed to be?"

"You weren't supposed to be the way we wanted you to be. Laura and I."

"Wanted me to be?"

"It's not important. Not tonight."

I leaned my body into hers. She tucked the curve of her hip into the flat part of my hip. We spoke to each other not in soft, uncertain tones but with the assuredness of old friends, the way we'd always spoken to each other since that time outside Laura's house, and now like declared lovers, uncomplicated and without metaphor.

Marian reached around and put her hand on my chest.

"Tell me you really thought this was the way it was supposed to happen," she said.

"Nothing ever happens the way it's supposed to happen."

"You had to come to Shady Grove to find that out?"

I put my arm around her waist and rested my hand on top of her thigh.

I told her, "I want to believe time starts now."

Marian said, "I want to believe you." She turned around. We kissed a strong, full-mouth kiss.

We made slow, careful love, like two strangers; the first awkward moment we'd had together, and the most self-conscious. And like first-time sex with anyone, at least anyone you love, it was doomed to disappoint. We didn't care, and we lay together in that creaking bed, laughing at ourselves. Then in the middle of the night, we made love a second time and all caution vanished.

We didn't get much sleep after that, lying in the dark, not saying much, and when we did speak it was just the smallest of talk, we were both too wound up.

About two hours before sunrise I sat up in bed.

"Come on," I said. "We're leaving."

Marian lay on her side, propped on her elbow.

"You're not making sense."

"We might as well go now."

She didn't move. "It's late. Where are we going?"

I was out of bed by now.

"We'll just get there early, that's all." I started getting dressed.

"What about the room?"

"It's paid for."

"I meant— Are we coming back?"

"You can sleep on the drive up." I tossed her jeans over to her.

Her hair was all tousled, and she didn't do it much good tousling it even more, as though that might clear her head and help her make sense of what I was doing, but at least she stopped asking questions and started to get dressed.

Twenty-two

I T WASN'T THAT I KNEW FOR CERTAIN I COULD FIND THE PLACE
in the dark, but most of the drive was straight on the
Thruway. Marian slept in the car, slouched in the front
seat, her head tilted to the side. There were a few times when
I wasn't sure if I'd made the right choice, if I knew Marian
as well as I thought I did, if this was the proper thing to do.
But whenever I looked over, there she was, there was Marian,
and I would think: You never thought it would happen and
it's happening . . . And I started humming deep in my throat.

By the time I reached our exit and came to the hard part,
it was dawn and all I had to do was follow the sun to the long
driveway through the woods, the open field and the yellow
clapboard house, where sunlight refracted through heavy
dew, dotting the ground with spectrums of moist color.

It was too soon to come to any conclusions. I had loved my
friend Laura, and my allegiance to her, sworn on duplicity,
had been long forgotten and required no forgiveness, but was

this her gesture of redemption? Bringing me to where I would meet Marian? Did she know this day would happen—did she possess that kind of intuition? Was it what she'd wanted? Did Buddy see God in the petal of a flower? Was the randomness he loved as simple as a four-leaf clover, and as magnificent? Was I doing no more than trying to shake Marian loose from Eliot and Shady Grove, or was this what love was like? And, as Marian might say, drawing a circle in the air, was *this* a part of *that*?

When I stopped the car, Marian opened her eyes, yawned, and squinted into the sunrise.

"Where are we?" Her voice was thick with sleep.

"We're here."

"Where's here?"

"Don't you recognize it?"

She sat up.

"Are we lost?"

"We're early. But it's okay. A man named Aubrey lives here. He knows we're coming."

"What time is it?"

I got out, walked around the car, and opened the passenger door.

"I want to show you something." I took her hand and helped her out.

We followed the path past the guesthouse with the cedar shakes, and a few yards farther around the back of the main house to the wooden dock, the boathouse, and the lake.

Marian stared across the water at the small island, where the gazebo caught some of the early light. She looked back at me, and then turned and looked over her shoulder at the house.

"I know where I am," she said.

"You know where you *were*," I told her.

"What are you talking about? Geoffrey, I know this place."

"It isn't here." I saw the tears build in her eyes. "That place that you hate," I said, "is gone. It no longer exists."

She wiped her eyes on her sleeve, looked again at the boathouse and the dock, and across the lake, then walked away. I stayed behind, watching her do a slow circle around the house, and, I assumed, behind to the guesthouse, built with wood from Buddy's cabin.

I could hear the soft shush her shoes made as she walked through the damp grass.

When she came back, Marian was looking at me in a way that I had trouble reading. As she came closer, I could see her lips moving, but I did not hear what she was saying.

She stopped a few feet from me, still looking around.

The wind rippled across the water. A stand of trees with their new growth of leaves swayed and bowed.

Marian put her arm around my waist, I put my arm around hers. She lifted her face to mine, and said, "It's time to get moving."

Acknowledgments

While the writing of a novel is a solitary process, it demands numerous conversations that could try the patience of a saint. I would like to thank my two saints: Joy Harris, who goes above and beyond the description of agent; and my wife, Marjorie Braman, whose creative insights, imagination, and tolerance are more than I deserve.

ML 3/2